They were both fast approaching the uppermost trees—Matt's quarry maintaining his eighth of a mile lead—when the mountain at the head of the ravine loosed a prolonged roar that set the steep hillside quaking.

Matt swung around in time to see a huge cumulus of snow billow out of the glaciated basin beyond the monastery. At the same time the evergreens were bowed by an icy wind. Swept off his feet momentarily, Matt managed to grab hold of a tree stump and pull himself to his knees. He wiped the snow away from his face and scrambled upward from tree to tree as a ferocious, swelling tide of mud, water, and massive chunks of ice began to funnel down the ravine.

Boulders the size of Volkswagens careened into view, and explosive reports filled the suddenly frosted air. . . .

Also by James Luceno
Published by Ivy Books:

RÍO PASIÓN
RAINCHASER

ROCK BOTTOM

James Luceno

IVY BOOKS • NEW YORK

Ivy Books
Published by Ballantine Books
Copyright © 1990 by James Luceno

Library of Congress Catalog Card Number: 90-90295

ISBN 0-8041-0628-7

Manufactured in the United States of America

First Edition: November 1990

For everyone who weathered the storm:
Tom, Brian, Millie, Matt, Pam,
Jack, Bill and Andy G., Joan,
Bill H., Norbu, Chandrabadur, and Nuong

"If your expedition turns out to be an adventure, you haven't done your planning properly."
—various sources on trail wisdom

Author's Note

Following in the footsteps of some twenty years of seekers, travelers, and trekkers, I have taken liberties with Nepal's cities, shrines, and mountains. May Nepal forgive all of us our trespasses.

Heartfelt thank-yous to Drs. Martin Alexander; Alan Fields, director of the pediatric intensive care unit at Children's Hospital National Medical Center, Washington, D.C.; and Arthur Kohrman, director of La Rabida Children's Hospital, Chicago, Illinois.

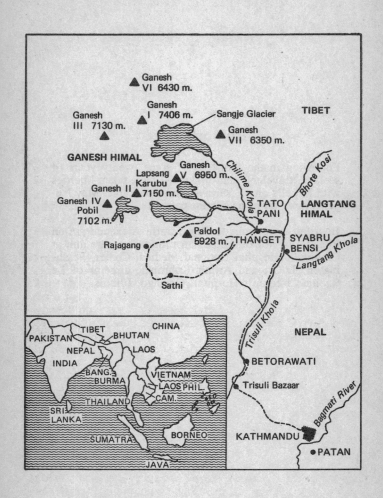

🪷 1 🪷

Dharma Bummer

Matt had combed Kathmandu from Thamel to Durbar Square and still hadn't found what he was after. He was lost in the Jaisidewal quarter—south of Ganga Path, west of Dharma Way—when he met the Tibetan.

His inclination was to continue heading south toward the Bagmati River, but some stray impulse had steered him east at the last moment into a narrow, crooked lane of small shops and three-story brick dwellings that took its name from a Hindu demiurge associated with bloody sacrifice. Women in blue saris leaned over to observe him from cantilevered balconies, and bright-eyed children as dusty as the street tried to converse with him in broken English.

Ragas and warbling Indian flute recordings blared from dark hollows and wood-framed glazed windows with extended lintels. Most of these were done in glossy turquoise, save for a few that were elaborately carved in Newari style. Tall sidewalks fashioned from slate flanked the lane, but nearly everyone preferred the street, which was little more than an upheaved ridge of square cobblestones forming a six-foot wide swath through the dun-colored earth. Taxis, rickshas, and three-wheeled *tempos* maneuvered through the throng, announcing themselves with horns and bells and whistled tunes. In the thick of it all stood a cow adorned with marigold necklaces.

1

Fecal odors dominated in the hazy autumnal air, and it occurred to Matt that all the world's fan-flung shit had ended up there in the street, directly in his path. Dog logs, human waste, cow pies . . . the whole kit and caboodle. Anything but retentive, the Nepalese seemed to enjoy seeing their shit on constant parade, but he was determined not to step in any of it this go-round.

The Vale of Kathmandu, he thought dismally. Cat Stevens and Bob Seger had sung about the place, when what it amounted to was fifty miles of crooked roads and a hundred and fifty square miles of open latrine.

He wondered why Kathmandu's roving bands of dogs weren't picking over the street's wealth of filth, supposing that most of them had gotten into the habit of foraging around Thamel or Freak Street, where trekkers dined on pizza and lemon meringue pie and did business with savvy Sherpa shopkeepers.

Yeah, the dogs had traded up, Matt decided, and he had been bequeathed the place: a dusty medieval stretch of offal and audio riot and demonic statuary.

Three kids propelling a bicycle rim along with sticks called out, "Hey, meester!" Matt gave a downward tug to his brimmed cap and quickened his pace. But by then the Tibetan he had spied lounging in the doorway to a spice shop was already alongside him.

"You want buy Tibetan belt?" the man said, hurrying to match Matt's long-legged stride. "This pure silver. Come from Lhasa. Very ancient."

Matt appraised the cloth-wrapped belt without slowing down. It was a cumbersome affair with a gem-encrusted buckle and a long chain that ended in a skirt-pin. Fresh from Lhasa himself, he needed only a moment to see that the thing was neither pure silver nor ancient. The seller, on the other hand, was authentic, his dark face all cheekbones and sun crevices.

"Some silver, mostly nickel," Matt said. "And younger than you and me."

The man smiled around large white teeth and looked up at him. "How old you think I am?" His shoulder-length brown hair was clipped straight across a furrowed forehead and tucked behind prominent ears with distended lobes.

Matt glanced at the Tibetan's large hands; tried to puzzle out how many years were disguised under the Chinese olive-drab sneakers and the Western trousers and shirts. "Fifty-five."

The man's smile broadened. "I seventy-two years." Matt nodded but didn't question it; he'd met eighty-year-olds in Lhasa who looked fifty. "So you want buy belt? I make good price."

"Already have one," Matt said, hitching up his sweater to show the strip of embossed brown leather that cinched his fatigues.

"For wife," the man persisted.

Matt shook his head. "Not married."

"For lovers then."

"Lovers?"

"Lovers, sure. Tall handsome American with movie star's face and spring of *tahr* in his step must have many women."

Matt stopped to laugh and the stranger joined him. The man explained that he had been a teacher in Lhasa. He and his family fled Tibet eight years before, and they had lived for some time in the refugee camp at Jawalakhel in nearby Patan. Recently he had found work with an antiquities merchant operating out of a well-known shop in Thamel. The belt, he confessed, was fifty percent silver and fifty percent nickel, but still a good buy at two thousand rupees—about one hundred dollars US.

"So why you were in Lhasa?" the man asked as they were sidestepping a procession of festively attired bicyclists.

"Traveling," Matt told him. "Wanted to see the Potala Palace."

The Tibetan eyed him suspiciously. "Ah, then you sightseer."

Matt frowned from under the bill of his cap. "Yeah, but a professional one."

"Not seeking spiritual wisdom?"

Matt rapped a knuckle against his forehead. "Fifty percent nickel," he said, grinning.

The man's initial puzzlement gave way to laughter. "Then what you look for in Nepal?"

Matt understood that by "Nepal" the Tibetan meant

Kathmandu. "Wine," he said, in a voice lowered in false conspiracy. "A dry red if we can find one."

The wine, Matt explained when the two had resumed their eastward amble, was for a dinner party scheduled for that evening at the Hotel Dorje. The guests of honor were eleven soon-to-be trekkers, recently arrived in Kathmandu under escort by Puma Tours, Incorporated, the adventure travel company that employed Matt as trip-development scout and sometime tour leader. When the Tibetan—who had introduced himself as Norbu—asked what a tour leader's duties were, Matt told him it was a little like being a teacher and a lot like being a salesman trying to peddle jewelry that wasn't always what it appeared.

"And if one is refugee?" Norbu asked.

"It helps," Matt replied after a moment's reflection.

Norbu said he knew a place that might have a bottle or two of wine and led Matt through a brisk street slalom to a lantern-lit sundries shop at the end of the lane. The shopkeeper was a Tamang with rheumy black eyes and a drooping silver mustache. He wedged a finger under a soft, fez-like cap to scratch at his shaved head while Norbu translated Matt's request in Nepali, the mountain kingdom's lingua franca.

Matt purchased a pack of Yak cigarettes for Norbu and the two of them smoked while the old man disappeared into an even darker back room, emerging several minutes later with two bottles of Heinz ketchup.

"Well," Matt said, turning one of the aged bottles in his hands, "we're probably closer than we think." If there was a Nepali word for wine, he didn't know it and guessed it wouldn't have meant much to the shopkeeper in any case. "Tell him we're looking for a red alcohol drink." He started to add *in a corked bottle* but thought better of it, venturing the old man would return with fermented honey beer.

Gazing around at the confusion of articles that crowded the shop's hopelessly bowed shelves, he asked himself whether a couple of bottles of *rakshi*, the local grain liquor, might do in a pinch. He and Jake could always tint the colorless drink with food coloring or some of that Heinz ketchup. . . .

The wine had been Jake's idea; Jake Welles at his tour operator best, bent as always on providing Puma Tours' clients with trips of a lifetime. Lately that had come to mean an inspired blend of soft adventure and transcultural contact, spiced with extras that might include fresh fish in Cuzco, strawberries in Bali, or wine in Kathmandu. But Matt had learned not to ridicule the perks. Jake had an instinctive feel for what it took to elevate a standard welcome dinner to a memorable travel experience.

Their friendship went back almost ten years, to 1976, in Peru. But with Matt now handling trip development in Asia and Jake overseeing marketing and sales from the company's head office in Denver, they hadn't spent more than two days together in the past year and a half. Puma business seemed to be taking over their lives, and it was just that that had prompted Matt to abandon his usual misgivings about group travel and take Jake up on his offer of a thirty-day carefree trek in the Himalayas.

"Matt," Norbu said, gesturing to the back room with the lighted Yak he had cupped in his right hand.

The shopkeeper stood beaming in the curtained doorway, clutching three bottles of wine vinegar to his chest.

"Close, but no cigar," Matt said. "Maybe we should help him look."

Grabbing an unlabeled bottle of mountain beer from a shelf behind the wooden counter, they ducked into the rear of the shop, where candles illuminated dozens of crates and burlap sacks stacked about a room that wasn't built to accommodate six-foot-plus foreigners.

"Make a good wine cellar," Matt said, with a hand against the brick wall.

Norbu picked up a large screwdriver and began to pry open one of the crates. Hunkered down in the cool darkness, Matt bit the cork out of the bottle of *chang* and poured beer for three into silver-lined cups turned from rosewood.

A few swallows of the potent brew set him back on his butt on the hard floor, exhaling a long, weary sigh—the aftereffects of a month of bad roads stealing over him. Or perhaps just the accumulated exhaustion of forty years of hard traveling.

A month ago Jake had given him the option of rendez-vousing with the trekking group in Kathmandu and accompanying everyone down to Chitwan National Park in the lowlands; or squeezing in a quick recon trip to Tibet, which was suddenly accessible via Nepal's northern frontier. Lhasa, the Tibetan capital, had long been the adventure traveler's wet dream, and Matt had felt the pull— the lure of untouristed places—in the same way that many of Kathmandu's expats professed to feel an almost gravitational attraction to the Himalayas.

With tourist flights between the two Himalayan nations still a year or so off, the overland trip was going to mean an ordeal by bus, but Matt considered himself a veteran of the long haul over mountain spines and sawtooth ranges and didn't anticipate any more than the usual hassles. He was, after all, one of the old-timers who had ridden yellow school buses through the Peruvian Andes before Marxist guerrillas had made travel unsafe in the highland pueblos. He'd endured the grueling Australia coast-to-coast and survived the infamous trans-Sulawesi. So what was a mere five days of Himalayan back roads?

And indeed the trip up to the Tibetan plateau had been uneventful; as was much of his week's stay in Lhasa. As it happened there was little to eat, a dearth of local guides, and the occupying Chinese had gone to devastating lengths to snuff out much of the magic that had earned Tibet its crowning place in the traveler's pantheon. So Matt had passed the time hanging out with other veteran overlanders in a small inn called the Migyu, which was Tibetan for yeti—the abominable snowman.

Even now in the spiced atmosphere of the shop's back room his nose could still conjure the smell of the butter lamps in the Potala Palace—now little more than a museum; and he could project himself into the government-operated hotels, with their untrained staffers, unlit corridors, and hundreds of unheated rooms. Puma tourers, he had decided in the end, weren't ready for Tibet just yet.

Then, on the return leg, a nasty change in the weather had shifted him down into low gear. Avalanches had wiped out the road between Nilamu on the Chinese side and Nepali customs in Kodari. In freak sleet and icy winds, the windowless bus found itself trapped between slides with a dozen foreign passengers who hadn't thought enough to pack along emergency rations or proper clothing. Matt shared what he'd brought and local farmers had contributed a few rock-hard potatoes and radishes dug from terraces on the arid slopes, but there wasn't nearly enough to go around.

The road repair crews still hadn't showed after two days, so Matt and a few of the overlanders decided to bundle up and make for the Nepalese border on foot. Two young kids from Indiana took severely ill on the way, and Matt ended up carrying one of them out on his back—a blond girl of about twenty-two, whose frequent intestinal bouts with Asia had reduced her to ninety pounds of skin and bones. The Chinese officials at the border were anxious to rid themselves of Matt's near-starving band, but the Nepalese insisted that any dying to be done was going to have to take place on China's side of the swollen frontier river.

Ultimately the guards had relented and allowed them to cross, but by then the two American kids were in serious trouble. For the next sixty hours Matt piggybacked the girl most of the way to Lamosang, deep inside the Nepal border, all the while trying to push memories of his late wife from his mind. She had died in Peru years back in a bus plunge from an all-too-similar notch road, in an all-too-similar rain. One that simply refused to let up, no matter how many imprecations were hurled against it.

But what he had begun to feel more than anything else was just plain *defeated*. The sudden weariness was the crescendo to a movement that had been building inside him for several years, during which time he had come to think of himself as something of a magnet for disaster— especially in the wake of events that had gone down in Peru, Mexico, and Indonesia. And though he had tried to lay low in the backwaters of the world, tragedy was continually seeking him out. Keeping in motion hadn't helped either, and he was wearying of the comings and goings, the spells of bad weather and rotten luck; tired of hard beds in closet-size hotel rooms, of temple tours, and intestinal ills. Tired of where the road had and hadn't led him.

And there he was: trudging through the mud with a cadre of gypsy freaks and overlanders in Afghani vests and Tibetan boots and Thai jewelry—the same ones who had been running scams out of the Migyu in Lhasa with their Foreign Exchange Certificates and contraband photos of the exiled Dalai Lama. And he couldn't help wonder whether he wasn't catching a glimpse of himself just down the road apiece: holed up in an ends-of-the-earth bedbug warren, comparing horror stories, and going lyrical about the good ole days of overland travel, the cheapest way *to fit it all in*—to *do* the whole world—collecting place after place, one experience after another, with nowhere to hang it all up, nowhere to use it all to some decent purpose.

So he'd asked himself somewhere on the slick mud stretch between Barahbise and Lamosang if maybe it wasn't time to come in out of the cold and take a safe and stable indoor job where he couldn't do himself or anyone else any more harm. If it wasn't time to quit the road, abandon the tour, ask Jake about installing him in some middle-management position with Puma Tours.

That was the real reason he was in Nepal, he told himself now, thinking back to Norbu's innocent query. He wasn't here to trek; he was here to tell Jake he'd finally had enough—

"We have, *sahib*," the shopkeeper announced suddenly, pronouncing the honorific "sahb."

Matt tried to second-guess what they had come up with—a cherry soda, perhaps, or a cooking sherry—and was astonished when Norbu placed a dusty bottle of red wine in his hands. A 1961 Bordeaux, no less. And there was an entire crate of it. Matt even thought he recognized the French vineyard label on the green bottle.

"Yes, *sahib*?" the shopkeeper asked.

"Yeah," Matt answered, marveling at the find. A dozen bottles of vintage wine had traveled halfway around the world to make a home for themselves in the dark back room of a nameless shop on a mostly dirt street where cows had the right of way, in a country that set its clocks fifteen minutes ahead of its neighbors. Had sat there for who knew how long just waiting to be discovered by a tired, jinxed, forty-year-old semi-professional wanderer from Montana who was only looking for a place to put up his feet.

Matt laughed out loud, thinking maybe there was hope for him yet.

2

Aliens

The Hotel Dorje was a solid fifteen-minute walk from the Jaisidewal quarter. Just across the Vishnumati River on the way to the hilltop stupa of Swayambunath, it was well out of the reach of the vivid chaos that reigned in the hub of Kathmandu. The only hotel further removed from the action was the Soaltee Oberoi, with its $150-per-night rooms and attached "Casino Nepal." But Jake hadn't selected the Dorje for either the location or the bargain-priced rooms, but for the gardens, the artistic decor, and the cheerfulness of the hotel's Nepalese and Tibetan staff.

Travelers who stayed in Thamel's guest houses would frequently make their way to the Dorje's rooftop restaurant for a sunset beer and linger to watch the city close down for the night, the encircling hills darken from conifer-blue to indigo. In winter the sun would stain the Himalayan peaks in pinks and russet, but in fall the mountains were often obscured by billowing white clouds left over from the monsoon.

Matt always felt there was something Mexican about the Dorje's layout—the name meant "thunderbolt"—and had heard a rumor to the effect that a Santa Fe architect had a hand in the hotel's design.

Since returning from Tibet, it had become his routine to nurse a drink while the sun was going down, then ease himself into warmer clothes and one or two follow-up drinks before striking out for food across the river. But with the welcome dinner scheduled to begin at seven-thirty, he instead had a drink sent to his room, where he tried to prepare himself mentally for what was going to amount to a month of enforced comradeship with the near-dozen strangers who had signed up for the trek.

Drink in hand, he was on his way into the Dorje's second-floor dining room now when someone called his name from the landing of the tiled stairway to the upper floor.

"Matt Terry," the resonant voice repeated as Matt swung around, trying to tie the man's handsome face and name together. He had been introduced to the group out at Tribhuvan Airport, but had yet to commit everyone's name to memory. "Karl Tower," the man said, sensing Matt's plight.

"Karl, right," Matt said, extending a hand. "I won't forget next time."

Tower pumped his hand. "Won't hold it against you if you do, amigo. Way I figure it there's eleven of us, and we've only got you and Jake and whatsizname—the naturalist—"

"Sinotti. Stu Sinotti."

"Stu, sure. Anyway, we've only got you three to remember."

It wasn't quite true, but Matt didn't bother to debate it. From somewhere upstairs came enthusiastic applause and a wild round of English and Nepali exclamations. "What's going on up there?"

Tower chortled. "Damnedest thing. The staff's watching a videocassette of *Aliens*."

Matt raised his eyebrows. "I thought that just came out in the theaters?"

"It did, partner, it did," Tower began in an accent Matt guessed might be Texan. "But somebody musta roped themselves a pirate print and run off a batch a dubs. Hell, I couldn't even see the thing back home the lines were so long." He lowered his voice. " 'Tween you and me and the bidet, you can't understand a goddamned line of dialogue from that dub. But it's no nevermind." He jerked a rigid thumb toward the beamed ceiling. "Staff's havin' a ball."

Tower explained that two science-fiction writers who had blown into town earlier in the week had rented the movie and the cassette player and were staging a party for the Dorje staff. Matt wondered briefly if the two were friends with science-fiction luminary C. Fredrick Roberts, with whom he had shared a misadventure on Bali a year back.

"Understand they've got some other movie called *Blue Velvet*," Tower added a moment later. Matt confessed that he hadn't heard of it either.

Tower's brown-eyed gaze was level; his forehead high, with a pronounced browridge. Dark reddish-brown hair fell over the open collar of a rayon shirt. He was Matt's height in low-heeled Dan Post boots; fifty, give or take; broad-shouldered, muscular, but thick-waisted. The hand Matt shook was callused, but whatever job Tower worked earned him enough to afford expensive clothes and five-thousand-dollar vacations.

The upcoming trek was not only the most expensive Puma offered in Nepal but also one of the most physically demanding; so Matt assumed that the eleven group members would be of a kind in terms of fitness and earning power. Stretches of the trek were so challenging that Jake had asked for physicians' statements from each of the participants, in addition to the usual requests for background information.

"See you're a drinking man," Tower said with a wave of Matt's glass. "What I've been wondering is how much everyone's planning on packing in."

"How much what?"

"Liquid entertainment. *Refrescos*. I mean, unless you can promise me a bar every coupla days, I figure on being well stocked."

Matt looked for somewhere to set the drink down, sorry now that he'd brought it along from his room. No matter how fit they all were, they were still going to be counting on him to know his way around, and appearing with a drink in hand at first meet probably wasn't the best way of instilling confidence. Even so, Matt's drinking didn't seem to bother Karl Tower any. And there was the wine

Jake asked for . . . "Depends on how you feel about home brew," Matt told him.

"This *rakshi* stuff, you mean—the corn liquor?"

Matt nodded.

Tower tugged pensively at a cleft chin. "Well, a couple of bottles of one-five-one rum and vodka wouldn't hurt any, would they?"

Matt assembled a slow grin. "No, I reckon not."

Six bottles of the lucky Bordeaux were uncorked and positioned at intervals along the rectangular tables reserved for Puma's group. Jake Welles, in pile jacket and wool slacks, stood at the head of the lot, doing what he did best.

"Most of us have already had a chance to get acquainted down at Chitwan," Puma's founder was saying, "but I want to take a moment to introduce you to some of our, uh, mission-essential personnel before dinner's served."

Jake drew a laugh from the group; a hoot from Karl, who was seated off to Matt's left at the foot of the table. The man on Karl's left was the doctor, the anesthesiologist, Matt reminded himself, Robert "Buzz" Bessman. Or was Bessman the software designer? And was that Mrs. Software or Mrs. Doctor to Bessman's left? The elderly woman farther along the table was Constance something or other—the one from New York with the dog, of all things. And across from her were the father-son-team, Doug and Chris Makey.

"*Sirdar*," Jake was saying, "is a Nepali word everyone thinks translates as head Sherpa. But what it actually means is 'one with the most headaches.' " He turned to his right as the table laughed. "Lopsang?"

Puma's Tibetan interpreter and logistics man rose and flashed the long table a shy but sparkling smile. Twenty-five, with a brown face, shiny black hair, and a broad nose, Lopsang had accompanied British, American, and Japanese teams on numerous Himalayan ascents. He had retired from mountaineering after his brother had died during an assault on Dhaulagiri I. Matt had trekked the Annapurna Sanctuary with him three years before and considered him to be one of Nepal's finest Sherpa leaders.

Jake waited for Lopsang to return to his chair before motioning to the bearded man seated at his left hand—a scowling six-footer who seemed to withdraw at the mere mention of his name. "Of course, you've all met Dr. Sinotti, our study leader."

"Stuart," Sinotti grumbled from the chair, hiding his mouth behind a glass of water. "Stu, if you must."

Jake made fleeting eye contact with Matt and checked a grin. Sinotti had walked the Himalayas for close to fifteen years, but they both knew that the only reason he agreed to act as lecturer on Puma treks was to finance further solo forays into the mountains. Forays that sometimes kept him eight months of the year as far from humankind as possible.

"And down at the other end of the table is Matt Terry," Jake continued, "who we not only have to thank for the cabs that were waiting at the airport, but the wine miracle he pulled off for tonight's dinner."

Matt stood to cheery applause. "Take a bow, amigo," Karl enthused in a loud voice, slapping a hand against Matt's thigh.

"Matt's our Group Program Coordinator. He's the one who scouts out new destinations for Puma in Asia, the South Pacific, and Latin America."

"That's fascinating," Constance said.

Chris Makey's comment was "awesome."

"And I sit behind a CRT for a living," the software designer grunted. "Let me know if you ever decide to resign, Matt."

Matt reached for his drink as he sat down.

"Now," Jake said, turning to the four women seated around the head table, "I think I'll let our climbers introduce themselves."

Matt watched the foursome over the lip of his wineglass, wondering which of them was going to stand up first. They were equally renowned, each a member of mountaineering's prestigious 8000-meter club.

Barbara Bass laughed as she rose. "Okay, I'll get things going. My name is Barbara Bass. I have my father to thank for my love of the outdoors, and I practically grew up on skis in Switzerland and Colorado. I have a law practice in Denver and Phoenix, and when I'm not in court, I'm out climbing mountains." At fifty, she was the oldest among them, with a globe of gray-streaked hair, and a leathery, Sunbelt complexion.

A second climber was already on her feet. "I'm Julia Tremont, and I suppose I'm either a professional mountaineer who lectures for a living, or a professional lecturer who climbs mountains." She inserted a pause for crowd reaction, giving a slight toss to long, auburn hair, clipped in silver behind one ear. "Actually, I've participated in several major international expeditions. . . ." And she went on to name them: On Everest, K2, Thalay Sagar, and Dhaulagiri's northeast face.

"That one reminds me of my ex-wife," Karl whispered while Julia was talking. "A little broader in the beam, maybe, but the same hair, same coloring." Matt thought he could read the hurt in Tower's pale eyes.

Kaylee McMahon, who stood up next, was every bit Julia's opposite. Lean, dark-haired, and dark-complected; a somewhat sad-eyed, self-effacing outdoorswoman, who seemed a curious mix of rugged cowgirl and desert flower. A former guide on McKinley and Rainier, she, too, had been a member of half a dozen international power teams. "I'm looking forward to our trek," she told the Puma group.

Last to speak was Candice Dekker, who, Matt had learned, was always Candice—never Candi or Dek—and was perhaps the most high profile of the group.

"For the next ten days or so we'll all be part of the same team," she said. "Once we're under way, I'll be happy to answer any questions you might have about mountaineering."

One of the climbing world's rising young stars, she was not only strong and surefooted, but articulate and well versed in all aspects of the sport. She wore her blond hair in a short, boyish cut, and had clear eyes and the fresh-scrubbed good looks Matt associated with centerfolds and breath-mint commercials. She was wearing a T-shirt that read: "EVEREST: '87—SUMMIT AN AMERICAN WOMAN."

The software designer—Travis Dey, Matt finally recalled—leaned over to Karl while Candice was introducing herself. "*Mount* an American woman's more like it," he said quietly, laughing into his hand.

By the time the *narkish kofta* had been whisked away by three sari-ed members of the Dorje's staff—their dark foreheads daubed with vemilion *tikas*—Matt had had an opportunity to trade quips with almost everyone at his end of the table and put a few more names and faces together. Audrey Dey, who looked as though she might have several years on her husband, was a former high school earth science teacher. Mrs. Bessman—Morgan, blond and slender and married to the doctor—was also apparently in-between jobs. The attractive woman seated with the climbers was Taylor Kohl, from San Francisco. To her right were the Delongs, Maurice and Dee-Dee, sociologist and psychotherapist respectively. Constance Battle's New York poodle was named Karma.

Karl Tower rambled on through dinner about Dallas and Austin, and between the two of them they had polished off a bottle of wine and half a dozen Star beers. Matt was feeling no pain.

Jake had a map of Nepal set up on the head table, and Stu Sinotti was running down the trip itinerary. "Buses will take us as far as Betorawati. From there we'll cross the Trisuli River and walk north to its confluence with the Langtang. Three or four days at most. Then we'll follow the Bhote Kosi for a short stretch before heading northwest along the Chilime Khola. You'll all be expected to carry at least twenty pounds, and the porters will handle the rest."

Travis Dey laughed. "We carried more than that in cub scouts." Audrey looked a bit piqued by the comment.

Sinotti stared at the software man for a long moment. "You're free to carry as much as you want." He returned to the map. "Now, allowing for altitude acclimatization, another four or five days should put us here, north of Paldol in the Ganesh Himal, where we're going to be crossing a seventeen-thousand-five-hundred-foot pass." He waited for the nervous laughter and comments to die down. "We'll make base camp at approximately fourteen-thousand feet on the other side of the saddle, just here, south of Lapsang Karubu, also known as Ganesh Two.''

Matt strived for long-distance focus on the map. His recon of the area had taken him up the Chilime, but not over the high pass.

''The climb team will separate from us there and continue north to Pabil—that's Ganesh Four—and establish their own base camp on the mountain's southern flanks. Time and weather permitting, we'll visit their camp to observe the initial stage of their siege ascent. Our return will take us in a circle around Paldol and finally back to Thanget on the Chilime.'' He scanned the table. ''Any questions?''

The target area was almost due north of Kathmandu, along one of the ancient salt-trade routes that linked the Tibetan plateau with the Indian subcontinent. When Jake originally asked for an out-of-the-ordinary Himalayan trek, Matt had suggested the Ganesh because the area was seldom visited by trekkers. The route would even take them into Tibet for a short stretch. The problem was that the Ganesh was closed to trekking parties; and that's when Jake had devised a plan to align Puma's group with a climbing team already in possession of a permit for the region. He'd learned about the climb the Women for Everest team was planning for Pabil, and after a bit of finagling had purchased a share in the permit, which actually entitled Puma's group to limited climbing privileges on Paldol. The eighteen-thousand-foot mountain was one of Nepal's designated Trekking Peaks, first climbed in the early fifties by Tensing Norgay, who would later accompany Hillary up Everest.

The trek broke down to ten days in, seven days at base camp, and thirteen days out, with Sinotti providing lectures on ethnology, natural history, and expeditionary logistics.

''One goal I would like to set for the trek,'' the study leader was saying, ''is that we all emerge from this experience with an appreciation of Nepal as a threatened environment—threatened in some sense by the very things we, as Westerners, have brought to these mountains. I'll ask you to disregard that the word 'trek' is African Dutch for a journey by ox-wagon in search of a new home, and that you come to think of it as a journey on foot to an enlightened attitude regarding our endangered planet.''

Matt leaned back into his chair, steepling his fingers in front of his face. It was Sinotti who had suggested that Puma begin to implement a new policy of ''ecotourism'' with the Ganesh trek. ''Low-impact'' was one of ecotourism's chief buzzwords; the idea was to leave as little trace of your passing as possible.

''Nepal is a few years behind India in developing an environmental conscience, so it falls to us to demonstrate our awareness of the issues to those whose lives we'll touch along the trail. That's why we decided against a trek to Everest base or the Annapurna Sanctuary, where in both cases trekkers hungry for home-cooked meals and hot showers are putting demands on the land and the indigenous populations. Hot water and cook fires require wood, which has already grown scarce in certain mountain regions. Where the trees have already been cut, the country people are forced to rely on dried livestock dung for fires, which deprives the soil of nourishing manure and its ability to retain water. Highland cattle—yaks— whether essential for dung, dairy products, or strong backs, need fodder. Hence, we end up with increased grazing, increased deforestation, increased erosion and watershed contamination—a vicious cycle.

''We can, however, show our respect for the planet by example. And one way we can demonstrate this is by coming out of the mountains with more than we've taken in.''

The group members regarded one another along the length of the tables. ''Do you mean that figuratively or literally, Stu?'' Buzz Bessman asked in a jovial voice.

''Quite literally, Doctor,'' the naturalist answered stiffly.

''Stu's talking about 'sahib's prayer flags,' '' Matt said quickly, barely managing to rise to the occasion. When everyone turned to look at him, he added: ''Garbage. We're all going to be packing out trekkers' trash.''

🏵 3 🏵

Lost Horizon

"I'm only saying you could have come up with a better way to phrase it," Jake was telling Matt the next morning. The group had a free day, and the two of them were on their way into town to purchase last minute supplies with Lopsang and the expedition kitchen staff.

"More delicately, you mean."

Jake nodded. "That, too." Then he laughed. "I mean, I watched everybody's face fall. I could see them imagining themselves humping out bulging green garbage bags."

"Covered with flies," Matt said. "The stench so thick it's visible from clear across the valley."

"The sanitation engineer's tour of Nepal."

"And we're paying five thousand dollars apiece to do this?" Matt added in a nasal rendition of every complaining client Puma had ever dealt with.

In truth it was the porters who were going to be carrying the trash on the way out, requiring only that each of the group members hump a few extra pounds of their personal gear.

They stopped on the bridge to enjoy a good laugh and spit over the iron railing into the café au lait waters of the Vishnumati. A funeral pyre was smoldering on the east bank, family members dressed in white, sons with scalps shaved, a good fifteen dogs waiting patiently for a shot at snuffling about the ashes for bones.

Kathmandu wasn't Benares or Varanasi, but at Pashupatinath on the Bagmati where the river looped around the airport, the willing tourist could experience a like scene: white-shrouded cadavers; priests arguing with families over the price of the wood or the clarified butter to be used in the ceremony; heads exploding in the flames; purifying baths on the steps below the pyres. Cremation as a spectator event, Matt thought. Asia.

"Sure isn't Bali," he told Jake while they were regarding the death tableaux. Cremation on the Indonesian island paradise being a cause for riotous abandon.

"Sure isn't," Jake said, turning his gaze on the surrounding hills and towering cloud scapes.

In bits and pieces since Jake's arrival they'd been catching one another up on a year's worth of highs and lows, dating back to the hijacking of the bus on Bali and the murder of the diplomat from Vanuatu. Jake had lost the short beard he'd worn for several years and added five pounds or so to a swimmer's frame; but at forty-one he was still in top condition.

Back in motion now, he was mostly talking business. Matt was searching for an opening to mention the middle-management position he was contemplating when his friend announced suddenly that he was getting married.

"Holy shit," Matt said, stopping to *abrazo* Jake while two cows sauntered by. "Congratulations, man. When?"

"No date yet. But soon."

"What made you guys finally decide to do it?"

Jake shrugged, running a freckled hand over thinning hair. "It's time. Besides, there's the whole kid thing."

"Oh, ML wants a kid, huh?"

"*I* want a kid," Jake amended.

"Oh, yeah, right," Matt said all too earnestly.

"It's not critical for her yet, but I don't want to wait till I'm too old to throw a ball around with the kid."

Matt did a quick calculation. "You're still a long way from shuffleboard age, Jake."

"Maybe. But I want us to be able to do things together while I've still got the energy. I want to show him some of the world we've seen before every place ends up looking like Aspen.''

"Or her."

Jake showed him a narrow-eyed grin. "You know what I mean. Anyway, I've had it with leading trips—except the out-of-the-ordinary ones. We have all the guides we need, and the way things stand now I've got my hands full with promotion and sales. I just want a family to go home to at the end of the day. No more of this hanging around the office until nine o'clock finishing up correspondence or getting in one last phone call.''

"ML's okay with giving up guiding?"

"She can't wait."

"And you figure marriage is going to get you home on time."

"I know it will." Jake laughed in a self-amused way. "Must sound pretty tame to you, huh? Setting up house, planning for the future."

Matt shook his head. "You forget I was married. I know what all that's about."

Jake studied Matt's face. "Guess I keep thinking you're the one who's forgotten."

Matt fell silent for a moment. "It's weird, man. See, I've actually been thinking along similar lines."

"About getting married?" Jake asked.

"No, not that. About making a change. Maybe coming back to the States and taking a job in the office."

"You?—in the office? Staring at a screen all day long?"

"Why not?"

"In *Denver*, Matt?"

"All right, so we open up a field office like the one we had in Palenque."

Jake threw him a skeptical look. "Where, for instance?"

"Hell, I don't know. Back in Bali maybe. Even here."

Jake shook his head. "There's no profit in it, Matt. You know how fast this business is changing. There's already forty trekking outfits in Kathmandu alone, and Bali's getting overrun. No, the deal now is to get product-oriented and corporate. To keep developing new trips and market them like crazy. If we're not expanding, we're standing still.''

Matt blew out his breath. "We'll be passing out Puma T-shirts next.''

Jake's laugh was heartier than it should have been. "Look, Matt, the fact is I don't need you in the office. I need you in the field. So unless you're telling me it can't be that way anymore . . .''

"I'm not saying that, Jake.'' Matt shot him a look. "Yet.''

"Uh-huh. So what happened to your plans to find the perfect place?''

"Maybe there isn't one's why. Seriously, man, my ass just isn't as hard as it used to be. Or my head isn't, or my gut isn't.''

"Yeah? What about the rest of you?''

"Jesus, Jake,'' Matt said, shaking his head, "don't even joke about that. That's all I need now.''

Kathmandu's morning heat was building. A noisy long-handlebarred tractor trundled by hauling a heavy wooden wagon. The dirt tract ahead of them was littered with plastic refuse and pyramids of human feces.

"You're just putting on the miles after that bus ride down from Tibet, and I don't blame you.''

"It's more than that.'' Matt worked his jaw. "After Mexico, Bali . . . I don't know, Jake, I'm feeling like a goddamned bad penny. I mean, any trip I lead should come with a warning from the surgeon general or something. You know what I'm saying?''

Jake's eyes were narrowed. "Come on, Matt, you've just been stuck in cities too long. You need a therapeutic dose of wilderness. Like Stu.''

"Now you're comparing me to a misanthrope. Terrific.''

"You'll see,'' Jake continued, undaunted. "This trek's going to do wonders for you.''

Lopsang and the cook staff were waiting for them in Thamel, chatting with a photographer with an ancient box camera and a fanciful, perhaps, life-size cardboard cutout of a red-haired yeti. The *sirdar* introduced Purbu, Num, and Pasang, all of whom Jake was meeting for the first time, although they had cooked for Puma on several previous treks.

The word "sherpa" was Tibetan for "easterner," but in Nepal it had come to mean two things: people of Tibetan stock from the plateau province of Kham, and porter in general. Strictly speaking, not all Sherpas were porters and vice versa. Home to many of them was Nanche Bazar, a treeless, terraced amphitheater village in Nepal's Khumbu region, southwest of Everest, birthplace to both Lopsang and Purbu.

Soft-spoken, limpid-eyed Purbu was the cook. He stood five-six in high-top sneakers, jodhpur-legged pants, and embroidered vest. His two kitchen assistants wore paisley fezzes—*topis*—tattered shorts, and loose-knit sweaters, frayed at cuffs and collars.

Lopsang had already secured forty lowland porters— Tamangs—who planned to rendezvous with the group in Betorawati, where the trek would have its official beginning.

The climb team had its own *sirdar*, cook staff, and porters, along with a Nepalese liaison officer, who had to be equipped and paid according to an official scale. A liaison officer was required for all the hundred-odd peaks on the permitted expedition list and essential for climbs along the northern frontier, where clashes had broken out between highland Nepalese and Chinese soldiers.

Matt and Jake went over their supplies checklist while Lopsang led the way to the old city marketplaces along Asan Tole. In stalls along a street where free-lance porters and ricksha drivers congregated, or in shops tucked away in narrow multi-storied buildings, one could have umbrellas repaired or disposable lighters refilled. In the open plaza itself, rice and vegetable sellers squatted by huge scales hung from ancient beams carved with serpents, and Hindu butchers displayed freshly packed blood and millet sausages. Behind smaller scales sat vendors of curry, saffron, cumin, ginger, and chili. Goat heads crowned fly-carpeted posts and bees swarmed the sweets stands.

Matt spotted several trekkers stocking up on peanut butter and native honey; on powdered milk, tinned butter, dry soup mixes, and chocolates. Where four years ago most of the tinned goods were Indian, many were Chinese now, a circumstance that contributed to growing tension between Nepal and its neighbor to the south.

But it was foolish to think of carrying canned food, or meat, or fresh fruit on a trek; and even the costly expeditions ultimately had to settle for *dhalbaht* as the tasteless daily staple—lentils and rice—which, after ten days or so, could seem a tamper-proof combination, resistant to the efforts of even the most creative kitchen crew. Jake had passed on a tempting wholesale offer from an outfitter that specialized in freeze-dried meals after Matt reminded him what it was like to share a tent with the noxious flatulence the meals never failed to generate.

As far as alcohol, Karl Tower had promised to help spread the word around the group that it was every person for him or herself.

Matt had little trouble picking out the tour operators in the bazaar, who could usually be found standing akimbo in the midst of plainly ritualistic bargaining sessions between well-dressed *sirdars* and stubborn merchants hoping for a few extra *paise* per kilo for their green beans.

Jake was adopting that posture now, while Lopsang and Purbu had it out with a one-eyed woman potato vendor. At an adjacent stall, a black-haired European in pleated trousers was arguing—in serviceable Nepali—with a spice merchant over a handful-size pile of pungent chili powder.

Matt edged closer to the argument and caught a phrase or two of muttered Italian. The man's wild gesticulations threatened to loosen the yellow sweater he had tied around his shoulders. The merchant kept shaking his head, growing more and more indignant with each of the Italian's hand motions. Exasperated finally, the Italian cursed and swept the chili from the scale with the edge of his hand. Matt expected to see *khukris* emerge from all quarters, but before a blade could be drawn, the Italian disarmed everyone in the vicinity by hurling enough rupees at the merchant to cover the cost of three times the chili they were arguing over.

Matt might have forgotten the incident entirely had he not run into the Italian again, back in Thamel, where he and Jake were completing the search for overlooked articles. A dozen aluminum ski poles—which made for durable walking sticks—were already leaning against the counter.

"How about seats?" Matt asked. "Were they listed on the personal gear checklist?"

"Seats?" Jake said in what sounded like disbelief. "We billed this as a wilderness trek, not a picnic."

"I'm not talking about deck chairs. But if we're not planning on breaking out the mess tent until base camp, it means everyone sitting wherever they can for the first ten days."

Jake made his lips a thin line and nodded. "Good point."

The small shop was as well stocked in trekking and climbing gear as any outlet in the States, but there was a pawn shop atmosphere to the place, with new and secondhand hiking shoes and backpacks and sleeping bags piled on every available surface. The owner was a stocky Sherpa youth with devilish good looks and a jet-black Fu Manchu mustache.

"What about umbrellas?" Matt said, once they had selected half a dozen portable folding seats.

Jake thought for a moment. "Umbrellas were on the list. But we better grab a couple just in case." Matt and the Sherpa began to rummage around. "What about sneakers for the porters?"

"Taken care of. Lopsang sent them on to Trisuli as part of the initial payment." Matt surfaced with four umbrellas and placed them on the counter alongside the seats. He and Jake stared at one another, thinking through contingency needs. "Pee pots," they said at the same moment.

They settled for an assortment of wide-mouthed plastic containers with screw-top lids. "Now," Jake said, letting out a breath as he regarded the stack of items, "anything else?"

Matt stroked his chin. "I know what I need. Air mattress," he said to the shop owner.

The Sherpa scanned him top to bottom. "Have one your size—ah, too late."

Matt swung around to follow the youth's raised hand

and saw the Italian. He had the rust-colored self-inflating mattress pad in hand and was unrolling it, measuring it against himself for fit. The Italian caught Matt's look and said something to his swarthy companion that set them both laughing.

"Hey, friend," Matt said, with an unplanned curl to his lip, "I don't suppose you'd wanna pass on that thing."

The Italian's smile collapsed. *"Lui e senza cervello,"* he told his friend.

Matt and Jake traded looks. "Something about your brain," Jake ventured.

"What about my brain?" Matt asked the Italian.

The man made a dismissive gesture with his hand and exchanged a few more words with his friend, who quickly reached for a wallet and laid six hundred rupees down on the counter.

"I have another," the Sherpa said, showing Matt a three-quarter length that would just about support him head to knees.

The two Italians laughed. "What doesn't kill you, mayka you strong, yes?" the new owner of the mattress said, offering a pearly-toothed grin Matt was suddenly eager to dismantle. *"Lui e uno scaricatore di porto,"* he added out of the corner of his mouth.

"Hey, Matt," Jake said, seeing murder in his friend's eye, "we'll find you another full-length. No problem."

"Sure, you find another," the Italian said, with another offhand motion. "Iffa not, I sell you this one when we return."

"From where?" Jake asked in a amicable tone.

"Ganesh," the other one said. "Ganesh'imal."

Matt had a dinner date with an ex–Peace Corps friend and Kathmandu expat named Linda. They had both been part of the same 1963 Peru Group–training sessions in New York, where, along with forty others, they were interviewed, profiled, sent into the Bronx to take housing surveys, and encouraged to score in the upper percentile on the Marine Corps Physical Fitness Test.

Linda had been close friends with Susan—black and proud and full of post-Kennedy earnestness—whom Matt would later marry in South America. Linda had re-upped once, then left Peru shortly before Susan's sudden death to embark on what would turn out to be a ten-year global odyssey—a trip that ultimately landed her in Kabul, where she met dashing, romantic Raymond with the mad poet's eyes, who had changed his name to Lucky.

Lucky had taught English in Kyoto and Manila, worked in refugee camps along the Thai border, and trekked in the Himalayas from Khumbu to Dolpo. He and Linda had eventually traveled overland to Kathmandu, where they now lived in a spacious three-story house on a tree-lined street off embassy row, just north of the Royal Palace.

Linda had made it a point to stay in touch with Matt through the years, her letters often trailing him from one place to the next until she had learned simply to forward everything through Puma Tours in Denver. Matt recalled a photo she once sent of herself in long braids, gypsy colors, nose ring, stoned on the steps of Borobadur in Java. But all that was part of a previous incarnation, she stressed over dinner, seemingly apologizing for the big house, the gardens and servants. Even Lucky was Raymond again and looking every bit the part of a successful expat entrepreneur. Still, Linda was the same lovely woman Matt remembered from twenty years ago, dressed in culottes and sandals, doing her best to teach the Andean highlanders about tube wells.

The house smelled of patchouli oil and anise incense. Dinner was mutton kebab, followed by apple pie, during which Matt consumed too many beers. Or so Linda's soft eyes told him in quick questioning glances. They discussed other members of the now widely scattered '63 Peru Group, most of whom, it seemed to Matt, had found their niches.

Linda took Matt's arm as Raymond led him on a tour of the house. He talked about his current project in Kathmandu, which involved training young Nepalese in the curious ways of Western tourists and trekkers.

"Tourism's the only thing Nepal has left," the well-fed American was saying. "Especially now that Tibet's accessible and Kathmandu's being bypassed for the real thing. Not that Lhasa has that much enlightenment to offer, with Chinese soldiers bivouacked on every corner.

The way I see it, China's found a way to conquer Lhasa's monks without lifting a hand against them just by opening up the city to foreigners. I think they used Kathmandu as their template.'' He snorted a wry laugh. ''But I suppose even a taste of Tantric Buddhism's better than the freeze-dried spirituality being peddled in Thamel.''

Raymond showed Matt where he conducted his English classes and explained that he was working on a way to send at least six young Nepalese to the States each year on get-acquainted tours.

To familiarize them with what they were going to be facing there, he'd borrowed a program frequently used in the Cambodian refugee camps and converted the whole of the house's enormous rear porch to a mock-up of a U.S. town, complete with post os ce, grocery store, police station, bus depot, and clinic. Cardboard and papier-mâche models of appropriate foodstugs and items were labeled in Nepali and English, and students were encouraged to act out scenarios involving typical encounters with salespeople, police os cers, what have you.

''I want to raise a whole new crop of *sirdars* who'll be able to anticipate *sahib*'s every wish. 'Cause let's face it, Nepal's going to sink or swim on tourism. And unless they learn to market what they have, the country's going to use itself up.''

That word again, Matt thought: *market*. Linda gave his hand a squeeze while Raymond continued.

''Not to detract from the egorts of the Peace Corps, but what did you people really leave Kathmandu with except a talent for baking pies and shooting heroin or chasing the dragon? Do you know there's afteen thousand heroin addicts in this city alone?''

''No, I didn't know that,'' Matt admitted.

''It's true. And before tourism, the main source of Nepal's income came from pensions for the Gurkhas. So it's no mystery the government charges big for climbing permits.''

''The higher you go, the more you pay,'' Matt contributed.

Raymond dashed him a sardonic grin. ''That's a lesson Nepal learned from the pushers who used to work Freak Street.''

The room fell silent for a moment. Matt could hear bats zipping about in the dark beyond the porch's shutters.

"It used to be that everyone came here in search of transformational experiences. Now everyone's hooked on aerobic spirituality." Raymond waved a hand in what Matt took to be a broad gesture to the mountains. "You've got people trekking, climbing, skiing, kayaking, bicycling, rafting, hang gliding . . . Pretty soon someone's going to start promoting the first wheelchair-accessible trek, or a skateboard tour of Helambu. I know a guy who's out there right now rigging the rhododendrons with these US-surplus infrared detectors and seismic intrusion devices hoping to find himself a yeti."

"Matt knows all about this, Ray," Linda offered, pressing Matt's arm against her ample bosom. "He's been all over the world and has had some really incredible adventures."

Matt tried not to let the wince show as Raymond aimed a tolerant smile his way.

"Yeah, I used to be into that," Raymond said. "But it gets kind of old, doesn't it? Racking up the experiences. I mean, what do you do with it all if you can't transform it into something meaningful? If you can't pass on whatever smattering of wisdom you've been able to glean from all the miles to someone who can use it?"

Raymond and Linda exchanged secret smiles.

"Hey," Matt said, turning out of Linda's arm to take a good look at her. "You're not . . ."

"I am," she said, smiling and lightly touching her abdomen. "Five months. It's a boy and he's going to be a Capricorn. Just like you." Raymond and Linda put their arms around one another.

Matt said, "Yeah? Well, make sure you give him a big backyard to play in so he doesn't decide to wander out of reach."

4

Aerobic Spiritualism

Matt kept staring at the staff cap long after Jake had had his laugh. Robin's-egg blue with a wide white brim, the cap read: "PUMA TOURS: GANESH HIMAL TREK, '86."

"What, d'ya get the idea from those Everest shirts the climbers wear?"

"No," Jake told him. "I've been planning this for a while." He took the cap back to admire it. "I had some made up for ML and Natalie to hand out in Mexico and Peru."

"I hope they don't say 'Ganesh Himal.' "

Jake ignored the sarcasm. "The ones for the Yucatan trip say, "MAYAN MOMENTS.""

"And what about ML's?" Matt wanted to know. "No, don't tell me. They say, 'INCA TRAIL.' "

"Trails," Jake said. " 'INCA TRAILS TO YOU.' "

"What?"

"As in 'happy trails to you.' " Jake tried to sing it.

Matt regarded him blankly. "You know, if we're going to keep this up, I'm gonna recommend we get some professional help with the slogans."

Jake seemed to take it under advisement. "You see why I didn't say anything when you joked about the T-shirt idea."

"I suppose this has to be done, huh?"

"Trust me."

29

"Maybe we should just airdrop leaflets, Jake. Like saturation bombing."

"Hey, if we could afford it, I would."

They were on the Dorje's rear patio, the supply boxes and bags that had crowded their hotel rooms spread out across the patio's terra-cotta brick. The morning was hot and dry, and those group members who weren't off temple-gazing in Bhaktapur were sunning themselves or sitting in the shade, reading.

Audrey Dey was wandering around in the garden with a guidebook in hand, and Constance Battle—much to the amusement of two of the Dorje's chambermaids—was throwing a stick for Karma, the poodle from Manhattan. "Karma's so used to Central Park," she had told Matt. "He doesn't know what to make of all this."

Constance and the dog would only be accompanying the group as far as Thanget. Arrangements had been made for their return to Kathmandu in the company of three porters and a cook who planned to rendezvous with the main group in Syabru Bensi the following week.

Lopsang and Purbu were sorting through the supplies and equipment, including the stateside foodstuffs Jake had been allowed to carry through customs: boxes of cashews, raisins, and Grape Nuts; packages of Slim Jims, NutraSweet Kool-Aid and Wyler's lemonade; jars of instant coffee and Tang; plastic packets of imitation maple syrup.

Purbu was making piles—lentils here, rice there, cooking oil over thataway—while the *sirdar* was weighing already-consolidated piles on a crude scale and assembling fifty-five-pound loads for the porters' wicker baskets.

Matt thought it would be a miracle if they fit it all in the truck he had hired to make the Betorawati run.

In addition to the foodstuffs, there were the tents, the cooking gear, the ground sheets and tarpaulins, all of which had to be meticulously labeled and packaged in marked loads. Matt was busy compiling a master list in Nepali and English, copies of which would go to Jake, Lopsang, and Purbu, so that everyone would know where things were. The *sirdar* had suggested further that the loads be coded to allow each porter to identify his or her individual basketful. It wasn't uncommon to have porters arguing over who was carrying the heaviest burden.

Much of the group's gear was down there as well—packed in duffels—except for clothes needed for the next two days, the items to be left behind for safekeeping in the hotel, and the personal gear everyone would be carrying in day packs: sunhats, toilet paper, extra socks, moleskin, binoculars, cameras, tape players, and the like.

And the booze of course.

Stu Sinotti was angry that Karl Tower was encouraging everyone to "stock up" and told Matt he hoped the drinking would be over and done with by the time the group reached high altitude, where alcohol could have potentially life-threatening dehydrating effects.

"I'm flatly against contaminating the wilderness with civilization's ills," the naturalist had lectured Matt earlier that morning.

On the far side of the patio was an even more mind-boggling array of equipment that comprised the climbing party's gear. Gambu, the Ganesh team's *sirdar*, was working on inventorying everything while he waited for the climbers to return from town with the kitchen staff.

Funding was a major part of any expedition, and much of that came in the way of brand-name gear from outfitters interested in seeing their boots or backpacks, ropes or crampons, make it to the summit with the team members. The photographic evidence from successful ascents was often used in advertising promotion.

And from the looks of things, Matt guessed that every major player in the outfitter market must have wanted in on the expedition funding. One glance revealed half a dozen logos: Kelty, REI, The North Face, Patagonia, Asolo, Lands' End, Moonstone, and Grand Design. It was like attending an industry trade show.

Matt thought about the trash heaps at Everest base camp—the discarded sneakers and boots, the holed sheet plastic, the depleted oxygen bottles, and empty tins—and wondered how much of the women's gear was going to remain in the mountains.

Shirtless, he was contemplating a bottle of Chinese ketchup—"tomoto sause"—when the climbers drove up in their rented Toyota jeep. Stocky Julia Tremont, mountaineer and lecturer, had the wheel, and Barbara Bass was riding shotgun.

Matt watched everyone clamber out—two Sherpas, five women—laughing, having a grand old time. The fifth woman was one of Puma's trekkers. Something Kohl, he remembered, seeing her graze her head on the Jeep's roll bar. She caught his eye, smiled, and headed toward the patio, pushing dark brown hair back from an oval face. Matt hadn't learned what she did for money back home, but guessed by the colors she wore that she was either a fashion designer or an interior decorator.

"We really didn't get a chance to talk the other night," she said, rubbing the top of her head. "I'm Taylor."

"Matt Terry," he said, shaking hands. Taylor's grip was firm; her nails were lacquered, worn at what Matt had once heard described as "active length."

Candice Dekker, in dungaree cutoffs and a body-hugging lavender tank top, was still standing by the jeep, stretching long, muscular arms in the air. Cowgirl Kaylee McMahon, the team's official photographer, was snapping shots of her with a weighty camera.

Karl Tower, reclined with a paperback in a square of dark green lawn, sat up to take notice and flashed Matt a grin from behind his book.

"God, this is all ours, huh?" Taylor was saying, gesturing to the gear. When Matt didn't reply, she turned to follow his gaze, her eyes knowing when she faced him again.

Matt understood the look and snapped out of his reverie. "No, uh, most of it belongs to the climbers. You're from San Francisco, right?"

Taylor nodded. "Is that how you keep us straight—by city of origin?"

"How do you mean?"

"Only that it must be tricky getting to know everyone right off the bat. I have this friend who's a schoolteacher, and she's amazing when it comes to remembering names. Me, I've got to practically write everything down."

Matt shrugged. "It's better if I don't try. Most of it usually ends up in short-term memory anyway."

"Really? So you just let everyone fade away when a trip's over?"

"Not all the time. But there are some people I've spent

an hour with that I remember better than people I've spent ten days with.''

"Yeah, I've had nights like that myself," Taylor said, failing to suppress a laugh.

She had dazzling blue eyes; layers of shiny brown hair. Five-six, he guessed. Slim but very shapely, in a denim skirt, red leather belt, and Hawaiian shirt. And everything about her—even the contagious laugh—seemed oddly familiar to him, almost as though they'd met before. "That's an unusual name you've got."

"I know. My parents named me after a movie star."

"Elizabeth?" Matt ventured.

"No, Robert.''

Matt drew a blank.

"*Quo Vadis, Knights of the Round Table, Ivanhoe* . . . Not exactly a big name anymore." She waited for Matt to say something, but he only nodded. "So," she said, blowing out her breath, "these roads can be a bitch, huh?"

"Depends on who's doing the driving."

Taylor glanced at Julia Tremont. "I'll make a note of that for next time." She paused. "Is the ride to Betorawati going to be as badass as the trip into town?''

"A lot worse," Matt said.

She twisted up her face in a way that made him smile.

"I suppose I should be getting myself in condition for the trek.''

"You could always climb Swayambunath," Matt suggested.

"That's the Monkey Temple, isn't it?"

"Three hundred steps to the top, and a great view when you get there.''

Taylor said something in a language Matt didn't understand. "Is my Nepali that bad?" she added after a moment.

"Say it again."

"Kun bato Swayambunath janccha?''

Matt listened and replied in kind, offering his best impression of a Tamang farmer and motioning with a hand: *"Baata jaane.''*

Taylor looked puzzled. "There from go . . . *That way!''* she exclaimed, with a note of discovery.

"Straight up the road," Matt told her.

"Thanks, Matt." Taylor gave him a sidelong look that might have been flirtatious. She was ten feet away when she turned around. "You think you might want to join me after you get all this stuff sorted out?"

"And this is my husband Maurice," Dee-Dee Delong was telling Matt a few minutes after Taylor left.

"Maury," Delong said, offering a stiff little wave at chin level. He was five-nine or ten, trim, balding on top. His sunglasses and Rolex watch made an interesting match. Dee-Dee was a couple of inches shorter, pretty but large-featured, with slightly crossed eyes. "We weren't going to disturb you," she said, "but we decided if it was all right for Taylor to do it, it was all right for us."

"It's fine," Matt said, reaching for his T-shirt and tugging it over his head. "What's up?"

"Well," they began together. "Go ahead," Dee-Dee said, deferring to Maury. "No, you go ahead," he told her. She patted his arm and looked up at Matt. "Are you familiar with corporate leadership training techniques, Matt?"

"Not really," he admitted. "You mean for executives?"

"Exactly. But you're aware, of course, that the techniques have a rather broad application. Leadership, after all, is just that."

"I'll take your word for it."

"What it comes down to, Matt," Maury took over, "is that we have a rather strong interest in interpersonal relations, and what we'd like to do is to get your views on leadership and group dynamics."

Matt managed a thin smile. "Jake's the one you should be talking to."

Dee-Dee glanced in Jake's direction. "Yes, but Jake's principally a businessman, isn't he? You see, what we're interested in is raw field experience. You have led treks before, haven't you?"

"A few."

"That's what we're after," Maury said, visibly encouraged. "The behavior of individuals in the absence of normal reclusive or seclusive outlets."

"Office environments are one thing," Dee-Dee was

quick to add, "but month-long treks are veritable laboratories for observing human behavior up close. No home to escape to after work; no fitness centers or local bars."

"No churches or synagogues, no weekly visits to the shrink."

Matt looked from face to face. "You'd be surprised how much personal time there is. Remember, we're walking for six or seven hours a day. Besides, we have separate tents."

Dee-Dee nodded, way ahead of him. "Still, you must have witnessed moments of stress, or outright agoraphobic panic."

"How do you deal with someone's sudden urge to go home when you're fifteen days from the nearest village, let alone airport?"

"Ask the climbers," Matt said, gesturing off to his left. "There's your laboratory. Mountaineers stay out for twice as long as we do."

"Too goal-directed," Maury said, after a moment.

"And from what I understand, base camp becomes something of a village. No, Maury's right, there's a mission ethic. We're talking about nonprofessionals under pressure."

Matt rocked his head from side to side. "We're not exactly a representative group. Everyone's fit and well educated."

"True," Maury said. "But so much the better." He regarded Matt askance. "What about you, Matt? You obviously spend an inordinate amount of time out on your own, in Asia or South America or wherever. How do you handle the stress of adapting to new rules of conduct country to country, trip to trip?"

"Maybe we should learn what stress warning signs to watch out for in Matt Terry," Dee-Dee suggested, with a laugh.

Matt was busy formulating an appropriate response when Taylor appeared on the balcony above the patio. "How much longer do you figure, Matt?" she called down from outside the door to her room.

"I'm ready now," he told her. Dee-Dee and Maury were wearing grins when he turned back to them.

"Well," Dee-Dee said, glancing up at Taylor, "at least now we know where to start."

Taylor was breathing hard by the time they reached the two hundredth flagstone step, fanning her face with a bare hand while she leaned back against the stairway's rust-pitted handrail. A couple of rhesus monkeys were scampering about in banyan shade, and a supplicant was ascending the steps, hands and knees wrapped in rags.

Taylor regarded the man mutely for a moment. "I'm being passed by a guy who's crawled here all the way from New Delhi or somewhere," she said at last. "Forget the Ganesh Himal. How am I going to make it out of Kathmandu?" She had changed into shorts and a tank top that read: "THE EXOTIC EROTIC BALL, SAN FRANCISCO."

Stone carvings of animals, the vehicles of the gods, were positioned at intervals along the ascent, their foreheads burnished by thousands of passing hands. Far below them at the base of the stairway, where beggars shuffled about in the dirt and the strewn remains of flower-petal offerings, stood huge columnar prayer wheels and Buddhas statues smeared with vermilion paste.

Taylor wiped sweat from her forehead with the front of her wrist. "So Jake tells me you were in the Peace Corps."

"Take a cleansing breath," Matt said, demonstrating the technique. "Pace is probably the most important thing."

She took his advice. "I kept telling myself I was going to start jogging . . . but before I knew it, the departure date was staring me in the face."

"With all those hills in your hometown you couldn't get in shape?"

She frowned at him. "We've got cars now, or haven't you heard?"

Matt laughed. "Don't worry about it, you'll get in shape on the trail. Besides, physical conditioning is only one part of it. You can build up muscle, break in your shoes, spend a thousand dollars on gear, and still come up against something unexpected. The main thing to remember is that you have to want to be where you are, or

else you're going to churn your feet or stumble. . . ."
He heard himself and let his words trail off.

Taylor was waiting for him to finish. "Zen and the art
of what—trail walking?"

"All I'm saying's that attitude's more important than
anything else. Otherwise we'd be telling our clients to
have their appendixes removed and their teeth capped
before a trek."

She made that funny face again, then gave him a lop-
sided look. "So how about it?"

"How about what?"

"How about, were you in the Peace Corps?"

Matt resettled dark sunglasses on the bridge of his
nose. "A long time ago in Peru."

"And you've been guiding for Puma since then?"

"Since eighty," Matt said.

"It's great, isn't it? Visiting all these exotic places and
getting paid for it."

Matt watched a group of tourists on the steps. "Depends. You meet a lot of people who like to think they're
in Goa or Kathmandu, and all you find are pockets of
Western living." He thought about handing over some
of Raymond's observations about the altered nature of
the quest but thought better of it.

"That *is* what everyone likes to talk about, isn't it.
The growing homogenization. The West's catastrophic
influence on the pure-spirited East."

"What d'you say we complete the journey?" Matt
said, motioning with his chin.

Taylor forced an exhale. "Okay. I'm ready."

The Swayambunath *stupa* took up most of the leveled
hilltop: a white hemispherical mound, topped by a golden
cube adorned with oversize blue-rimmed eyes. From the
cube rose an inverted cone of thirteen gilded rings said
to represent the thirteen degrees of knowledge, the ladder
to nirvana—itself symbolized by the thunderbolt and circular umbrella that crowned the shrine.

Flanked by twin bullet-shaped temples, Swayambunath—a burning lotus plucked from the draining waters of
Kathmandu's ancient lake bed—was one of the subcontinent's most revered monuments. Facing it across a peb-

bled terrace was a monastery, a *gompa*, surrounded by prayer flags fluttering in a warm, late afternoon breeze.

"If you want to hang out for a while, we can listen to the monks chant and blow their trumpets. It's worth checking out."

"Well, when you put it like that," Taylor laughed.

They chose a spot of wall to sit on and pointed out cloud formations and a hundred airborne kites.

The gaze of the almond-shaped eyes that looked out from the *stupa* was usually described as compassionate or omniscient, but Matt always thought it penetrating; somewhat demonic.

"Would you call that sky cerulean?"

Matt beetled his brows. "Blue's what I'd call it."

"I don't see how anyone could get homesick in a place like this." She took a deep, satisfied breath. "You ever get homesick, Matt?"

He wondered whether he should get into it or not. "Sometimes. But I don't feel the pull a lot of travelers talk about." Hearing the lie in his words. "I'm on the road most of the time. I haven't really had a chance to put down roots the last couple of years."

She regarded him, making up her mind about something. "You know, it's some people's notion that humans are genetically predisposed to travel. They say migration's in our blood; that we're all inclined to walkabout. It's the settling down that causes all the problems."

"Maybe. But I think there's also a time to call it quits and leave the hunting to the kids. Anyway, traveling used to be about new experiences; now its how outrageous you can be—the distance you'll go to find the edge."

"Traveler's angst," Taylor said. "I like it."

Matt shrugged.

"No, really. So you do miss home—even as an abstract."

"This is starting to sound like an interview."

Taylor smiled. "I'm sorry. Can't we just call it getting acquainted?"

"Sounds a little formal. But, okay."

She thought for a moment. "So what you're saying is there's perhaps a limit to travel's educational or *transformational* aspects. That it's not always good for us."

"Is that what I'm saying?"

Her eyebrows danced. "Psychologists like to equate wanderlust with unfulfilled sexual longing. What's your response to that?"

Matt turned to look at the *stupa*'s question-mark nose—a representation of the Nepalese number *ek*—one, therefore, unity. Pilgrims were prostrating themselves on the rounded stones of the terrace. "You seem like you've done you're share of traveling," he said. "You tell me."

Taylor smiled broadly, without showing her teeth. "Okay, we'll let that one go. So what would you say was the most adventurous trip you've been on?"

Matt laughed, scratching the side of his head.

"What about Bali?"

He turned to show her a dead-serious look. "What about Bali?"

Taylor seemed confused. "Well, I know about the bus hijacking. Jake told me you were the tour leader."

Matt shook his head in wonder. "What else did Jake tell you?"

"Nothing else. A diplomat was murdered, right?"

"First off," Matt snapped, "the man wasn't a Puma client. Second, there are adventures and there are tragedies—"

Taylor held up a hand, the other digging into her shoulder bag. "Wait a second. Do you mind if I use a tape recorder?"

"Tape recorder?! What the hell's going on?"

Taylor put her lower lip between her teeth. "Didn't Jake explain to you?"

"Explain what, Taylor?"

"Oh, shit, I'm sorry, Matt, I thought he told you." She quickly rezipped the bag. "I'm a writer. I'm on assignment for *Quest* magazine, doing a profile on Candice Dekker. I thought an interview with a professional guide might make a nice adjunct to the article. I asked Jake a few preliminary questions about you. . . . God, I feel so ridiculous! When you said this sounds like an interview . . . Shit." She laughed nervously.

Matt felt the "compassionate one's" eyes studying him, burning right through him.

◙◙ 5 ◙◙

Table Stakes

"**J**ust keep those damn things away from me," Matt told the ear man, loud enough to get a rise out of a pair European hippies seated below him on the temple steps.

In the brick-paved square below, advocates of Kathmandu's three religions—Hinduism, Buddhism, and Tourism—were conspiring to create a scene out of Hieronymus Bosch.

The ear man—a somewhat tall, slender Nepalese with bad skin and black-rimmed eyes—fell back bowing, bony hands held at chin-height in an attitude of prayer. "But Dawa no hurt *sahib*'s ears. Dawa's instruments very clean. Dawa very talented ear cleaner." Again he displayed the thin silver instruments he kept wrapped in red-and-black Nepalese cloth. "Dawa just remove wax buildup so *sahib* can hear songs the mountains sing."

"Wax buildup?" Matt tugged at his ear, scowling. "You think I've got these things lined with linoleum or something?"

Dawa winced but wasn't about to give up. From a filthy nylon day pack he extracted a cheap loose-leaf binder and opened it for Matt's inspection, revealing typed and handwritten letters photo-cornered to each page.

"Letters from *sahib*'s countrymen," Dawa said proudly. "From satisfied customers. Dawa cleans their

40

ears, they write Dawa from U.S.A. Look: Ralph Barnt, Kansas City. Sara Norwood, Eugene, Oregon.'' He turned a page. ''Eileen Dover, Kenosha, Wisconsin . . .''

''Eileen Dover,'' Matt muttered, shaking his head at the pun. He glanced at one of the letters. Were the authors customers or patients? He wasn't sure what to call them; any more than he was sure exactly what it was Dawa *did* with his gleaming tools. He only knew that he didn't want anyone with sharpened picks anywhere near his eardrums.

Look what damage Taylor Kohl had accomplished with far blunter instruments.

Durbar Square meant ''palace'' square, and nearly all the cities in the vale had one. Kathmandu's was a medley of pagoda-style temples, upward of fifty by count, dominated by the Taleju, within which resided the titulary divinity of the royal family. The only other structure of note was the Narayan, whose five-tiered plinth provided a display stand for vegetable and curio vendors, and a resting place for tourists.

Long before the ear man, Matt had been approached by astrologers, palmists, money changers, and kids in Hong Kong polyesters and knockoff Walkmans proffering hash oil, mescaline, cocaine, and heroin.

''Paper, *sahib*?'' asked a kid in dark glasses, showing Matt a smudged edition of *The Rising Nepal*, Kathmandu's English language daily.

Matt took a copy and fanned the flies away from his face while Dawa moved off.

A procession of saffron-robed monks had brought ricksha, bicycle, and tractor traffic to a halt in the square, where a cop on a stone pedestal was aiming frantic hand gestures at anyone willing to look his way. A sound of brass bells momentarily penetrated Durbar's midday cacophony of horns and hawking voices, reaching Matt in the same way a whiff of incense would occasionally infiltrate the dust and diesel smoke to remind him where he was.

A few of Puma's trekkers were meandering about, perusing blanket spreads of inexpensive souvenirs: bamboo pipes, prayer scrolls, rice-paper calendars, charm boxes, and tea bowls. The group had an hour more here before

Matt was supposed to take them to the Tibetan refugee camp across the river, where still other souvenirs were available. He planned to have the tour bus swing by Norbu's shop in Thamel by way of saying thanks for the crate of Bordeaux—and for the three bottles of Heinz ketchup Matt had only that morning procured for the trek.

Jake had explained about Taylor Kohl over dinner the previous night.

"Of course I told her to clear it with you first," he said in defense of his actions. *"And as far as Bali goes, she read the article that movie producer wrote for* The New York Times. *I only told her you'd been the tour leader on that trip . . ."*

"Yeah, but what does she want me to talk about?" Matt asked, not really expecting an answer.

"What you do," Jake said, *"your job with Puma. You don't have to narrow it down to Bali or anywhere. Who knows, maybe you'll start to remember why you've stuck with this job for the past eight years? The point is, it could be a way to market yourself. And if* Quest *picks up the piece, it'll mean terrific publicity."*

Matt realized that Jake probably had his best interests in mind, but the idea of being interviewed, made the focal point of some magazine article . . . If anything it seemed a stumbling block to defining who he was and what he wanted for the near future. Once before, in Guatemala, someone had offered him a shot at fifteen-minute fame, and he was no more comfortable with the idea now than he had been then.

And while it was true that the bus hijacking and the murder on Bali had made several prominent newspapers and magazines, there were things even Jake didn't know about the incident. About the involvement of French intelligence operatives, for one, and the link between the murder and the subsequent sinking of the Greenpeace ship, *Rainbow Warrior*.

Later—in the jungles of Sulawesi, Irian Jaya, and Borneo—Matt felt safely distanced from repercussions or reprisals, real or imagined. But a lingering sense of paranoia had accompanied him back out into the open.

What if Taylor Kohl wasn't who she claimed to be—a travel writer who'd sold articles on the Seychelles, the

Maldives, Bali, and Malta to *Outside* and *Condé Nast* and *Adventure Travel*? And what about the European tour leader he'd had the run-in with in Thamel? Matt had begun to ask himself. Maybe he'd been speaking *French* after all. Wasn't it a fact anyway that all Europeans spoke the languages of their neighbors?

And all these *eyes* in town, Matt thought. It took Karl Tower's voice to bring him back to reality.

"Matt Terry," the Texan repeated, edging through the crowd seated on the Narayan's uppermost tier, the big grin in place, a " 'scuse me, darlin' " for the handsomer women travelers. Tower's long red-brown hair was ponytailed, and the size thirteen cowboy boots had been replaced by high-tech hiking shoes with green logo patches glued over the ankles. "So what's shakin', amigo?" he asked, sitting down alongside Matt on the cool stone. He held a thin paper-wrapped package in one hand.

"Not much, Karl. What's inside the newspaper?"

Karl unfolded the paper and showed him an ornate *khukri*, the traditional curved-blade knife favored by Nepal's highlanders and Gurkha soldiers. "Hey, Bessman!" he shouted, spotting the physician wending his way through the vendors' spreads below. "What d'you pay for that thing?!"

Buzz held up a *khukri* similar to the one Karl had purchased and yelled up a price. Morgan, in raspberry-colored spandex bicycling shorts, patted her husband on the back, showing a strained smile. "He's working on a merit badge, too!" she called up to them.

A short distance away, Travis Dey, the software designer, displayed yet another knife, naming a lower price, with Audrey singing his praises. Karl then flourished his own knife and announced the lowest price of the three. "You people just don't know how to bargain!" he said.

The Bessmans and Deys laughed and waved goodbye.

"Fuckin' Bessman," Karl said, chuckling. "Man's got a regular pharmacy with him. Drugs and pills for you name it."

"We count on physicians traveling that way," Matt admitted. "Especially on treks."

Karl's large head nodded. "You notice how chummy those four are becomin'? What's your bet some swappin' goes down before this trip's through?"

Matt relocated the foursome in the crowd. Morgan was in fact walking with Travis. Audrey and Buzz were side by side at the base of the temple picking through a selection of mirrored shoulder bags.

"Saw you makin' off with Taylor yesterday," Karl said. "She's a pretty one, isn't she?"

Matt recalled the faces Taylor made and laughed in spite of himself. "Yeah, she is."

"How often you get yourself laid on these jaunts, Matt?" The Texan faced him with a roguish grin, thick forearms resting on his knees.

Matt cocked his head around. "What are you doing on this trip, Karl? You don't strike me as somebody who needs a thirty-day dose of wilderness."

Karl fell silent for a moment, then said, "True enough, Matt, I'm not exactly your back-to-nature type." He took a breath. "Fact is, my marriage went belly-up 'bout six months back. I saw Puma's ad for the trek in some magazine I picked up in the doctor's office or somewhere and figured what the hell. Thirty days of walkin' in the mountains, sure thing. Money wasn't a problem, never has been really. And I was missin' my wife so much I didn't know just what it was gonna take to turn me around."

Matt saw the hurt surface again in Karl's eyes. "But have you ever done anything like this before? I mean, you look fit enough, but it takes more than that to guarantee a good trip."

"I used to hunt a lot. I figure I can take the isolation. 'Sides, looks like we got the makin's of a good little team. I just hope I don't bore everybody with my moanin'. Sometimes I can't get her off my mind."

Matt wondered how much of the story he was going to have to endure over the course of thirty days. "Ever been up to seventeen thousand feet before?"

Karl grinned. "No way. I did a little skiin' in the Alps years back, but not much since. But don't read me wrong, Matt. I'm just lookin' to get away for a while and have some fun while I'm at it." He clamped a hand down on Matt's knee. "And speakin' a which, some of the gals

are plannin' on goin' over to the casino tonight. Ask'd if
I wanted to tag along.''

"Do it," Matt told him. "You'll get a kick out of the
place.''

"Yeah, sure, but I thought maybe you'd join us. You
know," he winked, "we might wanna try our luck.''

The Soaltee-Oberoi, which housed the Casino Nepal,
was an enormous brick rectangle constructed on a slight
rise just west of the city. The game room itself took up
a sizable portion of the hotel's ground floor and was
posted for foreigners only. The clientele was mainly Indians and their wives, who made sometimes weekly trips
from New Delhi and Calcutta to risk small fortunes at
roulette, baccarat, and wheels of chance. Karl took one
look at all the turbans, veils, and *tika* dots, and said,
"Shit, damned place reminds me of Vegas.''

They'd ridden up together in the climbers' rented jeep,
Jake, Taylor, and a few of the others following in a taxi.
Matt had hoped for a backseat position with Candice
Dekker, but found himself in the shotgun seat instead,
pressed against the passenger side door with an arm
draped around fifty-two-year-old Barbara Bass. Julia Tremont asked from the wheel if he was interested in driving
out to Vajra Yogini the following day while the group
was off on it's Royal Nepal mountain flyby. Matt said,
sure, why not, and asked if there was room for Jake, who
had wanted to visit the mountain shrine for some time.
Barbara suggested that the four of them leave around
"tenish.''

"You think they know what poker is around here?''
Karl was asking now, hands on hips as he scanned the
game room's crowded tables.

"I doubt it," Matt said.

"And I'll bet they play that damn French twenty-one.''

"Baccarat, right? Or is it chemin de fer?''

Karl regarded him with a twisted look, one boot tapping the carpeted floor. "Whatever it's called. One of
them freakin' James Bond games.''

Matt looked around for the bar or a cocktail waitress
and said, "So where's that leave us?''

The Texan shrugged. "Roulette, I guess.''

They split up to search for a decent table. Matt nego-
tiated a crowd of sullen Indians and laughing American
tourists and found a centrally located table with a few
empty seats. He waved for Karl, who joined him after a
moment with two drinks in hand. But by the time they
arrived back at the table, the Italians had already moved
in.

"Unbelievable," Matt said, indicating a fine-featured
man in the seat nearest the wheel. "First this dude aces
me out of a Thermarest mattress, now he gets our table."

"This one?" Karl said, pointing. "No sweat, I speak
eye-tie." He went over to the table and said, "*In culo
alla balena!* Up the ass of the whale," he told Matt while
the Italians were laughing.

Several people, including the tour leader, waved Matt
over. At least it was confirmed Italian, he thought, re-
assured.

"I got you fifty dollars' worth to start," Karl announced, as Matt bellied up to the table.

"Fifty?" Matt said too loudly. "Jesus, Karl, I don't
want to risk even *half* that much."

Karl was already laying down dollar chips across the
board. "Suit yourself, amigo. But you gotta play to win,
you know."

The tour leader watched Matt deliberate and finally
place a single chip on the eight-ten split. He commented
in Italian to Karl, who said, "You think so, huh? All
right, *paisane*, we'll just see about that."

Matt watched Karl cover an already top-heavy seventeen with a small stack of chips, straight up and on all
four corners. "What'd he say?"

Karl exchanged looks with the Italian. "Sez it's going
to come up seventeen. If it doesn't, he buys us drinks."

Matt narrowed his eyes and tripled his bet on the eight-
ten split before the croupier called an end to the betting.

"*Tornatene dalla mammina!*" the Italian laughed.

The white ball took a series of hops and landed in
seventeen's cup. The table cheered, and Karl reached
over to slap the Italian a high-five. Together, the two of
them spread an easy seventy dollars in chips around the
board, covering four-way corners, colors, and groups of
twelve. Matt stuck to the eight-ten split and lost again.

And again, on the next three spins of the wheel.

"Jus' not your night," Karl said, arranging his winnings into tall columns.

"Don't worry," the Italian said to Matt. "In the Ganesh, there's no casino." He explained to the table while Matt filled Karl in.

"You mean they're goin' to the Ganesh, too?" the Texan said, cowboying it up for the European players. "Well if that don't beat all. How'd they get permission?"

"Political pull," Matt said, guessing.

Karl was still shaking hands and rubbing cheeks with everyone when Matt slipped away, clutching the twenty dollars he had remaining. He was ready to let the Thermarest incident slide—even the market encounter, which was really none of his affair to begin with—but Karl didn't appreciate what it could mean to have another trekking party headed for the Ganesh. Between Puma's and the climb-team's porters, the trails were going to be crowded enough; and the addition of yet another group would mean precious little space for lunch stops and overnight camps.

Matt spotted Jake and Taylor standing by one of the baccarat tables and made his way over to them. The four climbers were seated around the table, but Julia Tremont and Candice Dekker were the ones playing. Julia had the shoe. The others at the table, including three well-heeled Indians and their silent, sari-ed wives, were observing the action with intense interest and placing heavy side bets with the bank—Julia in this case: the dealer.

"What's going on?" Matt asked.

"Grudge match," Taylor said, without taking her eyes from the table.

Matt saw that Julia's chips outnumbered Dekker's by five to one. "Seriously?"

She showed him a smile. "No, if course not. It's all in fun. But Candice is on a real losing streak for the players. Hey," she added, "are we still friends?"

"We never weren't," Matt said.

"Then you'll do the interview?"

Matt rocked his head. "I've got thirty days to think about it, don't I?"

Taylor laughed. "That's right. Only I hope you decide before then."

Matt said he couldn't promise anything and began to edge toward Candice's chair as the table applauded Julia's winning hand of eight. Kaylee McMahon was seated beside Dekker, whispering in her ear. A moment later it was plain that Candice and Kaylee meant to risk all their remaining chips on one last hand. Matt calculated the amount at eighty dollars; but something more important than money seemed to be at stake. Barbara Bass, the three Indians, and an Italian bet with the bank. The Indian wearing the largest ruby had more than five hundred dollars down on Julia's hand.

Julia dealt four cards from the shoe, and the table waited.

Candice stood on seven. Julia showed two picture cards and drew a nine.

Kaylee cursed while the bank was raking in its meager winnings and paying everyone else off.

"We can't all land the cover of *Mountaineer*," Julia said in a breathy tone, "but I guess some of us just know how to play the odds." She spread her hands over her stacks of chips, and the table applauded.

Candice returned a tight smile. "Oh, then it *wasn't* just luck and a Sherpa carrying an oxygen bottle that got you to the summit of Annapurna One."

Julia mustered a tolerant smile. "No, dear," she said after some of the sudden color left her face. "It wasn't just luck. Luck is being born with perfect teeth."

"That bitch," Matt heard Kaylee say in her partner's ear while the table laughed.

6

Le Sportif

Matt gripped the passenger-door armrest as Julia leaned on the horn and hurled the Toyota jeep around a horse-drawn cart filled with brass pots. The cart driver yelled something unintelligible and the approaching truck returned a deafening horn blast as the jeep shot past it on the narrow road. In the backseat, Jake—with one hand white-knuckled on the roll bar—was apologizing to Barbara for having fallen into her lap.

"Maybe Julia's just trying to bring us together!" Barbara said, loud enough to be heard in the front seat.

"Grab what you can, Barbara!" Julia shouted back, eyeing her friend in the rearview mirror. "We've got two months of Sherpas ahead of us!" She threw Matt a wink, tossing her auburn hair in the wind.

They were a few miles past the Bodhnath *stupa* on the road to Sankhu, a village in the hills northeast of Kathmandu. The final destination was the shrine of Vajra Yogini, perched on a hillside above the village; although Matt had begun to wonder whether they were even going to make it across the Bagmati in one piece. He understood now why Taylor had complained of a sore back after a few days of hard driving with Julia at the wheel. Things hadn't been too hairy on the Chinese and Japanese-built roads that ringed Kathmandu proper, but out here in the country at speeds in excess of forty-five

49

miles per hour each and every horse-drawn cart and pothole was a potential accident.

"You know, we're not on a first ascent, Julia!" Barbara added after a stretch of especially uneven road. She leaned forward to tap Matt on the shoulder. "She's legendary for this kind of craziness. It's just the way she takes a mountain: full-speed ahead. Siege tactics. Right, Julia?"

"I take everything that way!" Julia said, nailing Matt with that look again. He thought about fixed ropes and tried to imagine what she was like in bed. At the same time he wanted to turn around and take a reading of Jake's face; more so when the toe of Jake's running shoe commenced tapping out a meaningful signal on the door side of the passenger seat.

Matt felt Julia's deep-set eyes roving over him. Earlier on he turned to confront her, and she had held his gaze until something forced her attention back to the road.

The Puma group was on a Royal Nepal turboprop, which, given the clarity of the day, Matt thought might fly. If so, everyone would have a chance at viewing the Himalayas close up—at a distance of fourteen miles from an altitude of twenty thousand feet *while comfortably seated on board this pressurized aircraft*, as the airline brochure put it. Matt recalled the one successful flight he'd taken several years back, the nose and wingtips of the plane smeared in goat's blood after a sacrificial ceremony.

He experienced a moment of vivid recollection and closed his eyes, resting his head against the seat back to drink in a memory of argent snowfields, ice-blue glacial pores, cliff faces of metallic splendor.

His hands-on experience with mountains and mountaineers was limited to the few ascents he had participated in in Patagonia and the Andes north of Lake Titicaca. The team breakdowns that characterized those climbs had turned him off to group travel and kept him from accepting Jake's initial offers to join Puma Tours as a trip leader. He continued, nevertheless, to follow the exploits of mountaineers and was never less than amazed by the challenges they undertook, not only on the icy heights but in the realm of what Dee-Dee and

Maurice Delong would have termed interpersonal dynamics. But nature climbers seemed to be self-absorbed, competitive loners, who were forced to deal with others just like themselves to support their ambitions. In a sense they were no different from actors or a certain type of musician, but artists usually weren't sacrificing fingers, toes, or lives for their art. Death seemed to stalk these people, and it was no wonder readers devoured accounts of tragic expeditions with the same appetite they demonstrated for soap operas. One tended to become more fascinated with the human drama than the technical feats themselves. Climbs could almost be seen as war stories without enemies, in that the raw extremes of human behavior were continually surfacing. But that was adventure by definition, Matt supposed. He had decided, though, that should a climb opportunity ever present itself again, he would want to drop acid with his teammates *beforehand* to get all the bad stuff over with. . . . The Toyota tore across the Bagmati River, skirting a patch of dwindling hardwood forest as it began a climb into the hills. Houses in various stages of construction dotted the roadside, on-site molded bricks drying in the sun, men and women atop hand-hewn beams, at work with ancient hand tools. Kathmandu was spread out behind them, a honeycomb of tile roofs and obtuse streets against the verdant backdrop of the Mahabharat range.

The road followed the contours of undulating terrain—twisting in and out of drainages cut by streams that fed the Manohara River. At Sanku, a dusty little village that lay along the old trading route that once linked Kathmandu and Lhasa, they parked the Jeep in a secluded spot and commenced a steep uphill climb through dark conifers to the hidden shrine. Black-eyed children appeared from the woods, laughing at Julia's antics and marveling at Matt's seemingly absurd height.

Julia and Matt fell in side by side on the stone-paved path; she said she hoped they would have a chance to get to know one another on the trek, and he said he hoped for the same. He admitted to himself that her assertiveness and intelligence had put him off initially. But hell, most of the women he knew were far more educated than he was; and besides, he found her attractive and exciting company.

No one had made much of the incident in the casino. As Taylor suggested, the card game was all in fun, and as for the comments, well, that was the way Julia and Candice related to each other. Sure there was competition, but beneath it all the team was a tight-knit group, dedicated to advancing the women's movement in mountaineering and summiting an American woman on Everest in '87.

Up top, Jake and Barbara took wide-angle shots of the *stupas*, the directional Buddhas, the triple-roofed central temple, while Julia read aloud from a dog-eared guidebook. Vajra's Yogini's resident tantric deity was said to have been the one who persuaded Manjushri to drain the waters of the vale's primeval lake. There was a depiction of the goddess inside the main temple, flanked by two of her cohorts: Simhini the Lion Son and Byaghrini the Tigress daughter.

Matt fished in his pocket for the crisp good-luck dollar bill Brie had sent him from New York to deposit in a Nepalese temple before he set off on the trek. They had come close to being more than lovers on Bali, but careers and miles had come between them since. Her most recent letter—the one the dollar had arrived in—contained news of her not-so-sudden engagement to an advertising exec. Matt had grown wistful over it, kicking himself around some until he finally caught sight of himself. The choice had been there, and he'd passed on it.

Julia yelled "Lunch," and the four of them sat on stones and picked at chicken sandwiches assembled by the Dorje staff. For the first time Matt found himself actually looking forward to the trek.

Back at the Toyota an hour later Julia asked if anyone else wanted to drive. Matt considered making a grab for the keys, but held back when Jake said, "No, you drive. You got us up here all right."

"In record time, anyway," Barbara laughed.

"Records are what it's all about, Barb," Julia said, positioning herself at the wheel. "Meant to be broken."

She put on an exit show for the village kids, raising a cloud of dust as she powered the jeep through the gears and raced into the first of a series of sweeping, downhill curves. Matt thought he was imagining things when he heard her say they'd lost the brakes.

"What?"

Julia's foot pumped the brake pedal to no effect. "There's no brakes! Nothing!"

Matt saw her hand go for the ignition key and shouted, "No! You'll lose the power steering!"

They were screeching into the turn at close to fifty when Julia downshifted to second, nearly catapulting her three passengers out the open top. Barbara groaned as her head hit the roll bar, and Julia quickly upshifted to third, hugging the vertical wall at the inside of the curve and throwing everyone back into their seats.

Matt looked up to see them headed straight for a barbed-wire fence someone had thought to string along the shoulder—*to deter people from walking too close to the goddamned edge!* he had time to imagine.

Julia cut the wheel sharply right and the jeep's rear end drifted toward the drop-off. She overcorrected and sent them fishtailing down the road, right rear wheel slamming against a vertical wall of dirt and rock debris.

They were careening down into one of the drainages now, aimed for a narrow bridge across a waterfall and the serious hairpin turn beyond it. Matt thought they might have stood a chance if it wasn't for the procession. Perhaps forty people in all. Bearing a littered effigy of what was most likely Vajra's Yogini's tantric temptress. And they were smack in the middle of the bridge with nowhere to run.

"Downshift!" Matt and Jake screamed in unison. Which Julia did with a grinding of gears and a wail of protest from the Toyota's four-cylinder engine.

Matt squeezed his eyes closed as they plowed into the line. He heard the litter topple, he heard the panicked screams, the Nepalese invectives and imprecations; in short, he heard every sound but the one he feared: the unmistakable *whump!* of body contact. He spun around in his seat in time to see the final processioner spinning like a top, sari unwinding from the speed and proximity of the jeep's passing.

Julia's hands were welded to the wheel as the Toyota

left the bridge behind and bulleted toward the downhill hairpin. She had sense enough not to try for it.

Instead, they bounded off the road up onto a steep grassy hillside that popcorned everyone around in their seats but halved the jeep's velocity. *We'll make a jump for it at the crest,* Matt thought. Let the cursed Jeep reverse itself down into the river gorge for all he cared.

But Julia's instincts had another idea. And rather than allow the jeep to bleed its speed on the uphill incline, she twisted the wheel around to the left and sent them bouncing back downhill, aimed for the road once more with regained momentum.

This time the procession was ready for them. The Nepalese had double-timed it off the bridge and scrambled up into thick foliage above the roadbed, bringing the littered image with them. They pelted the jeep with everything handy—fruit, rice, small stones, pieces of wood. The young kids among the group were cheering and applauding wildly as the Toyota recrossed the bridge and flew into the uphill curve.

With a loud *splat!*, Julia caught something firm on the left side of her face and lost control of the wheel. The jeep veered into the embankment, tipped precariously to one side, and ground to a halt; only to topple then through a slow roll that landed it back in the middle of the road, bruised but upright.

Matt took a quick inventory of himself and craned his neck to see how everyone had fared. Jake and Barbara were unscathed; but Julia Tremont's right arm was bent at a most peculiar angle.

He had the presence of mind to realize he'd forgotten to leave Brie's lucky dollar up top.

"By the time we got a couple of rocks wedged under the wheels, the Nepalese were all over us waving fists in our faces. Somehow Jake made them understand we weren't a bunch of stunt drivers or drunk Japanese and that we'd had an accident."

Matt paused to fork a final piece of chocolate-cream pie into his mouth, trying hard to ignore the stiffness in his neck and lower back. "Julia showed them her arm and someone ran up to Sankhu to get help. Ten minutes later a couple of Germans showed up in a rental and we brought her over to the hospital.'' He fingertipped pie-crust crumbs from the plastic plate. ''You probably know more about the rest of it than I do.''

It was the morning after the accident, the day before the trek was to commence, and he and Taylor were in a Freak Street hangout called Custard's Last Stand—a combination pie shop, used bookstore, and curio bazaar, filled with odds and ends of satin, velvet, and silk. Those few hippies present were Nepalese.

Taylor continued writing for a moment, then jabbed a pen-tip period into her notebook page and leaned back from the table. She halved a hunk of lemon pie with her fork, but let it lie. ''Incredible,'' she said after a moment. ''You're all lucky to be alive.''

Matt gave a tight-lipped nod. ''So there's the companion piece to your story on Candice Dekker, huh?''

''I guess,'' Taylor said. ''You know, it's amazing: you start out writing one thing and you end up writing a different story entirely.''

''How's Julia doing?'' Matt asked.

Taylor blew out her breath. ''Well, of course she's upset about having to pull out of the expedition. But I think she's anxious to get back to the States and have her arm looked at by a specialist.''

''She can still lecture at least.''

Taylor made a face. ''How long do you think that'll last without new climbs under her belt.''

Matt shrugged. ''She's tough, she'll bounce back. Besides, Everest's the major climb and that's still what, a year or so off?''

''Just about. The thing is, Matt, the more ascents she participates in between now and then, the better her chance at a place on the Everest team. Ten American women have already failed in twelve separate summit attempts.''

Matt conceded the point. ''Sure you don't want that pie? Last chance till next month for lemon pie.''

Taylor took a small forkful and pushed the dish aside. ''Not a very auspicious beginning for our trek, is it?''

Matt was prepared for it. He tried for an even tone as he said, ''The accident had nothing to do with our group. You guys got to see the Himalayas, didn't you?''

"That's true," Taylor said. "But just how many accidents does this make for you? Have you been involved in plane crashes and ferry collisions, too?"

"Neither."

"How about avalanches?"

"One or two."

"Earthquakes?"

"A couple."

"Volcanic eruptions?"

"What's your point, Taylor?"

She smiled, holding back a laugh. "I'm just trying to calculate how many lives you've already used up."

Later that same day, Matt met with Jake for a drink at the Dorje's rooftop bar. Jake wore visible evidence of the accident in the form of a gauze patch on his chin and several black-and-blue fingers. Matt heard that Barbara Bass was similarly ornamented, but he hadn't seen her since the hospital.

He thought the accident might cripple the climbers' plans for the Pabil ascent, but Barbara had apparently placed a few calls to the States and interested a fellow woman mountaineer in assuming Julia's place on the team. Jake reported now that the woman had promised to try her damnedest to put a last-minute trip together. But if that didn't happen, the trio was prepared to go it alone.

"They are one hard-core group," Matt said.

Jake raised a Star beer to it. "Listen, Matt," he said, setting the bottle down in a determined gesture. "I was thinking about what you said about being jinxed and—"

"Hold on, Jake," Matt said, showing a hand. "I didn't rent the jeep. I didn't even have the goddamned wheel!"

Jake laughed. "That's exactly what I was going to say: that it should ease your mind some to know this one had nothing to do with you."

Matt studied a small puddle of beer on the bar and looked up laughing. "I'm starting to worry myself. You think Doc Bessman's carrying anything for paranoia?"

Jake said, "Matter of fact, Lopsang talked to a guy at the car rental company and they're claiming the accident was entirely Julia's fault. They're saying it was her driving. They maintain the brakes were just overhauled last week."

Matt dismissed it. "They're only saying that to milk what they can from Julia. It's like if we hit a yak: even if it wasn't our fault, we'd still have to pay for it."

Jake shrugged. "Maybe. But they've got repairmen ready to swear the brakes were tampered with."

Matt fell silent, allowing a sudden wave of apprehension and dizziness to wash through him. *It's not about me,* he told himself. *It had nothing to do with me—*

"Barbara's mad as hell about it," Jake continued.

But if it wasn't about him . . . "Jake," Matt managed after a moment. "What's Dekker's reaction to all this?"

"Candice? I don't know. Why?"

"I mean, where was she while we were out at Vajra Yogini? She didn't go on the flyby, did she?"

"I think she was here taking care of business with the liaison officer."

"But you don't know that for sure."

"No, I don't know that for sure," Jake said. "Why, what are you getting at?"

Matt wet his lips. "Remember that little showdown in the casino?"

"What showdown?"

"At the baccarat table."

Jake's freckled brow creased before he frowned in sudden realization. "You're not serious."

Matt's look was. "Why would the rental company say the brakes were tampered with?"

"You just said yourself they were looking for extra money."

"Yeah, but why not just say that Julia was driving too fast? Or that she'd burned out the brakes by riding the pedal? Why the hell would someone who rents a vehicle *tamper* with the brakes, Jake?" Matt heard the strident tone in his voice and reached for his beer.

Jake regarded him for a long moment. "You know, you have let yourself get addicted to trouble. Accidents *can* happen, Matt." He drew out the silence. "Look, three days from now we'll be thirty miles from here and this whole thing'll be forgotten."

"You think so, huh?" Matt said sullenly.

Jake closed a hand on Matt's shoulder. "I want your word on it."

7

Working Stiffs

Leeches

Stu Sinotti had asked them to burn their toilet paper; but Matt realized he had left his propane lighter back in his pack, which was resting trailside just now, at the outskirts of the village. Ecotourism. Leaving no trace.

Hitching up his fatigues, he decided that burying the paper would have to suffice. Besides, it would give him a chance to throw some soil on the leeches closing on his boot tips—slender hunchbacked tubes inching themselves over the edge of an irrigation ditch in a field of millet, homing in on human scent.

He figured everyone in the group was wearing a couple of the damn things by now. They weren't as plentiful in October as they were during the summer monsoon, but there were still more than enough to go around. They'd drop from the trees and the giant rhododendrons and work their way down your shirt, or hitch a ride on your hiking shoes and worm into your socks. It was one of the things everyone loathed about lowland trekking; right up there on the list with the stifling heat, the intense sun, the flies, and the choking dust.

Matt had worn his pants tucked into his socks for the whole of the afternoon's uphill trudge from the Trisuli River; but he ventured he had at least one leech in each shoe, possibly more. Just to be certain, though, he untucked his pants and plucked a small worm from the ground, placing it under the lip of his sock shortly before he regained the trail.

The group's faster walkers had already arrived, along with Purbu and the kitchen staff, who were off negotiating with the village elders for an overnight campsite. Jake and Lopsang had opted to walk rear guard that day to keep the stragglers moving. The climbers were still on the trail as well, burdened with gear, easing into their adventure.

Matt waited for an appropriate moment to discover the leech on his ankle. The black bloodsucker had only a moment to drink and the bite was a small one. "You better check yourselves," he said, going down on one knee to rid himself of the thing. "Just pull them off. Don't worry about leaving their heads behind. Dust them with salt if you don't want to touch them."

"Please *don't* use matches or lighters," Sinotti was quick to add.

"Unless you're into a Gordon Liddy trip," Doug Makey suggested, with a self-amused laugh.

Morgan Bessman made a disgruntled sound as she pried two bloated tubes from the back of million-dollar legs. "The great outdoors," she said in plain disgust. Matt was getting used to her bitching. She and Karl and Sinotti were carrying ski poles and wearing deep-pocketed hiking shorts and Puma Tours expedition caps.

The group's teenager eyed the blood smears on Morgan's calves and said, "Gnarly." His name was Chris, although he went by the name of Curls. He was fourteen, an avid surfer, seemingly at ease in the outdoors even without an ocean to challenge.

"The neologism for gross," Doug thought to explain, with a restraining hand on his son's shoulder. Doug was a private, self-described "government consultant" from LA, and something of a mystery. His broad forehead and prominent nose were sunburned, and he had a thing about shaving twice a day. The first day out, towheaded Chris told Matt that he and his dad had always gotten along well, even if Doug was something of a "buzz crusher."

Doc Bessman and Travis Dey were leech-free, having anointed themselves with Dibutyl Phthalate during the lunch stop. Buzz was short and powerfully built, even-tempered, and jovial. Travis—shirtless just now—was confrontational and heavy into uphill contests on the trail.

Constance Battle, in a long skirt and an "I-Love-New York" T-shirt, began a careful inspection of a desperately panting Karma. The dog was no longer the white, frolicking poodle he had been in Kathmandu, fetching sticks for the Dorje staff. Even at the group's departure, the chambermaids were still grappling with the notion of a dog with a trans-Pacific airline ticket and a frequent-flyer coupon.

Constance and Karma shared a roomy REI tent; but the poodle had spent most of the previous night barking, and several members of the group had voiced their complaints to Jake. No one had approached Constance directly; only four days out of Kathmandu and nobody wanted to come off as a party pooper—a buzz crusher. It took at least ten trail days before people began to reveal their secret identities.

"There's no need to treat the bites unless they show signs of infection," Sinotti was saying, taking obvious delight in scrutinizing Morgan's tanned legs.

The first of the porters were now arriving, dropping their loads and chattering among themselves. They were barefoot Tamangs from the hill villages of the Trisuli drainage. The name meant "horse trader" in Tibetan, and while the majority were Lama Buddhists, a few were followers of a more ancient, animistic religion known as B'on. The men had strong but spindly legs, and were dressed in filthy shorts and tattered T-shirts. The women were moon-faced—rosy-cheeked from exertion—and wore homespun skirts and blouses. They braided flowers into their long black hair, adorned themselves with brass earrings and nose-disks, and were prone to coy giggles whenever a *sahib* glanced their way.

They hauled their loads in tump-lined and shoulder-strapped wicker baskets, although a few old-timers favored roping the supply boxes directly to their hardened backs. Their personal gear—which seemed to include little more than towels and small blankets—was stuffed into plastic bags.

Matt had struck up a trek friendship with several of the professionals—eager, affiable men with rakish smiles and names like Pirim, Danbahadur, and Ram Tarang. He liked to watch them walk and tried to emulate their almost meditative pace; it was rare to see any of them churn or scuff the ground, or slam their toes into the exposed tips of trail stones.

The only problem Matt had with them was that they insisted on antagonizing Karma. One—his name was Tulo—was a regular trickster about it, joking with Matt that the porters were planning on dicing up the poodle for *mo-mos*—Tibetan meat-filled raviolis. Matt had warned him to keep the joke to himself. Constance and Karma had only a few more days with the group before their turnaround point in Thanget.

Matt rid himself of three more leeches and was helping lay out the group's duffel bags when Purbu reported that the schoolyard was theirs to use for the night—just as soon as the villagers could gather up their drying grain. Matt suggested tent sites and waited until the selections had been made before choosing spots for himself and Jake.

He tuned into scraps of conversation while he unpacked, taking note of comments and complaints. Save for the inevitable sunburn, intestinal distress, blisters, and downhill knees, the group was holding up well. Everyone was reasonably fit and convivial—Maurice and Dee-Dee Delong perhaps too much so—and Matt was cautiously optimistic. Taylor and Audrey were their weakest walkers, typically reaching camp an hour or so behind the leaders. But there was no saying that wouldn't change with time and miles.

Young Chris wandered over to ask if he needed any help. "You might wanna go around and help everyone tension their tents," Matt told him. "Then how about you and I check out the village later on?"

"Great," Chris said, and hurried off.

Matt smiled to himself. The kid looked up to him, and he liked the feeling. Liked that somebody could think he'd made something worthwhile of his life.

The sky was clear, the afternoon air warm, and Matt decided he would simply spread out a tarp, mattress, and bag instead of pitching his one-person tent. Even if it meant sleeping out in the open.

Three days of walking had worked out the residual stiffness from the jeep accident, but he had yet to out-walk the uneasiness raised by Jake's mention of brake-system tampering. The group's early morning departure from Kathmandu had prevented him from investigating the rental company's claim, and what with telephones left behind in Trisuli, there was no way of knowing how things had shaped up for Julia Tremont. He knew he should have put the incident behind him by now, and yet he felt compelled to dwell on it, to uncover any hidden truths that might be adhering to it.

First night's camp—after a nauseating six-hour bus ride through subtropical foothills—had been erected in a pipil grove at road's end. Unpaved and treacherously narrow in places, the road coursed through towns where snake charmers worked the street and the view inside every other doorway was a *National Geographic* cover. The hillsides and valley floors were terraced, lime-green with young rice, cabbage, and corn. The Himalayas were remote, peeking through towering white clouds massed on the horizon.

First camp hadn't been slated for Betorawati, but Jake and Matt wanted to give the climbers' porters a chance to push on ahead to avoid congestion on the trail. The team's liaison officer—Ang Samden Sherpa—was a swaggering ex-Gurkha physical fitness nut who commanded the porters like a military unit, demanding letters of recommendation and thumb-printed contracts from each of them. Samden was promising the climbers the most problem-free ascent of their careers.

Most of the Puma group had passed the afternoon in nearby Trisuli Bazaar, where street kids peddled warm Lemon Fanta and loinclothed men with spears posed for photographs in front of peeling Pepsi-Cola signs.

Trisuli's lake was laced with giardia, but the following day's camp afforded everyone an invigorating bath in the cold, wild river. A leveled rise above the water, the site was a veritable approach-run for hundreds of dragonflies which fed over the surrounding rice paddies. Unhappily the swim cost them sole proprietorship of the place, for the Italians arrived on-site at about the same time. Waning light and a lack of flat ground had forced the two groups into an uneasy alliance.

A baker's dozen of wealthy professionals from Milano

with four times the number of porters Lopsang and Matt had
hired to do Puma's carrying, the Italian group employed
solar-assisted generators to provide electric light and set up
huge safari-size tents which flew the Italian flag. Chefs in
tall hats prepared fresh pasta dishes, and arrogant sommeliers
served vintage wines. The folding tables in the mess tent
were covered with red-and-white checkered cloths.

By evening the site had become a sonic battleground, with
Steve Winwood, Willie Nelson, and Paul Simon's "Grace-
land" vying with Verdi, Puccini, and Madonna. The musical
volleys continued for well over an hour before Jake called
for a temporary cease-fire. With both parties headed for the
Ganesh Himal, he felt it imperative that an accord be reached;
so he and Matt sat down with Carlo, the group's fine-featured
tour operator, and an audio truce was declared. With transparent concern, Carlo had inquired how Matt was managing
on his undersized air mattress.

"Let's just say it won't kill me," Matt told him.

The truce held for the night. However, it was somehow
determined the following morning that several Puma clients had made improper use of the Italians' latrine tent—
their private hole in the ground, at any rate. Incensed,
Carlo demanded that his party had earned the right to an
unchallenged day on the trail—if for no other reason than
to avoid further contact between the two groups—but Jake
flatly refused to blow the day at the paddy camp and countered that the Italians could remain behind if they were so
distressed about having to share future sites.

While both groups were frantically breaking camp,
Matt devised a way out: Puma would simply cross the
Trisuli and stick to the western side of the gorge for the
trek north. The Italians would then be free to move at
their own pace along the usual route. An accommodation
was reached and the two groups separated amicably. Matt
had no idea then that a road was being blasted into the
gorge's eastern face.

Camp three—at six thousand feet, near a small Buddhist temple—was followed by a long day of yo-yoing,
which had brought them to the village schoolyard.

"Don't offer food that you've already nibbled or taken
a bite out of," Stu Sinotti was saying, hoping to acquaint

Cultural Taboos

the group with some of Nepal's cultural taboos. Pacing back and forth on the schoolhouse's wooden porch, the naturalist had almost everyone's attention. "If you're offered a drink from a bottle or a cup, don't let the vessel come in contact with your lips—just pour it straight into your mouth. Remember: as outsiders you're unpure."

"Do you drink from their cups, Stu?" Travis Dey wanted to know.

Stu heard the real question. "No, I don't."

The software programmer grinned. "I just thought since you didn't include yourself . . ."

Sinotti said, "We're equally unpurified, Mr. Dey," then paused to collect his thoughts. "That also means *we* should avoid the cooking areas, and that *we* shouldn't stand in front of anyone who's eating. If someone is sleeping or sitting on the ground, don't step over their outstretched legs, or show them the soles of your feet. And bear in mind what I've said about the appropriate use of the left hand and the importance of keeping *dhal-baht* and vegetables segregated on your plates."

The village's thirty or so dwellings had hipped roofs of thatch, and bamboo walls plastered with unpainted mud. The villagers were chiefly women and children and old men, who by sunset—which came early to the gorge's western face—were gathered around the tent city that had been erected in their midst. They were inquisitive but wary, preferring to maintain a respectful distance and point to things that captured their interest.

Matt assumed that most of the able-bodied men were out on expedition work, which earned them two dollars a day and sometimes kept them away for weeks at a stretch.

He had his ground cloth and sleeping bag spread in what he thought of as the camp's working-class neighborhood. Unobstructed views of the river gorge went to the larger tents belonging to the Bessmans, the Delongs, and the Deys. Behind them were Taylor, Karl, Doug, and Chris, along with Constance Battle and Karma. Jake, Stu, and Matt were somewhat closer to the schoolhouse. Purbu and the cook staff invariably slept close to their battered aluminum equipment, while over in the barrio, Lopsang and the porters were crowded together under makeshift tarp shelters. The *sirdar* had his own tent, but elected to sleep with his gang.

Karl was back there with them just now, passing out cigars and sharing *chilim* tokes of the black hashish he'd scored in Kathmandu. The porters seemed as amused by his easy-going manner as they were puzzled by his attempts at conversation. Taylor, on the other hand, could make herself understood about half the time, but the Tamangs would seldom do more than tease her in return.

The climbers, with their colorfully logo-ed geodesic sleep and supply tents, had created a kind of satellite camp outside the stone wall that enclosed the schoolyard. Kaylee and Candice shared a tent; Barbara Bass had a smaller one to herself.

Dekker and McMahon were listening to Stu's lecture from camp chairs in front of their tent. Candice was dressed head to foot in Grand Design burgundy pile; Kaylee in exercise tights, poly-silk shorts, and a nylon parka. Despite what might have been better judgment, Matt was eager to question them about the jeep accident, but there had been no opportunity to do so. When he wasn't busy with trek tasks, they were.

He watched them until he was satisfied they had lost interest in Sinotti's lecture; then he did some final arranging of his gear, slipped into rubber thongs, and wandered over to their side of camp. Candice's greeting smile made things easy.

"I've been meaning to tell you guys how sorry I was about Julia."

"Thanks, Matt," Candice said, handing him a stuff-sacked sleeping bag to sit on. Kaylee appraised him with narrowed eyes, but offered an enigmatic smile when he looked at her.

"How bad's her arm?"

"Seriously bad." Candice ran long, tapered fingers in an upward stroke through the back of her short hair. "Her husband's supposed to be flying in from Bangkok tomorrow."

"Jake says you found someone to replace her."

The women exchanged looks. "We hope. We won't know for sure until the mail run to Thanget." The climb team had left one of their Sherpas behind in Kathmandu to grab any last-minute letters or telexes and literally run them up to the village the following week. A second mail delivery would be made to base camp the following month.

Matt picked up a twig to toy with. "Did you and Julia know each other well?"

"Pretty well. Kaylee knew her a lot better than I did."

Matt glanced at the darker woman. He couldn't help thinking she was sitting in Candice's shadow.

"I met her when I was doing ski patrol in Sun Valley. We kept running into each other at Snowbird, Telluride, Grand Targhee, all over the place." Kaylee touched the tip of her tongue to her upper lip. "We did Ranier and McKinley together and ended up in South America on a few climbs."

Matt demonstrated his interest with a thoughtful nod. "How about Barbara?"

"We've climbed in China," Kaylee said flatly.

"Barb and I have known each other for years," Candice said. "She's one of the people who inspired me to climb."

Matt kept his eyes on Kaylee while Dekker spoke, but there was nothing to discern in her eyes. "Think the three of you can go Pabil alone if you have to?"

"It's hardly K2," Kaylee said. "Shit, the *two* of us could do it if we had to."

"With a lot more work," Matt said.

Candice rocked her head. "Well, we'd have to approach it alpine style. Fair means. Carry all our own gear. Keep moving. Up and down."

"Not just on the mountain. I mean, someone's got to take care of business: pay the porters, watch over base camp, that sorta thing."

"That's what we're paying Ang Samden Sherpa for," Candice said in a dramatic voice.

Matt guessed the liaison officer and the Sherpas were at least two days—two stages—ahead of the trekking party by now. He managed a laugh and drew a line in the dirt. "Right. Heard you got stuck dealing with him while we were out at Vajra Yogini that day."

"Not me," Candice said. "I went shopping."

Matt studied both of them for a moment.

Kaylee spoke to it. "That was me. We always try to split up the work load and build in as much individual free time as we can. We think it's better when we're not always doing everything together.''

She looked at Candice. ''That's what I think gets so many men's teams off on the wrong foot. The guys hang out together doing their male bonding thing, and before they know it, they're all trying to dazzle each other or establish some kind of pecking order. Everybody starts getting on everybody else's nerves and they end up carrying all that dumb ego shit onto the mountain with them. Then, of course, they get homophobic about relating and opening up to each other and it interferes with the climb.''

Candice watched her partner and turned Matt a broad grin. ''You know how *men* can be, Matt.'' Kaylee joined her in a laugh.

''I know how people can be,'' he told them.

He went over the conversation as he relaxed under his sleeping bag gazing at satellite traffic above the gorge. Purbu and a few of the porters were whispering and laughing around the remains of a fire, but most everyone else was asleep. Or so it seemed from the symphony of snores and wheezes that filled the night air. Dogs were raising hell in the village, but Karma was on good behavior in Constance's roomy tent.

So maybe there was nothing more to the jeep accident than bad luck and poor judgment, he told himself as the Seven Sisters were rising into view. Why anyway would the climbers want to sabotage their own expedition? It was as crazy a notion as disabling your own brakes.

But he understood plain enough why he was so obsessed with seeing it that way: because it kept him from thinking that he'd been the accident's real target.

He cursed himself. Jake was right to leave it alone. It was just added weight to hump into the hills; a load of paranoia left over from a previous incarnation. He was sure ex–Peace Corps Linda would agree.

A deep breath of night air calmed his thoughts momentarily. Things were going to work out fine, he assured himself. Including the three-quarter-length sleeping pad most of him was resting on.

As long as the weather held.

8

Starch Trek

Matt thought that if he was ever going to move back to a small town it would have to be one where people said hello to one another on the street.

"*Namaste,*" he said, greeting four Tamang women coming up the trail in the opposite direction. Bent nearly double under ten-foot lengths of hewn timber and earth-brown baskets filled with shale and water-smoothed rocks, they wore colorful cummerbunds and necklaces of turquoise and coral.

"*Namaste,*" they returned, almost singing it between breaths. "*I salute the god within you.*"

Matt had volunteered to take the point once again, preferring a brisk pace to a lazy one. Midline the porters were continually overtaking you on the narrow downhills, sneaking up on you with their sullen, whistled warnings.

It had been another long morning of contouring; drainage after drainage, the slopes above the trail forested with deciduous hardwoods and evergreens. Fording runoff streams was becoming second nature, and Matt thought he would soon arrive at the Zen point he was seeking, when the pace would determine itself and his steps would come in measured stride, each foot falling precisely where it should, no churning or scuffing, no break in the rhythm.

He reasoned that by centering himself on trail technique he could leave all the bad shit behind him.

Road crews were at work across the gorge—colored dots on the denuded slopes—and every so often a thunderous explosion would echo out over the swift river. When he was done with the gloating, Matt allowed himself a private concern, thinking about what the Italians were up against over there.

He was carrying sixty pounds of gear in an effort to strengthen his legs and lungs for the climb to the high pass. The climbers wore equivalent amounts; Barbara Bass going everybody one better by jogging each morning before breakfast. Taylor, too, was packing more than she had to. Matt had seen her earlier on walking with Candice, then off on her own dictating notes to her voice-activated tape recorder.

Matt supposed the Tamang women were headed to the village he had passed a mile or so back—a spotless little hamlet nestled in a verdant drainage below terraced fields of wheat, corn, and rice. Cows and chickens wandered the narrow streets, and wild *ganga* grew in profusion along the trail. Kaylee had stopped to photograph a sprocket-bottomed prayer drum turned by a stream of clear water diverted from the ridge; the stream continued down slope to pour through the slate roof of a mill shed. There wasn't a doorway or a window frame in the village that wasn't intricately carved, and resting on the lintel above the entrance to a shrine, Matt had noticed three upended flashlights, placed there like a trio of votive candles.

It was just outside the village that he had encountered a Tamang man traveling with his young son—past and future images of each other in khaki shorts, embroidered vests, soft fezzes, and gnarled walking sticks. The father had a sparse mustache and a bit of steel-wool beard.

Matt walked with them, wishing he could understand more of the running commentary the father was offering on plants and rocks and special places along the trail. He recognized that there was some sort of oral tradition at work; that the father was showing the kid the sights, as it were. But more, that he was instructing his son in the ways of the world, passing on the learning he had been taught, the wisdom he had accumulated with all the calluses, age wrinkles, and laugh lines. Sometimes that even included Matt and the strange baggage he carried, whatever it was he stood for as foreign symbol or harbinger of things to come.

The boy would nod his head respectfully as he listened, stopping occasionally to touch or sniff at a particular plant. At other times the pair would stand atop an outcropping of rock and the father would aim a knowing forefinger at distant places and speak of serious matters.

Watching them, Matt drew into himself, recalling the mountains and prairies of his Montana youth. The succession of trailer camps, and bar-strewn cities, the pulp mills, and wilderness camps that came part and parcel with his father's search for work and an acceptable place to settle down. His mother, strong-willed, adapting to every last-moment change in plans with a resigned smile. Matt could still recall her telling Emmett that he should take a job as a hunter's guide or a cook if he loved the Bitterroot so much; that all the moving from place to place, the haulage work, the bar-tending, and oil-camp rigging was just so much wasted energy. And he recalled how her slow death had sent his father adrift in a place he hadn't visited before—one he couldn't traverse with the issue-compass he'd carried on his key chain since the war.

Emmett's search had seemed to grow vague afterward, even though he'd always maintained it was only his own peace of mind he was interested in. That every man and woman had to do whatever it took to solve the problems that drove them to wander. That settling of any kind reeked of compromise and ultimately had a defeating effect on people.

His father stopped talking to him after Anna's death; it was as though he'd judged whatever he had to teach worthless. When he did speak, it was to tell Matt that life was mostly bullets, and that he had to cut his own escape through it; that he especially shouldn't listen to the sorry sounds of some drifter who'd never made a place for himself—despite the survival skills he'd bequeathed Matt on journeys that took them through wild, wild country.

So Matt had settled down to high school baseball, and later a taste of college. He'd turned his hand to tree skinning and platform rigging and somehow found himself in New York City with a bunch of eager-faced kids from New England universities who were going to change the world—or at least Peru's little corner of it. And then there he was in Peru, lost again until Susan.

He could see that he'd been following in Emmett's footsteps since Susan's death; but that didn't alter things any. Brie might have turned him around if he'd given her half a chance. But stronger than his feelings for her was a fear of the legacy he'd be passing on. Movement was in his blood, and maybe he was meant to end the line.

The snow-platted massif of the Langtang Himal loomed abruptly into view around a sharp turn in the trail and Matt lifted his face to the cool breeze, sensing an inflowing of renewed strength and enthusiasm. The Tamang father suggested a rest spot in a circle of poplar shade, and for the next hour Matt was treated to a series of wide-eyed expressions as one by one the Puma group rounded the bend and drank in the gleaming northern view.

Karl clapped Doc Bessman on the back and offered him a snort from a hip flask. Travis Dey and Morgan took out their cameras.

"We're finally getting there," Taylor said, shrugging out of her day pack and collapsing in the dusty shade.

Chris's only comment was: "Holy snow."

Jake called a lunch stop and everyone sated themselves on boiled potatoes and *chapatis* with jam and peanut butter.

Later, Matt and Taylor fell into step on a stretch of level trail that wound through pine forest. In front of them, Karl and the anesthesiologist were comparing the surroundings to places in Texas and Utah.

High clouds had moved in and the blasting had touched off a massive avalanche low down on the opposite face of the gorge. Within minutes the river had gone muddy with debris, and the foliage was dusted with fine red powder.

At times Nepal seemed positively preoccupied with road building; and while rumor had it that gold had been discovered in the Ganesh, the road's more likely destination was the Tibetan frontier—the border with China, from which Nepal was receiving more and more of its imported goods. If nothing else, the new road would one day allow visitors to begin their treks from the high country. For at least as long as the bridges held up.

"There wasn't even a road into Kathmandu before 1955," Matt said from beneath a bandanna he'd tied across his nose and mouth. "Porters used to carry jeeps across the mountains from India on litters. Now Nepal wants to link up every town in the country."

"So what's wrong with that?" Taylor said, one hand gripped on a ski pole, the other covering her mouth.

"So sooner or later the place is as parceled up as a national park. Without the garbage cans," he added.

"You sound like Stu."

"Why's everybody keep comparing me to him?" Matt muttered. Taylor was panting hard and he passed her a canteen of water.

"Cacohydrophobia," she said, refusing. "Fear of drinking foreign water."

"It's treated with iodine," he told her. "Anyway, you have to learn to keep your fluid intake up. Especially when we start gaining altitude." She told him she was feeling a lot stronger than when they'd climbed Swayambunath together. It was just her knees.

"Try bending your legs on the downhill." He demonstrated the posture and she laughed.

"Matt's attempt at equipoise."

"Even if it does look idiotic. You shift your weight. Lower your center of gravity like the porters do."

Taylor gave it a try. "Why are they always laughing at me when I'm just trying to be friendly?"

"To get a rise out of you. They're just entertaining themselves." He shrugged. "No TV out here. They've gotta do something to make the trek interesting."

"Like scare Karma every chance they get, and try to trip Audrey?"

Matt cut his eyes to her. "Who tried to trip Audrey?"

"That one you're always talking to—the one with the red sneakers. The honey gatherer."

"Tulo," Matt said, frowning. "I'm going to have to put a stop to that."

"You really should."

"So how's the profile of high-profile Candice going?" Matt asked after a moment.

"That is some profile, isn't it?"

"I don't know. Too much cheek, too much chin."

"You think so?" She brightened somewhat. "It's going all right, I guess. But she's hard to figure. One minute I think she's the perfect spokesperson for women's mountaineering, the next I feel like I've heard it all before. That everything about her is packaged—from the buzzwords right down to the Grand Design thermal underwear."

"You've seen her in her Grand Design thermal underwear?"

"Gender has its privileges. Actually, though, I'm learning more about everyone else than I am about her. Except you, of course." She held up a hand before he could speak. "I'm not pushing, mind you."

Matt lowered the bandanna to reveal an attentive expression. "What's everyone telling you?"

"Aside from the fact they want to kill Karma?"

"Don't worry about it. He's going home soon."

Taylor thought for a moment. "Well," she laughed, "there's Stu's story about his divorce."

And she went on to explain how Puma's study leader had returned to the States from one of his six-month trips in Nepal only to find several articles of unfamiliar clothing hung in his closet. He didn't want to question his wife about the clothes, but when she wasn't forthcoming about what she'd been doing while he was away, he simply took to wearing some of the mystery apparel. At first his wife pretended not to notice, but eventually she slipped and started calling him by different names, and it came out that she'd been carrying on three separate affairs.

"No wonder he stays in the mountains as much as he can," Matt said.

"Interesting thing was they were all ski bums and climber types." Taylor glanced over her shoulder and lowered her voice. "He hates mountaineers. On principle and otherwise."

Matt scratched his head. "You sure you got that right? I mean, I've known the guy for three years. He never said anything to me about hating climbers."

Taylor shrugged it off. "You just have to know how to ask."

"Except with Karl."

"Oh, poor Karl," Taylor said. "His ex-wife should get together with Stu's for a battle of the nags or something. At least the way he tells it."

"He told me Julia reminded him of her."

"Really? He said that to me about Morgan. But maybe that's in terms of attitude." Taylor chuckled. "God, there's a fish out of water if there ever was one. I can't figure what made Buzz think she'd enjoy herself on this trek. She's at home in tanning salons and nail-care centers."

"Helluva strong walker," Matt said.

"Yeah, well I would be too if I could spend every day playing tennis and swimming and walking up and down Rodeo trying on chichi exercise outfits."

Matt laughed. "Am I detecting a little 'attitude' there?"

The thin line Taylor made with her lips didn't hold, and she laughed. "Actually, she's all right. She's real open and honest. If I could get Candice to be that frank, I'd have it knocked."

"She just wants to climb mountains," Matt offered. "Could be nothing more to her than that."

Taylor was shaking her head. "Uh-huh. There's a lot more to her than climbing. Besides, 'because it's there' doesn't answer it anymore." She put finger quotes around it. "You gave me the idea yourself when you were talking about the lengths people go to to realize a goal. It's not enough that you're *doing* it anymore: it's *how* you're doing it.

"People want to see style, you mean. They want you to go to the moon without oxygen."

"It'll get to that," Taylor said.

Matt watched her for a moment. "You this serious about all your assignments?"

Taylor confessed that she wasn't. "But I've decided that I need to get this one right if I'm going to stick to covering climbing events. What I really want is a crack at covering next year's Everest bid—from base camp anyway. I know the team's going to be looking for a book to come out of it and I'd like to be the one to write it. The field's dominated by men, but I know I can write as well as any of them."

"So you and whatever woman gets picked for the Everest team are going to be breaking new ground."

" 'Summit an American Woman,' " Taylor said, quoting the climbers' slogan.

Matt refrained from repeating Travis Dey's lewd rejoinder. "You know who might have an interesting slant on things? Dee-Dee and Maurice."

"Oh, please," Taylor said. "If I have to hear one more thing about stress indicators and group dynamics . . ."

"Delong Theory," Matt said.

"Delong*champs*," Taylor amended, straight-faced. "They're French, you know."

A near-vertical, four-thousand-foot switchback descent to the Trisuli Khola landed them at the crossroads village of Syabru Bensi. It was raining by then and the porters were complaining, so Jake and Lopsang called it an early day at a level but trash-strewn area fronting a police barracks that had fallen into disuse. The one-room building sat atop a stone-wall shelter that had been erected by soldiers brought in to investigate a helicopter crash several years back. The rusted remains of the chopper still littered the steep mountainside above the river.

While the tents were going up, Purbu and his staff whipped together a tasteless dinner. The weather put a damper on things and the trekkers picked at their food. Audrey excused herself entirely and ducked into her tent well before dark. She had been strangely silent all afternoon and Matt began to wonder if it was something other than trail sickness that was bothering her.

Stu Sinotti's lecture wasn't helping matters any. "Because all this *filth* is considered a status symbol," he was yelling over the Trisuli's icy tumult, stomping around in crushed tin cans, empty film canisters, and unidentifiable refuse. "Trash means that foreigners have visited here; that *progress* is on the way. *That's* why they don't clean it up!"

The Puma group remained silent, huddled together under the veranda of the dilapidated building with their congealed noodles and cold tea. Tethered, Karma was barking nonstop at a dozen dogs orbiting the area for scraps or handouts.

Matt knew there were sometimes a few bottles of Star beer to be had in Syabru Bensi and said as much to Karl. Doug Makey stood up on the Texan's "What are we waiting on?" and the three of them splashed off toward the iron bridge that spanned the river.

"I'm sorry I didn't listen to you about stocking up in Kathmandu," Doug told Karl at the edge of the village's grid of cobblestone streets. He was sporting a Puma cap, Gore-Tex jacket and rain pants. Matt and Karl were carrying umbrellas and flashlights. "But right now I'd settle for *rakshi*. Even if it does taste like vinegar and dishwater. Anything it takes to keep me from hearing that damn dog all night long."

So that was it, Matt thought. Earlier on, the "government consultant" had been arguing with Chris over some detail concerning tent stake placement. Matt had Doug figured as a lot to live up to, a lot to live down.

"Why not drop one of those Valiums the doc's carrying?" Karl suggested.

"Those I'm saving for higher ground, Karl."

Owing to the rain and the dark ridges that rose at the end of each street, Syabru had a claustrophobic feel; but the village's proximity to the Langtang Himal guaranteed it a steady flow of visitors. In one lantern-lit store Matt struck up a conversation with a German geologist doing soil studies in the mountains, and in another he met two Dutchmen who had just packed their friend out of the valley on a bamboo litter—the lymph glands in his groin so swollen from leech bites he couldn't walk.

The search for Stars ultimately brought them to a trekkers' hotel called the Yak-Inn, where they found Carlo, the Italian tour operator, hunched over the last beer in the house.

"I might have known," Matt said, trying to wrap it in a smile.

Carlo's dark eyes glared at him in candlelight. "And you didn't know about the road, eh, *traditore*?"

"I didn't, man. I'm really sorry about that."

Carlo regaled them with horror stories about the eastern rim trek. How the explosions and resultant avalanches had completely obliterated long stretches of trail; how one of the Nepali road crews had tried to direct them right into a blast area; how he'd almost lost two clients to the river's fury.

Using pinky and forefinger, Carlo formed horns with his right hand. "This-a, for the rest of your trip."

"Hey, doesn't that mean *cuckold* or something?" Karl asked.

"It's just a hex," Matt said.

"Justa hex," Carlo said, continuing to jiggle the gesture.

Karl thrust out a hip and jabbed a thumb against his right buttock. "You can *besame khola*, Carlo," he announced, mixing several languages but making his point. "You can just kiss this, *paisano. Proprio uno stronza.* And I hope you burn your sauce."

Smiling, Carlo brought his other hand into play. *"Vaffanculo!"*

"Fucking eye-ties," Karl persisted, even after Matt and Doug had hustled him out. "And they're even worse on skis."

It was the middle of the night and still drizzling when Matt was jolted out of sleep by a dogfight that erupted just outside his tent. He sat up so fast his forehead smacked the mini-flashlight he'd hung from the ceiling loop.

By the time he disengaged himself from the sleeping bag and scrambled through the zippered netting, the fight had spilled over into the kitchen section of camp, where Purbu and Pasang were banging wooden spoons against pots in an effort to chase the curs off.

Someone aimed a flashlight on the fight and only then did Matt realize that one of the snarling dogs was Karma.

Someone else with a decent arm finally caught the attack dog on the rump with a fist-sized stone and sent it yelping for the perimeter of the camp, where it was immediately set upon by several others that resembled it, short muzzle to bushy tail.

Karma was whimpering, down on his side trying to raise his tongue to a hacked-up rear leg. Constance Battle took only a moment getting to him, but one look at the leg and she was frozen in place.

"But I had the tent zipped up!" she wanted everyone to know. "I even closed the rain-fly!"

Lopsang had to scold half a dozen porters who were yucking it up on the barrack's veranda. "*Mo-mos*, Matt!" Tulo kept yelling.

Most of the group members were awake, some peering out from the doorways of their tents, others standing barefoot in the rain under umbrellas. Doc Bessman, attired in a pale green surgeon's outfit, came over with medical kit in hand and went down in a puddle to attend to Karma's wounds.

"We've got a problem," he told Jake, one hand to his brow in the beams of several flashlights.

⚖⚖ 9 ⚖⚖

Yo-yoing

Everyone was sorry to see Constance go. At first Matt thought Buzz was exaggerating the seriousness of Karma's wounds simply because he wanted the dog off the trek; but by sunrise it was obvious that Karma was in deep trouble.

The poodle was up to date on rabies vaccinations and such, but the puncture wounds the village mongrel had inflicted were in real danger of infection. Doc Bessman thought there might be internal injuries as well. So while Matt and Jake spent an hour cobbling together a bamboo litter, Lopsang searched Syabru Bensi for someone willing to take on Constance and Karma for the return trip to Kathmandu. One thing was clear: The streets of New York City—perilous though they might be to humans and dogs alike—could be kinder on occasion than the mountains of Nepal.

Jake got the group going by eight o'clock after an hour of trash collecting, and by ten, under sunny skies, Constance and the poodle were on their way, left in the capable hands of the *sirdar* of a Polish climb team returning from a successful new-route ascent in the Langtang.

Matt hung around to oversee their departure, then stuffed his personal gear together into a day pack and set off along a west bank trail that paralleled the river. North of the Trisuli-Langtang confluence the river was

called the Bhote Kosi, which, like all the major rivers
of the subcontinent, flowed not from the Himalayan
range, but from the more geologically ancient Tibetan
plateau.

The trail snaked through tall grass, still wet from the
rain, and patches of nettles, whose stinging hairs were
forever attaching themselves to the unmindful trekker.

And if anyone were offering a prize for unmindfulness,
Matt figured he had it cinched. A near-sleepless night,
Karma's wounds, the revelations about the French Delong*champs* with their stress experiments, Stu's animos-
ity for climbers, Doug Makey's anger, Tulo's jibes . . .
all of it had combined to hole-shoot his trail rhythm. He
was stumbling every tenth step, scuffing his feet, slamming his toes into rocks. He felt a good twenty pounds
heavier, despite the fact that the porters had relieved him
of his pack for the catch-up march.

He was so preoccupied, in fact, that he didn't see the
pit in the trail until he was practically right on top of it,
and then only managed to avoid it by hurling himself into
the wet nettles of the upslope side. When his breath returned and he had picked himself up, he parted the thigh-
high grass concealing the trail to have a closer look at
the pit. Someone had levered a large stone out of the trail
and done a bit of excavation work to enlarge the hole to
a depth of almost a foot and a half. Matt located the stone
a couple yards below the trail where the land sloped down
to the river.

Good for a sprained ankle, Matt thought as he was
filling in the hole with small rocks. Maybe a broken leg.
Water at the bottom suggested that the hole could have
been there for days. But someone could have slopped
water into the hole to make it look that way.

Pratfalls were the sort of thing the porters found comical, but outright excavation seemed a bit extreme, even
for them. And, of course, there was no way of telling
just who the digger had had in mind. If the hole had been
dug for him, however, it indicated that someone had deliberately slipped out of line and waited for everyone else
to pass the spot by. Either way, it meant the trekkers had
a dangerous trickster in their midst.

* * *

Matt caught up with the group at the Chilime Khola bridge, an hour's walk above Syabru Bensi. He found Jake sunning himself on a boulder a quarter of a mile upriver. Some of Puma's trekkers were washing clothes in the frigid waters—shirts and socks and shorts strewn about on the glacial rocks. Taylor had her tape recorder out and was talking to Audrey Dey. The rest were attending to blisters, reading, or napping. Chris—who Doug claimed had once slept through a sizable earthquake—was apparently the only one who hadn't been disturbed by the midnight dogfight.

"Did Constance have anything to say?" Jake asked as Matt was taking off his day pack.

"That she was sorry for all the inconvenience she'd caused. That she hoped she could trek with us again sometime."

Jake looked over at him. "Without Karma."

"Without Karma." Matt recalled the jokes that had circulated in private after the dogfight: *Our Karma's ruined. We're leaving our Karma behind*—

"Did you get a look at the tent?"

Matt nodded. He'd volunteered to break down Constance's tent while she was busy packing her duffel and making soothing sounds to the poodle.

"And?" Jake asked.

"And I guess he could have nuzzled the front door zippers open and bellied out under the rain-fly."

"So you don't think the porters had anything to do with it?" When Matt didn't reply immediately, Jake said, "Come on, out with it. I know the way your mind works."

Matt held his gaze. "Were you walking point on the way up here?" Jake nodded, and Matt told him about the excavated hole.

No one had reported anything to Jake, but then why should they? What trail in Nepal didn't have pits and snares and traps. Some farmer could have pried the stone loose thinking he'd found just the one for his front door stoop, just the one to crown that length of wall. As far as anyone dropping out of line, Jake thought he remembered Doug and Karl and Taylor all making pit stops.

Matt could see that he was getting nowhere and

dropped the subject after telling Jake that he wanted to keep a close eye on Tulo and some of the other porters.

Then they turned their attention to revising the trip itinerary yet again. Jake's recommendation was to allow the group a few hours by the river and to push on only as far as Thanget instead of trying to make Tato Pani—"Hot Springs"—which would have entailed an afternoon climb of several thousand feet. The Italian trekkers weren't a concern, since Lopsang had learned they were laying over a day in Syabru to recuperate from their harrowing experience on the east rim.

Matt heard someone scrambling over the rocks and looked up in time to see Stu Sinotti's large head bob into view. "Prepare yourself," he told Jake.

Jake swung around but didn't get a word out before Sinotti barked: "Did you or did you not advise these people about washing in the river?"

"I warned them it was cold, Stu," Jake began.

The naturalist's gray eyes bulged. "Cold?! Who gives a damn about the temperature? I'm talking about the *soap* they're using!"

Matt winced.

"I thought we had an understanding, Jake. I thought I made it clear you were to insist on biodegradable products only! K-Karl . . ." he stammered. "Karl is down there washing his socks with a goddamned bleach!"

"Calm down," Matt said, pushing himself up on his fingertips. "I'll talk to him about it."

Sinotti was still glowering at them. "Tell him I won't stand for it, Matt. Tell him he can do what he wants in Texas or wherever he comes from, but that kind of behavior is simply unacceptable here. Either he agrees to the ecological terms of the contract or he's out. Let him find some other trekking agency in Kathmandu that shares his disregard."

Karl apologized, explaining that it was the only soap powder he could find in Kathmandu. "I mean, for chrissake, Matt, they're selling the stuff right there in the marketplace."

"I know," Matt said. "That's the problem."

Closer to the underside of the bridge, Candice Dekker

was free-climbing the pitted face of an enormous boulder. Dressed in loose-fitting hot pink short-shorts and a red-and-white diagonally striped sleeveless top, she looked like some sort of Amazonian insect against the granite face of the rock. The sport was often referred to as "bouldering," and Matt thought its advocates an even match for bicyclists when it came to sport-specific outfits and hot colors.

Boulderers and rock enthusiasts would mention places like Buoux and Smith Rock, and talk about five-point-one-three-level ascent routes, second-generation spring-loaded cam clusters, hangdogging, and yo-yoing; but Matt wasn't sure he could tell flash from genuine crack technique.

Kaylee was kneeling at the foot of the boulder readying her camera. "Can you get some more flex in your left calf?" she called up to Candice, experimenting with different angles.

"Product photos—for the expedition sponsors," Matt explained as Jake sat down to partake of the heads-up view.

A mating of ninja sneaker and ballet slipper—and all the rage among Paris ramp models—Candice's shoes were called "French Toes." Cherry-red and mint-green Cordura uppers, Stealth rubber soles, an inner band of Kevlar . . . Trademarks to add to the brand names that adorned the climbers' gear, Matt thought. Thinsulate, Gore-Tex, Polypropylene . . . The shoes' rubber ankle wafers read Grand Design, as did the logo on Candice's shirt and purple chalk bag.

Matt and Jake watched her spread-eagle herself against the boulder's porous face, leg and arm muscles taut, chalked fingertips and shoe tips gripped on invisible ledges, buttocks tensed—

"Callipygian is the word you're looking for," Taylor said, appearing out of nowhere with an arm load of laundry. "A shapely derriere," she explained. "Well, at least close your mouths, guys. You look like you should be wearing raincoats." She gazed up at Candice, turning back to them with an appreciative grin. "Although I've got to admit, you picked a good view."

Jake and Matt slid apart to make room for her on the

rock, and the three of them watched the climber in silence, the whir-click of Kaylee's camera off to one side, the roar of the Chilime at their backs.

"In fact," Taylor continued, after a long moment, "your reaction's exactly the one Grand Design is counting on. I should tell Kaylee to take shots of your faces and send them along with her product photos."

Matt said, "What's with Grand Design? She have a personal contract with them or something?"

"They all have personal sponsors. It's part of receiving backing for expeditions."

"Marketing," Jake said, as though in love with the sound of the word.

"In a nutshell. The next time you guys see a Grand Design logo, what are you going to be thinking of?" Taylor's hand indicated Candice. "Candice Dekker's . . . shorts. So imagine how some U.S. outfitter would feel about having the company logo in a photo taken on top of Everest."

"Especially if an American woman's wearing it," Jake said.

Taylor smiled. "Right again. And especially if that American woman also happens to be gorgeous, articulate, and photogenic. A company might run into trouble trying to market a line of cosmetics, but there's a lot that can be done with outdoor apparel and soft adventure hiking shoes—not to mention technical gear. Climbing ropes, crampons, all that."

"Are we getting a foretaste of the magazine article here?" Matt wanted to know.

Taylor made a face at him. "In a way. But only because I'm still trying to separate the person from the packaging. You think about mountaineers like Reinhold Messner, _living in castles_ and doing car ads. Mountaineering's no different than rock 'n' roll or movies when it comes to product promotion. And a lot of American equipment companies are dying for a new personality to market—preferably a woman."

"Like Candice," Matt said.

"Or Kaylee. Or Barbara, for that matter. They're all bright, intelligent, attractive women."

Matt drew a mental picture of Candice standing at the

top of Everest, then silver-haired Barbara; but he kept his mouth shut.

"Getting a woman to the top of Everest could be worth ten million dollars to an outfitter."

Matt frowned. "Providing they have a climber willing to sell herself just to get backing."

Taylor shook her head. "That's not all there is to it. Successful climbers hit the lecture circuit—schools, oil companies, financial firms. That can pay two thousand a shot. And you figure sixty-five, seventy-five talks per year . . . It's not a bad income."

Matt took a moment to absorb it. "So if women have that much juice in the current market, you'd think climb leaders would be falling all over each other to get them on an Everest ascent."

"Well, now you're over into something else," Taylor said. "Some teams have enlisted women *only* for the cash and the equipment sponsorship. Others have decided that connections—either for permits or sponsors—are more important than ability, and a lot of strong women climbers have been overlooked."

Jake said, "Ask Barbara about that one."

"Why her?" Matt asked.

"Because Barbara's one of the ones with political connections. Her husband's a congressman or something."

"Not quite," Taylor amended. "But he is a Reagan appointee and that counts for a lot of 'juice' when it comes to raising money and cutting through the permit red tape."

Matt rubbed the stubble on his chin. "But she's as experienced as Candice or Kaylee, isn't she?"

"I never said she wasn't." Taylor watched Candice for a moment. "That's why this Ganesh expedition got so much attention early on. The four of them organized it as a woman's climb to prove they could get the funding and the gear without having to rely on some high-profile male climber with a dozen eight-thousand-meter peaks under his belt. They even passed on offers from the TV networks because they didn't want to turn the climb into some exploitative media event—even though coverage would have helped underwrite expenses. The idea was to demonstrate that there *is* camaraderie among the women's contingent. That it's not all infighting and backbiting, as a lot of the men have been saying." Taylor shook her head. "Unfortunately, K2's eclipsed a lot of the initial interest in the climb."

They fell silent for a moment. The mountaineering world was still reeling from the recent summer tragedy, when the so-called "savage mountain" had claimed the lives of thirteen climbers.

Finally Matt said, "Too bad Julia's no longer with the team, huh?"

Jake threw him a warning look over the top of Taylor's shoulder, as if to say don't give her any ideas.

"I only mean it's a shame she's going to miss out on all the *camaraderie*," Matt said, returning the look.

The route into the Ganesh Himal veered northwestward along the white-water Chilime Khola. It was easy walking on wide paths glinting with mica schist and trail garnets; through fields of marigolds and red-tipped sorghum; past Buddhist shrines flanked by guardian figures and sanctified with bas-relief images of Swayambu and Bodhnath. Tattered blue-and-white banners flew from long poles along the ridge line, fluttering block-printed blessings to a clear sky.

The group was in good spirits after the rest stop and Matt kept expecting to feel Karma brush past him on the trail, barking and breaking for the lead. Even the porters were singing. With the poodle gone, however, they had to concentrate their efforts on Taylor and Barbara for comic relief—the climber's habitual jogging amusing them no end.

Matt wondered how long it was going to take for them to get around to Audrey Dey, who had neither Barbara's strength nor Taylor's talent for comical faces. But maybe then Travis would start walking with his wife instead of pairing up with Morgan all the time.

Matt passed the first part of the walk looking forward: trying to imagine his next move if Jake nixed the request for an office job, or if the office job just didn't work out. How was anyone back in the States who wasn't an investment counselor or a stock trader making ends meet with Reagan still in office and drug money controlling the streets? Was there even a place for someone who'd taken twenty years off to get a glimpse at the rest of the world?

Matt figured himself a decent carpenter; he knew his way around tools. He was fluent in Spanish and Bahasa Indonesian, and he could get by in a half dozen South Pacific island languages. He had had a good deal of paramedical training, and he supposed he had enough idealism left over from the Peace Corps to see him through a stretch of social work in some inner city. He could sell camping gear; work for a wildlife concern. There was enough money in a bank back in Denver to assure him an apartment, a phone, a television. But what were the rules for dropping *in*? Unless maybe the answer was to marry rich. Father and parent a couple of kids with someone like tan and lovely Morgan Bessman. Play the house husband; take the kids to Little League practice; spend summers at the shore. He could cook, he could sew on his own buttons; and after years of dropping tents and cleaning propane stoves, he had nothing against housework. . . .

He gave it a minute and shook his head in disgust; nothing like making long-range plans when you were busy dodging bullets and nasty holes in the road.

He cut back his pace and waited for Chris Makey to come abreast and they eased into a conversation. They'd already had a few trail talks about surfing. Chris would tell him about the waves he'd ridden in California and Hawaii, and Matt would talk about straight-up places in Indonesia and Australia. The teenager had confided that part-time-dad Doug was worried about him pissing away his life. Worried about grades; about girls; about drugs; about hanging out.

"I mean, it's not like I've ever dissed him or anything," Chris said now. "It's like he's just worried I'm gonna end up movin' to Manhattan Beach or somewhere and crashing with a bunch of granolas, surfin' and doin' weed all day long."

"Is that what you want to do?"

Chris flipped ash-blond bangs away from his eyes. "I'd like to do what you do. Travel around, get into adventures . . ."

Matt put a hand on the boy's shoulder. "It's even wilder than it looks, Chris."

"Yeah, well it's better than working in some office like my dad does."

"What's he do, anyway?" Matt asked, on alert after Doug's anger with Karma.

"I don't even know. I mean, we like usually only see each other on holidays and stuff. But this summer he was on some business with his geeknoid Washington friends. Then he comes back and lays it on me that he's pulling me out of school for like two months so we could take this trip. I was like: 'Bite moose, man. No way I'm going to *Asia* for two months.' "

"You still feel that way."

Chris thought it over. "I don't know. It's pretty fresh over here. I mean, ralph on the food, but it's not as cheesy as I figured it'd be."

Matt took it to mean that the kid wasn't having a bad time. "So your dad lives in Washington. But you don't know what he does."

"Yeah, but he's not like in politics or anything." Chris added a hop to his step. "Hey, Matt, wouldn't it be rad if he was like a CIA agent or something?"

Thanget was mostly a Tibetan village of fieldstone houses and clean dirt streets. Thatch roofs had given way to slate and cedar shakes battened by long poles weighed down with river rocks.

The group pitched their tents in a spacious grass courtyard formed by an arrangement of tin-roofed buildings that served as clinic, police post, district headquarters, and dumping ground for hundreds of empty birth control pill boxes. A volleyball net was strung in the center of the yard, and ample wood for cook fires was neatly stacked under a porch with oak support posts and bamboo handrails.

Children held out their cupped hands for one rupee, one *paisa*, one pen; but quickly tired of the game and began wrestling in the grass. Tibetan women—monkishly attired in brown robes, striped aprons, headbands of colored twine, and flat-topped embroidered caps—showed up with handcrafted items to sell. They were mysterious, ethereal, unknowable; nothing like the earthy Tamangs who loved to sing and tell dirty jokes.

While supper was being prepared, Matt and Lopsang presented their Ganesh trekking permits to the local official, who meticulously recorded the information in a large black ledger. Ang Samden Sherpa had already cleared the way for the climbers and left word that he and the porters would be waiting for the team somewhere between Tato Pani and the alpine meadows below Paldol. Thanget was the last official outpost between Syabru Bensi and the wild country of the Tibetan highlands.

When Matt emerged from the police post half an hour later, an argument was in progress in the courtyard. Before he could make any sense of it, Jake pulled him aside, saying, "We may have to do something about Stu."

The naturalist was wagging a thick finger in Buzz Bessman's face and lecturing him about field medicine. The doc had the medical kit open by his feet, and behind him was the usual line of porters with blisters, coughs, running sores, and intestinal ailments. Behind these few, however, stood at least two dozen villagers without appointments.

"This has to stop right now," Sinotti was saying. "You think you're helping them, but you're only making matters worse."

"I'm just treating a few blisters and toothaches, Stu," Buzz said in a calm voice.

"I have no problems with the blisters. If you feel you need to brush up rudimentary procedures during this trek, fine, that's your choice. But I must ask that you refrain from dispensing aspirin or any other medications."

Bessman's hairy arms flexed under the short sleeves of his surgeon's shirt. "Have you seen the inside of that so-called clinic?" he asked, pointing. "I've got more in this bag than they have in that entire medicine cabinet."

Sinotti's hands shook. "Then donate your medicine to the clinic. But leave it to the doctors who staff this place to prescribe it."

"And meanwhile these people should go right on suffering, is that it?"

Matt stepped in between them with both hands raised. "Everyone just calm down," he began. "Stu, just back off for a minute." He turned to Bessman. "Buzz, here's the deal: We're only going to be here overnight. You hand out an aspirin for a toothache and somebody just might have a pain-free night. But then you're not here for the follow-up. And it's worse when the aspirin doesn't work because whoever's taking it starts to lose faith in the stuff. Then when some nurse or doctor shows up to administer pills, the people throw them away."

"Man's got a point," Travis Dey offered from the sidelines, where he was standing with the fair-haired Morgan.

"Who asked you, Travis?" Buzz said.

Matt heard Morgan's laugh, but the doc either didn't hear it or chose not to respond to it.

"I've watched porters *trade* antibiotics some well-meaning physician has given them to treat coughs and infections," Sinotti said. "And I've seen even bigger fools hand out Good 'n' Plenty placebos. 'The pink ones are for very bad,' " he mimicked, " 'the white ones are for not so bad.' These are adults," he added, gesturing to Bessman's would-be patients, most of whom were grinning by then. "If they haven't learned to take care of their own feet, they shouldn't be working as porters."

"Here, here," Travis said. "Well put, Stu."

Helpful guy, Matt thought, biting back a remark. Buzz had his mouth open to say something when a beaming Barbara sidled into the circle, displaying a buffalo-horn bracelet on her wrist. "*Look* what I just found," she announced to everyone present. Matt took a look at Stu's face and aimed a gesture of surrender Jake's way.

Someone asked Barbara how much she had paid. "One hundred rupees," she said, proud of herself. The Tibetan woman who sold them had apparently put up quite a fight. From the pockets of her jacket, Barbara produced a hand-woven belt and a silver bracelet set with a blood-red stone. "I also got these. Aren't they magnificent?"

Sinotti glanced at them and issued a snort of disapproval. "Wonderful. You probably bargained her right out of her family heirlooms."

Barbara showed him a perplexed look. "She didn't *have* to sell them, Stu. She could have refused, you know."

"Oh, she was supposed to turn down your money? She's supposed to hold onto a bracelet that won't fetch a *paise* in Thanget, but's going to put a hundred *rupees* worth of food on her table if she sells it to some *mem-sahib*? So what if it's a piece of her family history? So what if it's one of the few valuables she got to take with her when she fled Tibet—"

"Screw you, Stu!" Barbara snarled. "You weren't there when I bought this. I know what they're getting for these in Kathmandu, and let me tell you something: This poor Tibetan refugee of yours was one smart business-woman. And frankly, I don't give a damn what you think." She shook her head in frustration and forced a breath. "I need a run," she said a moment later. "There's a path just behind the compound. Anyone care to join me?"

"I'll go," Travis said. He swung to Morgan and urged her to come along. "Be serious," she told him.

Matt whirled on Sinotti when the trekkers and porters had dispersed some. "You and me are gonna have a talk," he seethed, just loud enough to be heard.

📧 10 📧

Fair Means

Matt and Stu walked in silence, the sun disappearing behind the Ganesh highlands. West of Thanget where the Chilime forked, the grain-green land was adorned with shoulder-high *mani* walls—linear heaps of stone tablets, capped with mounds of sun-dried ganga. By custom one passed to the left of them, offering up a stone or a prayer of supplication to the godhead.

"I can't take much more of it, Matt," Sinotti said at last. "I'm sick of taking groups out here."

"Yeah, well, there's a lot of that going around," Matt told him. "But we're here, and these people have paid a bunch of money for our services."

The naturalist scowled. "I won't compromise my ideals—especially with people like Barbara, who should know better."

"Cut her some slack, will you? She bought a couple of trinkets. You've got everybody walking around on eggshells, afraid they're going to do something to set you off."

Sinotti kicked a stone off the trail, then muttered an apology. "But we're part of a much bigger problem," he wanted Matt to understand. "We're here to walk and climb in these mountains and—"

"Stu," Matt cut him off. "Save it. Look, maybe you were right to lecture the doc; but I'm only reminding you

92

that you were hired to talk to everyone about plate tectonics and climate zones, not beat them over the head with ecotourism. If you figure you can't do it . . .'' Matt shrugged. ''It's no more than you demanded of Karl. Or Buzz. You understand?''

Stu stopped short to turn on him. ''I'll do my job,'' he said, raising a forefinger but changing his mind about deploying it. ''But it's you and Jake and Barbara and the rest who don't understand.''

''I say we give him to base camp to get his act together,'' Matt told Jake later on. ''If he doesn't, we send him back with the porters.''

Jake set aside a plate of noodles and boiled potatoes. ''I don't know. The price included a lecturer.''

''So we get Candice or Barbara to talk about mountaineering. You and I can entertain them with travel tales. We'll talk about Peru—''

''Or Mexico?'' Jake said with a wink in his eye. ''Or Bali maybe?''

Matt frowned. ''Better than finding a Swiss army knife sticking out of Stu's neck one morning.''

''I'll think about it,'' Jake said, exhaling.

Matt contemplated his carbohydrate plate. He was fast losing his taste for the fare, but knew better than to pass on the essential calories the noodles and potatoes provided. In the end, he shoveled the concoction into his mouth without thinking about it.

The evening air was chilled and he stopped by his tent to suit up in vest and cap before heading for the fire. Karl, Doug, and a few of the others were sipping coffee, tuned in to Willie Nelson, or Candice, who was responding to Taylor's questions. Over the tips of the flames, Matt studied Doug Makey for signs of intelligence community tampering. He'd had dealings with the mind-set before and could sometimes identify it. Doug certainly didn't look or act the part of a government man, but then operatives were difficult to make in the Reagan era.

Eventually he settled into the spot Morgan Bessman abruptly abandoned, next to Travis Dey. He leaned over to ask the software designer how the run with Barbara had been.

"Trail's a bit rough in places," Travis said quietly, "but it's a good jog. Winds through a patch of birch and alder behind the camp."

Matt followed Dey's finger. "Where's Audrey?" he asked a moment later.

"Where she always is: in the tent."

Travis's expression warned him away from the subject, so Matt turned his attention to the interview. The climbers' mail runner had arrived from Kathmandu with news that their replacement teammate wasn't coming after all. Julia Tremont and her husband had left for the States. The Sherpa had no word on how she made out with the rental company.

"Women climbers are just going to have to accept the fact that a lot of expeditions are inviting them along because of their sex and not necessarily because of their ability," Candice was saying. She was sheathed in pile, crowned by a red beret. "Every team needs funding, and if a woman's presence is going to make it easier to find sponsors, then so be it."

"Have you found yourself invited along for sponsorship?" Taylor wanted to know.

Candice nodded. "And I've made it clear that I'm not interested in doing trade routes on brand-name peaks just so a bunch of climbers can add another ascent to their resumes."

"So you think an ascent should be a 'creative statement,' as someone has termed it?"

"Absolutely."

"But what happens when you get to the mountain? As a woman climber are you given a fair shot at the summit?"

"That depends on who you climb with. Unless the expedition is exceptionally well led, there's bound to be complaints about hauling supplies just to support one or two climbers' bids for the summit. But I've been on expeditions lately where two teams are sharing a permit and both have women climbers along. Suddenly everybody's so into this 'summit a woman' thing that it becomes a game for one team to get 'their women' to the top before the other team gets to summit *theirs*." Candice shook her head. "I'm beginning to hate the whole Everest business. I just wish one of us would get to the top and close the lid on this thing once and for all.''

Taylor slipped a fresh cassette into the tape recorder. ''It seems to be a commonly held notion—among men climbers, at any rate—that women aren't as adventurous at high altitudes. That we're too concerned about losing fingers or the tip of our noses to frostbite.''

''Yeah, I've heard that crap, too. And you hear these same men talk about how they've seen us practically kill ourselves trying to prove that we're as strong as men. That they've never been on a mountain with a woman who could pull her weight. But as far as I'm concerned, the men who are saying this have forgotten why it is they climb. Or maybe they've been climbing for the wrong reasons all along. Ego needs and competition shouldn't be what climbing is about; and when men say that we're 'killing' ourselves up there, they fail to understand that it's the *mountain* we're challenging, not their fragile egos.''

Taylor smiled in the firelight. ''Getting back to basic fears and differences in technique, just where does personal vanity fit into any of this? Or does it?''

''I don't know of a woman climber who's turned back from a summit attempt because she was worried about her looks. I mean, of course it's a concern; but I haven't heard it expressed by women any more than men. And if you've ever seen the way people look when they return from an eight-thousand-meter climb through blizzard conditions, you know no one's doing it to cultivate a cover-girl complexion or a centerfold figure.

''The fact is most people don't climb for the publicity or the product photos. I'll admit a metal-tipped nose wouldn't make it in promotion ads, but I've never let my fear of that—or lost toes—get in the way of my climbing. All this *seems* important now because certain climbers have become high-profile spokespersons in magazines and whatever. I just don't care about any of that. I know I'm in for trouble as soon as I start buying into the hype.''

''Then why do you climb?'' Taylor said.

''Oh, God,'' Candice said, ''that's the one I always have trouble fielding. 'Because it's there' doesn't explain

it, but I do think it *expresses* it. People talk about the
high you get from being on the edge and the sense of
accomplishment. But in the last analysis—even with a
support team—a climb is an individual endeavor with very
differing personal satisfactions. And maybe one of the
reasons for the schisms that come about, is that each of
us knows these intensely private moments are going to
have to be externalized and shared."

Later, the Tibetans and the Tamangs staged an im-
promptu get-together. The villagers were decked out in
dragon bracelets, pectoral ornaments, and strands of coral
beads. The women porters sang old standards and danced
a hip-hop step in opposing lines. *Rakshi* was passed
around—poured from brass-strapped wooden bottles into
silver-lined bowls.

Puma's group entered into the merriment, drinking and
partying themselves silly. On the front porch of the police post, Doug Makey danced with Candice to Robert
Palmer's "Addicted to Love," while Chris played air-
guitar on one of the ski poles. Jake danced with Kaylee
and Barbara. Stu, Lopsang, and the kitchen crew stood
off to one side, clapping out of time. Karl asked the Bessmans and the Deys to join him in some black hash.

Determined not to move for the rest of the evening,
Matt was stretched out in front of his tent with a canteen
concoction of overproof rum, *rakshi*, and NutraSweet
Grape Kool-Aid. But it wasn't long before Dee-Dee and
Maurice Delong sought him out. They were higher than
he was.

"Touchy scene this afternoon between Stuart and Dr.
Bessman," Dee-Dee said. "I thought it particularly interesting that you stepped in."

Matt took a pull from the canteen. "You figure I should
have let them argue it out."

"The results might have proved more enlightening."

"In terms of establishing a hierarchy," Maury chimed
in. "A pecking order."

Dee-Dee was smiling. "Really, Matt, if you're going
to keep intruding . . . I mean, I realize it's your job and
all . . .''

"Try to think of us as rats dropped into the same cage, all scrambling for position," Maury started to say.

"I do," Matt told him. "It's just that I see it more as a maze. And believe me, I've been through this one before."

Karl was red-eyed stoned when he wandered over. "I finally got a bead on it, partner," he announced without preamble. He made an inch sign with thumb and forefinger. "With a bit of help from Dee-Dee. See, the problem was I kept putting my wife on one of those pedestals everybody's always talking about. And the higher I put her, the more shit I got in return. And ya know why?"

"Why?" Matt asked tiredly.

" 'Cause she didn't feel like she belonged up there's why. She had a low self-image. So what she needed wasn't somebody telling her how special she was, but somebody booting her around, playing to just what she thought of herself."

By the time Taylor plopped herself down beside him on the nylon tarp, Matt had most of the canteen drained. She took a sip of the mix, twisting up her face when she handed the canteen back to him. "Gawd, that's awful-tasting stuff."

Matt nodded. "Like cough medicine."

"Romilar," Taylor slurred.

"One of 'em."

"Stu," Taylor said, and began again. "Stu is afraid the Tibetans are going to end up xenoiatrophobic." Matt tried and failed to repeat the word. "Fear of foreign doctors," she explained. "Of course, he's got a case of hypselotimophobia himself when it comes to the handicrafts—fear of high prices."

Matt stared at her. "Came all the way over here to tell me this, huh?"

"No." She held up a finger and blinked her eyes. "No, I've got a story for you." She laughed and drew a breath. "Seems Barbara and Kaylee were on a climb in China together. This was a couple of years ago and they had to fill out these ridiculous customs forms when they arrived, because the Chinese were dead set against allowing anything in the country that might undermine the moral fiber of the people. So what does Barbara do but get a hold of

Kaylee's customs declaration form, and she writes down under transistor radio and flashlight and all that, 'one battery-operated vibrating marital aid.'

"Well," and Taylor laughed again until tears ran from the corners of her eyes, "when the customs officers read Kaylee's form, they practically tore her pack apart looking for the thing. They actually threatened to strip-search her to see if she was wearing it!"

Matt recalled the flat tone Kaylee used when she told him she had climbed with Barbara in China.

"You don't think it's funny?"

"Sure it's funny."

"So funny you forgot to laugh, right?"

He laughed then and they turned to watch the dancers. "We need a nun with a ruler to get between Travis and Morgan," Taylor said. "And check out Doug and Barbara. Turns out they have about a dozen mutual friends in D.C. The small-world syndrome. But Doug doesn't know Barb's husband. Different political circles, you understand."

Jake was waving them over to the porch; but Matt only grinned back and raised the canteen in salute. "What's the matter, you don't dance?" Taylor asked.

"Be a miracle if I could stand up," he told her. He tipped the canteen to his lips, shivering as he set it aside. "I listened to you with Candice. Good job. The Feminist Mountaineer's Manifesto. Your editors'll eat it up."

"So when are you going to let me do you?"

"*Do* me?"

She gave his arm a whack with the backs of her fingertips. "You know what I mean."

"Interviewaphobia," he said.

"You're just worried about being found out."

He tried to focus on her face, which kept bobbing around in his *rakshi*-ed field of vision. "Found out by who?"

"That's the part I can't figure. Sometimes you seem like a regular guy; other times it's like you're carrying the world around with you."

"I don't smile enough, is that it?"

Their shoulders touched as she reached past him for the canteen. He could smell lilies in her hair.

"Come on, Matt. Look around us: We're in *Nepal*!"

"Save that for your travel articles. Only promise me one thing. That you won't begin: 'Nepal is a land of contrasts. . . .' "

Taylor fell silent for a moment. "Don't you like being out here?"

Matt let the sounds of the porters' songs wash over him. The moon was a fuzz of light peeking over the mountains.

"I know you do," Taylor continued. "So maybe what you don't like is being out here with *us*." Again she didn't wait for an answer. "I was wrong. You're not like Stu at all. You're more like Candice. What you get out of wandering is personal, and you just don't enjoy sharing the experience."

Matt forced his eyes open, as though to see things clearer. "Tell me my phobia," he managed. "And how much money the cure's going to cost me."

Taylor said, "I like you, Matt. Doesn't that entitle me to some rights?"

"Property rights," Matt said. "But you can't touch what you can't see."

"You're like a rock 'n' roller singing about how terrible it is to be on the road, even while you're busy making plans for the next tour. You're thinking you've either got to settle down somewhere, or continue wandering on your own, and you can't bring yourself to do either. So in a way, we're all you've got."

"Is this what altitude does to you, or are you naturally nosy?"

Taylor laid a cool hand against his cheek. "Poor Matt," she said, leaning her face close to his. "It's like the song almost goes: 'I'd rather have the blues than what you got.' "

He remembered crawling into his tent and passing out after the party had wound down. He thought he remembered kissing Taylor, or Taylor kissing him, but it might as well have been a fragment of a dream.

He'd tried to rouse himself when the porters commenced their morning hacking rituals, but it was no go. A bit later, with faint light filtering into the tent and the zipper and Velcro movement beginning, he heard Barbara try to whisper Travis awake for a morning run. And later still he heard her trying to interest Chris in joining her.

"No way, man," the teenager moaned, "the rack monster's got me for another hour."

It was Pasang who brought him around, unzipping the front door and saying, *"Chiya, sahib."* Matt got one eye opened and trained it on the man's dark face. "Tea, *sahib,*" the cook's assistant repeated, showing Matt a smile absent several teeth.

Matt struggled into fresh socks and shirt, overcoming his nausea little by little with sips of the highly sweetened brew, and slipped out to greet an overcast day. It was of some solace that everyone in camp appeared to be equally hung over.

"Rugged night," he said to Jake, whose head was poking out from his tent.

"Is it over?" Jake asked in a pained voice.

"Far as I can tell." Matt crawled over to Jake's tent and signaled Pasang to bring two cups of coffee.

"What are we facing today?"

Matt squinted at the ridge line north of the Chilime. "Thirty-five hundred feet of uphill for starters. Then an hour's contour and we're at the hot springs."

Jake sighed and lowered his head to the dew-spotted tarp. "A light at the end of the tunnel."

Matt gave it a long moment. "Listen, Jake. At some point we've gotta talk seriously about this office job—"

"Oh, no," Jake said, up on elbows all of a sudden. "Now what?"

Matt pivoted on his ass and found Barbara and Karl hobbling into camp, arms around each other's shoulders. It was difficult to tell who was supporting whom.

"Not my morning," Barbara announced, as Lopsang hurried over to help her sit down. She bent down to inspect her bruised knees and laughed at herself. "Got these big feet of mine snagged in the bushes. I'm glad no one was around to see it."

"I was out at the latrine," Karl said. "Saw her limping in."

Pasang arrived with the coffee and Matt conveyed a cup over to Barbara. "That'll teach you to jog."

"I'm fine. It's just road rash." Her T-shirt and shorts were wet and smudged with mud.

"Let me look at those knees," Doc Bessman was saying, squatting at Barbara's feet. She toughed it out while the physician completed a gingerly inspection of the damage. "I'm going to get my kit," he told her.

It was then Matt noticed the short swath of abrasion on her left shin, just above the lip of her wool sock. "You say you got tangled up in the bushes?"

Barbara took a sip of coffee and nodded. "The trail's overgrown in a few places. I must have caught my foot in a root or something. I nearly fell flat on my face." She showed him the heels of her hands. "Road rash."

Matt looked at her shin again. "Same trail as yesterday?"

"Same one. I suppose I should have waited until it was lighter out."

Matt held her gaze. "I want to see where you fell."

🏵🏵 11 🏵🏵

Hot Water

Matt parted the ferns where they met over the footpath and touched a hand to the damp ground. Barbara's and Travis's running-shoe prints were still visible from the previous day, as well as the scuff marks and grooves Barbara had left half an hour before.

"I don't see the point to all this, Matt," Barbara said from a few feet away. "I snagged my foot and fell. Here," she added, gesturing to the path where it made a sudden dip out of the fern ground cover and twisted down into a birch-studded hollow. "I'll bet we can find where my hands hit."

Matt straightened up, clapping dirt off his palms and glancing both ways down the mostly hidden path. The air was cool and mist was lingering at treetop level. A white-rumped swift darted out of the hollow with something dangling from its beak. Barbara's eyes tracked the bird, then came to settle on Matt as he was stepping into the ferns off to one side of the trail to examine the trunk of a birch sapling. "Who knew you were going to be jogging this morning?" he asked after a moment.

Barbara climbed up out of the hollow with short steps, her bare knees and shin painted with antiseptic. "Why don't you just tell me what you're after, Matt?"

He forced a grin. "I heard you wake up Travis and

Chris. But who else knew you were going to be out here?"

"Oh, for Christ's sake," she said, looking over her shoulder toward camp. "Shouldn't we be dropping the tents instead of playing twenty questions out here?"

He rustled the ferns over the path with his hands, shaking loose a brief shower of droplets. "There aren't any exposed roots, Barbara. Or creepers. I mean, I can see where your foot slid out. I just can't find what tripped you."

"So I tripped over my own feet, Matt. It wouldn't be the first time."

"You weren't curious enough to check for yourself?"

Her laugh was a mix of amusement and exasperation. "Picture me down on my face with my knees smarting, Matt. I was thinking more about getting back to camp than scolding one of the ferns."

Matt scratched at his cheek. "Yeah, guess you're right. But humor me for a minute: Travis knew, Chris knew . . . Who else?"

Barbara puffed out a cloud. "Fine, Matt. Candice knew, Buzz knew, Karl and Taylor knew . . . Ask who *didn't* know?"

"But who knew the route—aside from Travis?"

She shook her head. "I can't help you there. But it's a straight run from here to the campsite. You can see the latrine tent from the bottom of the hill. I suppose anyone could have seen us come in yesterday afternoon."

Matt paced down the path until he had the latrine tent in sight. The path ran several yards behind it but merged with the latrine trail just short of the clinic courtyard. "Was anyone awake when you left camp?" he asked as he was climbing the hill.

Barbara laughed. "Which one of us is the lawyer here?" They stared at each other for a moment before she relented. "Most of the members of our traveling TB ward were awake. Tell me you can sleep through their hacking."

"No way."

"Stu and Kaylee were awake. And I think I saw Doug heading for the latrine." She folded her arms. "Now, unless you have further questions for the witness-slash-victim . . .''

"Just one: Have the porters been hassling you?"

"Of course they have. You know how they are. But I've dealt with their nonsense before. I just rib them right back." Her brow furrowed as she regarded him. "I hope you don't think they had anything to do with this?"

"Just checking;" he told her.

Matt watched her limp off. What was it, he asked himself, that made people ignore the signs? Maybe it was better not to know where the bullets originated. That way you didn't have to spend half your life ducking; you just kept your head up and hoped for the best.

When Barbara was out of sight, he squatted down to take hold of the crudely fashioned stake someone had concealed among the ferns bordering the path opposite the birch sapling. The stake had been pounded into the soft earth at an oblique angle, but the force of Barbara's fall had yanked it forward in its hole and it was standing nearly vertical now. A three-foot length of thin, hemp rope was knotted under a V-notch two inches from the stake's rounded top. It was the rope that had given Barbara the shin burn. The knot was a kind of porter's hitch, frequently used to secure cargo to pack ponies and yaks.

Tugging the stake from the ground, Matt wasn't surprised to discover that it was close to two feet long; nor that it had been cut from a well-used Tamang walking stick. The recent sharpening and notching had been done with a *khukri*, rather than some small bladed knife.

The young birch was similarly notched. Matt assumed that the rope had been slipknotted around the base of the tree; that it was meant to have come undone once Barbara tripped it.

He slapped the stake against the palm of his hand, wondering if he'd erred by not showing her the thing. Pretend like I didn't tell you, he could have told her. I'll keep an eye on your back and we'll flush out this whacko. But she might have gone running to Jake or Lopsang, and that was surely just what the trickster wanted.

Presently he untied the rope and gave the stake a toss. Coiling the rough hemp around his fingers, he shoved it into the inner pocket of his vest and returned to camp.

* * *

Halfway through the morning ascent—under the pretext of ridding himself of the vest—Matt stepped off the switchback trail and zipped open his pack. The slate rooftops of Thanget and the wooden bridge across the Chilime were visible two thousand feet below, the river a ribbon of white-flecked silver.

The trekkers filed past him with barely a word—Buzz and Karl up front, Taylor and Audrey lagging way behind. Faces flushed, feet dragging; everyone was getting a real workout. Matt's own temples were throbbing, though less from exertion or altitude gain than *rakshi* hangover.

Lopsang appeared around a bend in the trail a few minutes later, a walk-in-the-park look gracing his handsome features. Matt pulled him aside, but waited for a cluster of porters to go by before he explained himself.

"But what is Tulo and this?" the *sirdar* asked, handling the rope like a snake charmer.

"Maybe nothing. I just want him to have it."

Lopsang shrugged and slipped Vuarnet sunglasses back down over his nose. The sun was giving the day its best shot, but the weather hadn't improved any. Matt could smell rain on the wind coming out of the Ganesh. Across the Chilime, fresh snow powdered the southwest ridge line at twelve thousand feet.

They were discussing the weather when Tulo trudged into view, knobby hands hooked on the leather tumpline that wedded him to his basket load. His expression was placid until he noticed Matt and Lopsang sitting by the side of the trail; then he smiled, nodding his head in servile acknowledgment. The Sherpa waved him over and Matt handed him the rope as the line of porters came to a halt. Speculation broke out as to whether Tulo was about to be rewarded or admonished.

Tulo accepted the rope as though it were a strand of prayer beads, and the porters' chatter dissolved into confused mutterings.

"He asks what you want him to do with it," Lopsang told Matt. Matt gave Tulo his best penetrating gaze. "I want him to think of me when he handles it."

Lopsang translated and Tulo grinned. "He wants to

know if it is a gift.'' Tulo said something over his shoulder and laughter erupted along the porter train.

''Tell him it's for luck.''

Tulo smiled up at him, wrapping the rope around his hands and giving it a forceful tug. *''Danyabad,''* he directed to Matt. ''Thank you.''

Matt didn't return the smile. ''Ask him where his walking stick is.'' The Sherpa and the Tamang conversed for a moment, and Lopsang said, ''He says it broke in half and he threw a part of it in the Trisuli. Yesterday morning, at the bridge.''

Tulo's reaction was just what Matt had expected. Or close to it, he told himself, back into the switchbacks now, one foot in front of the other. Winded. Because all this thinking was throwing his rhythm off.

Letting Karma loose—all right, that would have been like the wiry Tamang. But setting up a trip-wire for Barbara or whomever it was meant to bring down? Tulo just didn't fit the bill as a psychopath.

And did Karma *figure into it at all?*

Was there even a connection between the dog and the snare? The snare and the hole in the trail? The *modus operandi* was the same. But as some literary detective had once pointed out, there was simply too much evidence at the scene of the crime. It seemed far more likely that someone was deliberately implicating the porters.

And wasn't it after all the trekkers who had done most of the complaining about the poodle? Doug Makey for one. Then there were all the recent arguments and revelations: Stu was angry with Barbara; Kaylee had once been the target of a Barbara prank. Taylor said that Sinotti had a thing about climbers. Barbara confirmed that both Stu and Kaylee were awake when she left for her run. But then Travis Dey knew the trail better than anyone else; he'd run with her the previous evening. And yet he was supposed to have accompanied her, and given his trail fascination with Morgan Bessman who knew what Buzz and Audrey were feeling toward him?

What about the Delong*champs* and their self-confessed

interest in stress reactions? What about Karl for that matter? He'd been on the scene, and there was that *khukri* he'd purchased in Kathmandu. At the same time Travis and Buzz had purchased theirs . . .

Matt shook his head in an effort to clear his thoughts and only ended up jumbling them. He knew he'd have to tell Jake eventually, when he was feeling less proprietary about his suspicions.

Including the jeep accident, the snare had been the *second* attempt on Barbara's life. So perhaps someone on the trek didn't want Barbara participating in the Ganesh climb. Just the way that same someone hadn't wanted Julia along.

But counting the jeep accident, there had been two attempts on his own life as well.

By Tato Pani, Matt had decided the problem was one of insufficient sight. The pattern was eluding him, so perhaps it was a new maze after all. At the very least he needed a third eye like the one depicted between arched brows on Swayambunath's gilded cube. One to watch Tulo, one to watch Travis Dey, and one to watch Stu.

When all he wanted to watch were the four young Tamang women scrubbing each other down at the far end of Tato Pani's concrete rectangle of near-scalding iron-rich water.

The hot springs bubbled from a mountain cleft of hard-wood forest and meager pastureland; the baths were the size of a small-town public pool with a uniform depth of three feet. Off to one side was a one-room smoke-stained teahouse—a *bhatti*—and opposite it a kind of trading post for the piratical-looking highlanders whose sheep and cattle grazed on the steep hillsides above the baths. The animals had brought flies to the place, but hot water being the commodity it was in Nepal, no one seemed to mind.

The black-haired Tamangs were luxuriating in the pool when Matt arrived and dropped his pack, and they had been at it for over an hour, scouring each other's scalps and groins, rubbing each other's arms and legs and backs until the skin virtually glowed pink. They were dressed in little more than saris, which they tied above their

breasts like sarongs and hid behind as the washing got
under way. The net effect approximated that of a strip-
tease, or an erotic fan dance.

For Matt, the scene recalled the Teej Brata festival
he'd witnessed only a month or so back in Kathmandu,
when women from throughout the vale had converged on
Pashupatinath dressed in scarlet saris and golden wed-
ding dresses. There, in lascivious fashion, they stripped
and bathed in the muddy Bagmati, beseeching Shiva and
Paravati for continued conjugal contentment, while the
men ogled them through binoculars from the opposite
bank.

The four Tamang were as thrilled by the attention they
were receiving as Puma's male contingent was enthusiastic about bestowing it.

But then Candice and Taylor and Morgan—although
seemingly unaware of it—were eliciting the same reaction from the porters, who were fascinated to the point
of immobility by the Americans' ability to wash themselves without removing their bathing suits. Matt thought
it might have something to do with the sight of hands and
arms and soap bars slipping around under all that form-
hugging Lycra spandex.

The highlanders, on the other hand, were content to
sit on their haunches smoking cigarettes and *chilims*, and
observe the entire scene with a faintly clinical objectiv-
ity. Chris, too, was disinterested. His back turned to everyone, he was standing in the waves the women were
creating, knees bent and arms outstretched, making
swooshing surfer noises to himself. Kaylee was shooting
him from a distance, not far from where Barbara was
nursing her sore knees.

A strange thing had happened when the American
women first appeared from the maintenance shed where
they'd changed into their swimsuits, and Matt was still
trying to figure what if anything he should do about it.
Morgan had emerged in an electric-blue string bikini,
followed by Audrey Dey, in a plain suit with an attached
pleated skirt that was anything but flattering to her figure.

Audrey was rounder and softer-looking than Morgan,
but she carried herself with an innocent grace that was
equally appealing. Audrey's eyes had traveled from Mor-

gan to Travis—who was also watching Morgan—and on to Matt. Both Matt and Audrey had then turned to Travis, then to Morgan, then back to Travis before locking in on each other once again.

The older woman's expression was pained when she spun on her heels and disappeared back into the shed. She was off by herself now, angrily waving her Puma expedition cap at the flies.

Surrendering interest in the Tamang women, Matt put his pants on over his wet swimsuit and was headed in Audrey's direction when a commotion broke out in front of the teahouse.

Tulo came stumbling backward out of the doorway, waving his arms and shouting at the cruel-faced high-lander who was pursuing him, brandishing a sheathed *khukri* and an aged walking stick. The Tibetan was dressed in baggy pants, a black-belted cloak, and red wool boots that reached his knees.

A circle of porters and locals quickly formed around the pair, contributing their own voices to the argument. Matt couldn't make out what was being said, but he could see—through waving fists and over the tops of dozens of *topi*-ed heads—that Tulo was on the defensive. The Tamang was being accused of trying to steal the Tibetan's *khukri*; the highlander even pulled an eyewitness forward to give an account. Several of Puma's porters were back-ing Tulo up, but not one raised a hand to protect him when the Tibetan suddenly batted Tulo on the side of the leg with his heavy stick. The Tamang went straight down, curling himself in the dirt with hands interlocked on his injured knee.

The Tibetan continued shouting for a moment more. Then he waited to see if anyone was going to take issue with him before he stomped back into the teahouse.

"These people are rough ones," Lopsang said, ap-pearing at Matt's side out of the dispersing crowd. "Very coarse. Many bandits."

"Did Tulo try to steal the knife or not?"

"Oh, he did. He says he lost his knife along the river."

Matt's eyebrows arched. "First he tells us his walking stick broke, now it's his knife?"

The *sirdar* shrugged. "Tamang not careful with their things. Always replace them."

"*Mis*place them."

"That, too."

When Matt looked next, one of the older women porters was standing over Tulo's prone form, cursing him out. "Tulo's mother," Lopsang explained.

Matt did a double take. "His mother's one of our porters?"

The Sherpa nodded. "Oh, yes. She says now she will have to carry Tulo's load and her own. And that he has disgraced her." Lopsang chuckled to himself. "For getting caught, I think."

12

Cloud Forest Camp

The rugged ascent and the hot water took a toll on the group, and, what with rain moving in, afternoon stamina was in short supply. Several people were suffering from sore throats and diarrhea as well. (The kitchen staff was taking all the usual precautions—boiling the water for twenty minutes, soaking the vegetables in an iodine solution, generally trying to keep everybody's hands out of the pots—but sometimes even those measures failed.) Lopsang had hoped to catch up with the climbers' Sherpas, but Matt and Jake instead called camp in a fallow field an hour beyond Tato Pani, at the edge of a cloud forest that rose steeply from the north bank of the turbulent Chilime.

Under threatening skies the group foot-tamped level sites in the furrowed ground and passed the remainder of the afternoon applying moleskin to blisters and silicon sealer to the tent seams. Battening down the hatches. The rain commenced at 5:00 P.M., but broke half an hour before sundown, when gilded views of the Langtang's snow-capped peaks appeared high in the eastern sky through holes in the clouds. With the clouds moving askew to the horizon, it was almost as though one were standing on the upslope of a bowl and looking across to the opposite curvature; normal perspective was inverted,

111

and the result was a bewildering vertigo, a kind of space-station interior dislocation.

After supper, Stu gave a rambling lecture on plate tectonics, explaining how the India plate had crashed into the Asia plate, raising the Himalayan range. Later on, Morgan—one of the few who wasn't down with something—offered back rubs to the diehards around the fire. Buzz, Doug, Chris, Taylor, Dee-Dee, and Maurice had long since crawled into their tents. Karl said he would take a rain check. Travis took Morgan up on it, but only after Audrey announced in an aggrieved voice that she was turning in. Jake and Matt moved away from the fire to talk.

"Okay, so maybe she *would* like to see Travis in a body cast," Jake said. "That still doesn't mean she has the know-how to whittle down a walking stick and rig a snare using a porter's hitch. Besides, she and Travis were both inside the tent when Barbara asked him if he wanted to run. I'm sure of that much. Unless you're going to tell me she rigged the snare during the party."

Matt had told him about the stake, and after a heated go-round about accidents and circumstantial evidence, Jake had at least agreed to dismiss Tulo and his mother as soon as the group reached meadow camp.

"I know, I heard her in the tent this morning," Matt conceded. "But who's to say she can't wield a *khukri* with the best of them? Maybe her father served with the Gurkhas or something. I mean, what do we know about these people anyway, Jake? Just what they tell us on their application forms. And you can't figure someone's going to list 'psychopath' or 'homicidal maniac' under special interests or wilderness skills." He held up a hand to silence Jake's rebuttal. "No, I don't really think she rigged the snare expecting Travis to go out jogging. But there's shit going down we should attend to."

Jake shook his head. "Morgan Bessman's not our concern. Even if she is Travis's. We're all consenting adults."

"But she *will* be our concern if this group starts to come apart emotionally on the high pass."

"If."

"I'll give you the if. But it wouldn't hurt to get one of them to talk about it."

Jake made a sweeping gesture with his hand. "You want to play therapist, be my guest. But I think you should leave it to the professionals. Talk to Dee-Dee if you want. Maybe she can talk to Audrey."

Matt frowned as he stood up. "I've got no intention of playing therapist. And I've got my doubts about Dee-Dee's credentials."

At the Deys' tent a moment later, he zipped the rain-fly open and closed, as though ringing a doorbell. "It's Matt," he said to Audrey's who's that. "Mind if I come in?"

She stammered, "Matt? Um, why sure, um, just give me a second."

The dome tent was illuminated by a fat candle burning in a small brass-plated lantern. Travis and Audrey had matching mummy bags opened on full-length Thermarest mattresses. Although the bags could be zippered together, they weren't; and where there were wildlife guidebooks on Audrey's side of the tent, there were grip exercisers on Travis's.

Matt left his rubber thongs outside the door flap and settled himself cross-legged at the foot of the tent, hunching over just a bit. "Thought you might want to play some cards," he said, showing her a hand-oiled deck he'd been carrying around for several years.

"Cards?" She laughed. "I'm not much good."

"Hearts okay?"

Audrey stared at him, then shrugged and propped herself on an elbow opposite him. She was wearing quilted-cotton thermals and down booties. After a few minutes of silent play, she asked over the top of her cards, "Matt, is this something like an official visit?"

"Sort of," he admitted. "I just wanted to know how you were feeling. No sore throat or pulled muscles?"

"No, thank God." She looked away from him. "I've been lucky, I guess. And I'm very impressed with the way you and Jake are running things." She exhaled audibly and set her cards face down. "Matt, I know you're wondering about what happened at the hot springs—"

"If I'm trespassing . . ."

"No. You're not. I didn't mean to fly off the handle tonight, but it must be obvious to everyone by now that Trav is . . . *smitten* with Morgan. Back rubs," she snorted. "I just have to learn not to be so affected by it. But it's difficult when you find yourself in the midst of strangers and your emotions are on display twenty-four hours a day." Her eyes teared up.

"Of course, it's not like they can run off together." She made light of the idea. "We're like a small town, aren't we? Everyone involved in everyone else's business. In my more rational moments I don't even care about Trav's flirtation. He *is* hitting that magic forty-five," she said, as though it explained something.

Audrey had to be fifty, fifty-two, Matt thought. "I'm closing on that myself."

Her smile was tolerant. "Look, Matt, I don't know how much you're really interested in all this. I suspect it's part of your job to watch over everyone's emotional condition—maintain group integrity or however you term it. But you see, Trav and I married young. Well, young for him. We have two grown kids back home in Spokane, and this is the first time we've been away together in a long time. Away *alone* I should say." She sighed. "We were supposed to go to Tahiti last year, but Trav decided we didn't have the money—after he'd bought himself a little Japanese sports car, at any rate.

"I don't know for certain that he's been faithful to me all these years, but it really never concerned me because I think for the most part we've been happy together. As happy as any couple can be nowadays. He's always been a hard worker, and I've tried to be a supportive wife. I started teaching again a few years ago and that's sort of helped me over the trouble spots of turning fifty. Travis, though . . . Trav is just beginning to realize that he's forty-five and he's got two grown kids and that there's this whole new set of dilemmas confronting him all of a sudden.

"About six months ago when he got it in his head that we should see the Himalayas, I was thrilled. He started going to the gym and working out, all that stuff, and he bought me a membership, which I used all of *one* time. He lectured me about how I was setting myself up for hard times once we got here, and I guess he was right, seeing how I'm the slowest person in the group. God, even Constance was stronger than me, and she was sixty-eight. And look at Barbara. We're the same age and I could never do what she does.''

She paused to consider something. ''The thing is, I did get in shape in my own way. I walked, I read about the culture, the language, the religion. I didn't come here to conquer the mountains or rush through every day's stage like it was a marathon. I'm content to walk at my own pace. I enjoy seeing morning glories and butterflies and crab apple trees and all these beautiful wildflowers. But Trav came here to prove something to himself. And along came Morgan.''

Audrey shook her head and studied her hands. ''What is she, thirty-three, thirty-four? Oh, I don't suppose her age even matters. What matters is that she's sexy and strong and she knows how to wear clothes. I was never that way. I could never *be* that way, you know? I mean, I don't know what her story is with Buzz. She's his second wife, so maybe Buzz has already been where Trav is now. Anyway, Morgan's treating Buzz just the way Trav is treating me. It's like these two people have suddenly found each other and Buzz and I are evil presences or superfluous people or something. At first I thought she and I could be friends, but now she doesn't say two words to me. Lucky for me there's Barbara and Karl and Doug. I can't say much about Candice and Kaylee, because it seems like they're on their own separate trip most of the time.''

''They're getting ready to climb a mountain,'' Matt heard himself say.

''I'll tell you something in confidence, Matt: It may look like Trav and Buzz are getting along just fine, with all this rum and *rakshi* drinking and hashish, but they're not.'' Audrey rolled her eyes. ''God, I'll never smoke that stuff again. It just made me dwell on everything and feel really far away from my home and the things I love. I think Karl was just trying to help loosen up the situation, but it backfired. Morgan was . . . I don't even want to go into it.''

She hugged her knees to her chest. ''But Trav doesn't

like Buzz. And I think Buzz is starting to get upset about these flirtations. You saw the bikini Morgan was wearing. It's not that I wouldn't wear a suit like that if I had her figure, but I'd at least have sense enough to know where and when to wear it instead of flaunting what God gave me in front of all those Nepalese. They probably think she's some kind of American goddess.''

"Don't kid yourself," Matt told her. "They have other ways of making up their minds about people."

She said, "I'm sure you're right," showing him a faint smile and turning over her cards one by one. "I'm starting not to care about it. Let the two of them have their little high-altitude fling if that's what they need from this trip. I'll move into a separate tent if I have to. I'm just eager to get to base camp so I can take walks on my own and finish these novels I've been meaning to read for twenty years now."

"There'll be plenty of time for that," Matt assured her.

Audrey reached over to squeeze his hand. "Thanks, Matt. And by the way," she added as he was getting ready to leave. "I like Taylor a lot."

"Yeah, she's a lot of fun."

She nodded. "In fact, I think you two make a terrific couple."

Matt sat by the camp fire until almost midnight, shifting his attention between the tents and the tarp shelters. The fires were dying out and the porters were beginning to huddle under towels and threadbare blankets. It was only the rain that finally drove him into his tent.

It was still drizzling in the morning when they began their walk into the cloud forest—a dark magical place of bearded lichens, maple, and laurel, alive with the sounds of gurgling cascades and thunderous rapids. There were twisted, mossy oaks and cedar at the higher altitudes, concealing a thick understory of juniper, rhododendron, and ilex.

Three hours along they encountered a group of Japanese mountaineers returning from an unsuccessful ascent in the Ganesh. The climbers' lips were cracked and their faces were nearly black from the unshielded sun, save for what goggles and sunglasses had spared them. Some of them looked like victims of radiation—which they were, in effect—and they talked about how the weather had turned on them and made mention of freak storms that were dumping early snow on the Ganesh passes.

One of the men recognized Candice and they insisted on posing with her for photos and getting autographs. They then marched off toward Tato Pani, singing a happy Japanese song.

The Japanese mountaineers' liaison officer told Lopsang that the climb team's Sherpas were camped in a small clearing about five miles upriver, where the valley narrowed and the Chilime took a vertical plunge from the highlands through a notch of glacial rock.

It was pouring by the time the Puma group found them, and everyone seemed in miserable spirits. Everyone except Ang Samden Sherpa, who was actually doing push-ups under a tarp lean-to as Matt approached the camp.

"Ah, at last you arrive," the muscular Nepalese exclaimed, leaping to his feet and striding toward Matt in state-of-the-art hiking shoes and a clean gray-pile jogging outfit. "Now we can all move on together."

Gambu, the climb team's *sirdar*, showed Matt a pleading look.

Matt set his umbrella down, took a long look around the evergreen clearing, and immediately decided to call it a day. "I don't think so," he told Samden, loud enough to be heard above the rain. "We've had a real slog from Tato Pani and a couple of our people are sick."

Puma members were plodding in, muddied to the knees, some under umbrellas, others layered in Gore-Tex jackets and forest-green rain pants. No one was smiling. Least of all the Tamang porters, who were shivering under their basket loads and sheet-plastic slickers.

"Ah, but we're almost there," Samden countered, in a futile attempt to work up enthusiasm among the new arrivals. "By sunset we can arrive at the meadow." He gestured broadly to the Sherpas, most of whom were glaring at him. "My men are all prepared to leave. I myself will carry the loads of your sick ones."

"Forget it," Jake told him. "The weather's going to

be worse up there than it is here.'' He backhanded raindrops from the tip of his nose. ''Besides, our porters
aren't equipped for this. I'm not risking hypothermia just
to make a few more miles.''

Candice, Barbara, and Kaylee voiced agreement. ''You
and Gambu go on ahead if you want to,'' Barbara said
to Samden, practically shouting it. ''We'll overnight here
and catch up with you tomorrow.''

The liaison officer threw Lopsang and the hapless porters a disparaging glance. ''Lowlanders,'' he muttered.
And with that began to order Gambu and the Sherpas into
formation.

Jake crowded under Matt's umbrella and they walked
through a quick survey of the site. ''Well,'' Matt said in
a resigned tone, ''time to pick your puddle.''

⌘⌘ 13 ⌘⌘

Wild Country of the Soul

Matt awoke with the shakes; something was going on in his lower GI tract he didn't want to think about—roilings and rumblings, an internalization of the thunder rolling around the Chilime valley. He unfurled the watch cap down over his face and drew himself into a ball inside the sleeping bag, laying motionless for a few minutes, gathering strength.

The rain had continued throughout the night, torrential at times, and the nylon walls of the tent were beaded with water. A small pond had formed under his feet and saturated the lower third of the sleeping bag where there was no air mattress to keep it off the rubberized floor. Matt imagined Carlo lying high and dry somewhere down valley on his full-length Thermarest and tried not to fume.

He heard someone sloshing toward the tent and thought it might be Pasang or Num bringing tea, but it turned out to be Stu Sinotti.

"Did you instruct the porters to gather wood for a fire?" the naturalist growled. He was wearing high rubber boots and a Gore-Tex fisherman's hat.

Matt looked up at him from the doorway of the tent, squinting and reaching out to retrieve his thongs. "Of course I did. I figured we better have a load on hand in case the rain didn't let up. Which it hasn't," he added, after a head-rattling report of thunder intensified the violence of the downpour.

"I want you to see something," Sinotti said, marching off in the direction of the porters' shelter.

Matt fished a T-shirt and reasonably dry shorts from a Ziploc plastic bag he kept inside the tent. The kitchen staff was just beginning to deliver tea to the trekkers when he crawled outside, the morning air penetrating, a challenge for sweater and rain jacket. Where the ground wasn't slicked with puddles it was spongy and waterlogged.

The smoldering fire the porters had going under the angled tarps had already been fed the better part of a once-healthy oak; but even so there was little warmth to be had.

"They cut down an entire tree!" Sinotti said in angry disbelief. "An entire tree!"

Matt made several false starts at replying. Looking at the porters he could only think of sick puppies, pressed together in a confused, abandoned litter. A few of them were pale and slack-featured, and shivering uncontrollably. "Your tree's the least of our problems, Stu," he managed at last.

Sinotti balled up his fists and huffed. "Most of them sold the sneakers we purchased for them. And half of them didn't think to pack along anything warmer than a bath towel."

"I'm gonna get the doc over here," Matt said, turning to leave.

"And what about this tree? Who's going to nurse this tree back to health? You see what we do? You see what our vacations cost, Matt? You see?"

Huge pots of water were boiling over the cook fires in the kitchen tent. Pasang and Num were running barefoot deliveries of bowls of steaming oatmeal to the group. Matt found Jake and Lopsang standing under a striped golf umbrella in front of Jake's tent.

"We're going to recon the upper valley," Jake said, warming his hands around a mug of instant coffee. "Lopsang thinks there might be a few shepherds' huts up there. Might give us a place to store the duffels and gear. We could break camp as soon as the rain lets up."

"Yeah, like next month," Matt said, even louder than was necessary. Jake called him a pessimist. Matt shrugged. "I want Buzz to have a look at some of the porters. Then I'm going to rig a better shelter for them."

Jake nodded and set the cup down. The *sirdar* handed Jake the umbrella; they exited the clearing, and Matt made directly for the Bessman tent.

"Shivering, apathy, confusion," he was telling Buzz a few minutes later, crouched down at the doorway under the brown rain-fly. "I don't think any of them are hypothermic yet, but you'd know better than I would."

The anesthesiologist was struggling into trousers. Morgan was still inside her bag, applying color to high cheekbones with a soft, stubby brush. The spacious tent was stocked with catalogue-camper gadgets: battery-powered book lights, Cordura toiletry kits, collapsible cups, and plastic wash basins. "So the doctor gets to go on his rounds after all," Morgan said, staring into a square of burnished aluminum mirror. "You've made his day, Matt."

"And just what does it take to make *your* day, Morgan?" Buzz said, snapping closed his vest with a vengeance.

She showed him a weary look. "Please, Buzz." She turned to Matt. "Just how long are we going to be cooped up in here? I'm beginning to feel like part of the food chain."

"For the rest of today anyway."

"Wonderful."

"Do you want another Lomotil or not?" Buzz said from the door. Matt's gut cramped at mention of the drug and he almost asked for a pill.

Morgan went back to applying her face. "Don't trouble yourself, Buzz. You wanted an adventure, here it is. So get out there before it slips away."

Matt spent two hours chopping wood and improving on the lean-to the porters had constructed. Buzz urged that three of the porters be dismissed immediately; so Matt paid them off and sent them on their way in dry shirts donated by Doug and Karl.

He began his home visits with the Deys, who hadn't

left their tent all morning. Audrey was reading Proust. Travis was working on his grip. The vibes were so heavy inside the tent that Matt felt better off in the rain.

Doug and Chris were both inside their bags reading *Zen and the Art of Motorcycle Maintenance*; the cover of Doug's copy was green, Chris's was blue. The teenager was also wearing foam headphones, his Walkman cranked so loud Matt could hear the brilliant shriek of Eddie Van Halen's guitar.

Peppermint incense was smoldering in the Delong's tent and some sort of stripped-down disco music was throbbing from twin speaker cubes. Dee-Dee was wearing white silk ski thermals; Maury's were blue. The couple invited Matt inside and asked about the forecast.

"We could be here for a few days."

"A few days," Maurice mused, gyrating to the music. "You here that, babe? This tent's our port in the storm."

Dee-Dee ran a hand along his forearm. "It's the moment we wanted. Nothing to distract us." She looked at Matt. "We're going to acclimatize by meditating."

A television jingle erupted from the speakers, playing over the disco beat only to fade away in echo.

"Acid house," Maury told him.

Matt nodded uncertainly. Maury and Dee-Dee were gazing at each other in a dreamy-eyed way that usually meant drugs of one sort or another. 'Ludes, Matt thought, until they offered him a hit of Ecstasy.

Maury made an X with his forefingers. "MDMA, Matt—a variation on mescaline and methamphetamine. You can't beat it, you can't bum out." His grin had a maniacal edge to it. "It's a totally up experience, Matt. Rain or shine."

Matt declined. "Looks like you guys got a corner on happiness right now." A Richard Nixon voice-loop stammered along to the music's aggressive bass line.

"It's here when you want it," Dee-Dee told him. "It'll make you feel *gggoood*, Matt. Wouldn't it be great for the three of us to feel *ggoood* together? I'll bet we have a lot in common."

Matt looked at Maury, but Maury was staring at Dee-Dee. He thanked them again and eased toward the door. "Uh, do me one favor, though," he said from the other side of the mosquito netting. "Promise me you won't go passing that stuff around the camp."

Karl was in Taylor's tent playing gin rummy. It seemed the one genuinely tranquil spot in the campsite. "That's 'cause there's no gettin' this one down," Karl commented, motioning to Taylor with his heavily stubbled chin.

She snorted and laid down a trio of queens. "A little rain's supposed to bum me out? Not likely." Legs curled up under her, she was wearing black tights and a hooded red sweatshirt.

"Especially Himalayan rain, right?" Matt said.

She stuck out her tongue. "Your clients should all be so accommodating."

"No argument." Matt peered out the door in the direction of the climbers' tents. "Anybody seen Candice?"

"I think she's in her tent," Karl said in a distracted way. "Kaylee was snappin' photos of her in different foul-weather outfits."

"What about Barbara?"

Taylor said, "I think I saw her getting ready to jog."

Matt's stomach wrenched. "With those knees of hers?" he shouted before he could stop himself.

Taylor looked up from her cards. "What's your problem?"

Matt traded quick looks with her and hurried outside, wondering which trail Barbara had taken. But just then he heard her laugh, and a moment later she entered camp with Jake and Lopsang. She was already headed for her tent by the time Matt reached them.

"How do things look?" he asked Jake, with an eye on Barbara. Kaylee—bearing two steaming cups in hand—intercepted her halfway along and they disappeared into the North Face dome together.

"It's snowing up there," Jake was saying, motioning behind him.

"Any shelters?"

Jake shook his head. "Nothing we can use. Besides, Lopsang figures we're going to be socked in for three or four days."

Matt whistled. "That long? This place is going to be a lake by tomorrow afternoon."

"Still, we're better off with rain than snow."

Matt rocked his head. "Then we better erect the mess tent. We've already got a couple of potential cases of cabin fever."

"I might have a better idea," Jake said. "What would you say to going back to that potato field and checking out the conditions? Without a pack you could make it there and back in a couple of hours. If it looks good, we can move tomorrow. That way we'll at least have Tato Pani close by. If worse comes to worse, we go back to Thanget."

Matt mulled it over for a moment. A walk was just what he needed. "Give me five minutes to change, ten minutes to grab something to eat, and I'm gone."

Matt's attitude and physical well-being began to improve the moment he left camp. The trail was slippery and running with water in places, but he found the conditions suited to his needs. The uphills required controlled breathing and stamina, while the downhills demanded balance and surefootedness. And for the three hours it took him to reach the southeastern edge of the cloud forest, he thought only of the terrain and his progress through it.

He could see the Italian tents with their colorful banners long before he arrived at the fallow field. A fine windblown drizzle engulfed him as he emerged from the trees, but patches of blue sky holed the clouds down valley. A few of the trekking party's porters monitored his approach, and Carlo was on hand to meet him as he walked into camp. Mario Lanza was singing.

"You lost," the Italian tour leader said. He was dressed for après-ski.

Matt couldn't tell whether it was a statement or a question. He studied the layout of the campsite for a long moment, and judged there would be just enough ground for the Puma group if the Italians agreed to consolidate their tents somewhat.

"You ask us to make room for *you*?" Carlo's laugh had a certain Mediterranean panache. "After you ohmosta send us to our doom on the Trisuli? *Ti sei bevuto il cervello?* Go back to your forest lake.''

Matt recognized the word ''brain,'' but not much more than that. ''Come on,'' he said, close to losing it. ''Where's that Italian warmth I've heard about. *L'amore*, or however you say it. There's plenty of room here for all of us.''

Carlo smiled. ''You can go to Tato Pani, then.''

Matt actually liked the way he pronounced it, but was too enraged to give it more than a passing thought. ''We can't make Tato Pani in a day in this muck. You know fucking well this is the only decent place to end a stage.''

Carlo threw his hands up in a dismissive gesture. ''Too bad, eh?''

Matt glared at him, nodding his head.

''An' don't think about just showing up.'' Carlo indicated the two dozen Tamang porters and group members who were observing the exchange from fifteen feet away. ''We can make trouble for your group.''

Matt sighed and launched a weary laugh. ''The spaghetti western comes to the Himalayas.''

''I say you let me go find Ang Samden,'' Matt told Jake back at camp. ''With our porters and the climbers' Sherpas we could go back there and . . .''

Jake watched him. ''And what? Raze their campsite? Make off with their women?''

Matt shoveled a spoonful of lentils into his mouth and looked up from the table laughing. ''It'd be news, though, wouldn't it? Battle of the trekking groups.''

Jake's grin stopped short of a smile. ''Nepal gets any more popular, it could come to that someday.''

The mess tent was a high-ceiling, army-surplus affair with a ridge pole and a dozen guy wires. The supply-box tables could accommodate fourteen if need be, but Puma's group leaders normally encouraged their charges to eat in shifts to allow for a bit of elbow room. Everyone had eaten by the time Matt returned from his mission. It was just after 6:00 P.M. and still raining.

The trekkers had remained in the tents most of the afternoon, save for Stu and Karl, who had gotten into a shouting match after Stu learned that the Texan had presented the unhappy porters with a *Playboy* calendar. Just to keep them warm, the way Karl had explained it to Jake.

It was warmth that was on Matt's mind as he contemplated the soaked interior of his own shelter in the weak beam of a pocket flashlight. The sleeping bag was draped over a cord he'd strung lengthwise across the tent, but it was going to take a full day of sunshine to dry the damn thing out. The Thermarest mattress was floating in two inches of water. Nothing to do but bunk with Jake for the night, he decided.

He dragged the mattress outside, dug a stuff-sacked poncho liner from his pack, and was headed over to Jake's tent with everything underarm when Taylor met him in the dark.

"Checking into a hotel?"

"It'll seem like one after what I've been sleeping in."

"I was just about to invite you over."

He couldn't make out the details of her face. "That's right neighborly, ma'am. What exactly did you have in mind?"

Taylor pushed wet hair back from her forehead. "I've been trying to remember if I kissed you the other night."

"As opposed to me kissing you?"

"No," she said after a moment. "As opposed to me kissing someone else."

"Well, everybody's still up," Matt told her. "We could take a poll."

"I suppose. But I'm not sure I'd take the word of anyone in this group. Except for Chris, maybe."

"In that case we owe it to ourselves to talk about it."

"We do. We absolutely do."

Two hours later, lying wrapped around each other on the loft of the open sleeping bags, Matt figured he was as warm as he'd been in three days. As warm as he'd been in the baths, and twice as relaxed. He only wished he'd shaved while he had the hot water.

A game of cards had been their preliminary to love-making, meaningful eye contact and suggestive jokes. He caressed her shoulder in a friendly way and she put a hand atop his. They kissed with mouths wide open, lips barely touching, tongues darting, tentatively, teasing. Stuttered exhales as the warmth built in each of them; hands holding back from exploration, kneading, flexing.

In the end they'd made an adult, eighties choice and kept things confined to mouths and hands and pleasure spots—a self-imposed restriction that had only heightened the intensity of their passion. An adolescent promise of even more wondrous delights to come.

The blue walls of the octagonal tent were running with condensation. Two flashlights shone down on them from ceiling loops, broad spotlights suffusing the interior with a warm glow. Taylor was stretched out in a sleeveless top, white socks, and panties. She had small breasts with upturned nipples and a flat tummy. Her slim legs and underarms hadn't seen a razor in some time.

"Lots of room for one person," Matt said, looking about from the crook of her arm. He was wearing an ikat shirt he'd picked up in Borneo months back.

She nuzzled his hair. "And I suppose you'll be wanting to move a few things in now."

"I just need one drawer. Maybe a couple inches of closet pole. I don't have much of a wardrobe."

"First I want flowers."

"They'll have to wait for Kathmandu. The Nepalese have a saying that picking wildflowers and scolding children are the two worst things anyone can do."

Taylor pinched his arm. "An easy out. I'm glad we did this," she said after a moment. "Fantasies'll only take you so far."

"Depends on the fantasies."

She took her arm out from under his head and planted a line of kisses down his chest, lifting his shirt and laying her cheek against his belly. "At first I told myself, no way. This was going to be a solo trip. But I changed my mind after you kissed me in Thanget."

"I did that?"

"Go ahead and deny it, but you did. You tasted like *rakshi* and grape Kool-Aid, but your lips felt good. Anyway, I was watching you at Tato Pani while you were busy ogling those Tamang women and I thought, so much for promises."

"I wasn't ogling. I was observing."

"Of course you were." Taylor stroked his thigh as he stroked her hair. "Want to know what made me change my mind? I started to notice things about your body. Like your eyes and your shoulders. And your feet—you realize you've got third-world feet?"

"I do a lot of walking. That's what's spread them out."

"And all your scars."

"It's living in the tropics. Cuts don't heal the same." Matt wondered if she was going to get around to mentioning the thinning hair, the love handles, the touch of cottage cheese under the skin, the hair growing out of his ears. Only last month a molar had worked itself loose and fallen out, just like that.

"And you're lean, like the Nepalese."

"It's not always easy to eat right in Asia. You know how it goes: If I'd known I was going to last this long, I would've taken better care of myself."

Taylor laughed. "That's good. Can I quote you?"

"You can, but it's not mine."

She looked at him. "Don't get me wrong, Matt. I think you look great."

"I could say the same, but that wouldn't half tell it." He hugged her and felt her smile against his skin.

"What's this scar?" she asked, gently fingering the wrinkled circle low down on his left side.

Matt's thumb glided over the spot. "A souvenir from an overeager *jefe de policia* in Panama. Lots of years ago."

"A bullet wound?" she asked in a surprised voice.

"A small one."

"Before Puma?"

"Way before."

Taylor went up on her elbow to regard him. "Matt, tell me something: How often do you hook up with somebody on these trips? I'm asking as a friend, not a new lover. I mean, do you have a partner somewhere? And I hope the answer's no. I don't want to be messing around with some woman's man."

"It's no. You could've asked me."

She nodded. "I thought about it, but I couldn't figure a way to have it come out sounding right."

"What about you?" Matt said.

"Not really. I was married, but that's been over for five years. Which is just about average for this crew."

"What a bunch, huh?"

"Karl and Stu are divorced. Doug is separated. Candice and Kaylee are divorced. Constance was divorced. Travis and Audrey are touch and go. Buzz is working hard on number two—and from the looks of things, I'd say he's failing."

"He picked Morgan before she was ripe."

"Oh, she's ripe enough. She's just a bad apple." She lifted her head to regard him. "Forget I said that, okay?"

Matt nodded. "Well, Jake's about to be married. And Barbara's hung in there. And of course there's Dee-Dee and Maurice."

"Have they offered you any Ecstasy yet?"

"This morning."

"I think they're after a group grope."

Matt fell silent for a moment. "So you said 'not really.' You've got someone back in San Francisco pacing the hallway worrying about you?"

"Doubtful. I went through a dating stage after my divorce. I even joined a computer dating service." She chuckled. "I decided there had to be one man for me in the Bay area. So I went out on thirty-two one-night dates looking for him."

"You found thirty-two straight guys in San Francisco?"

She narrowed her eyes at him. "Don't be crude. And besides, that was over a course of six weeks. And I didn't go to bed with one of them. I didn't even find one of them I *liked*. But I learned quick enough how absurd it was to be *looking* for somebody. So I started to accept travel assignments. Since then, most of my relationships have been more like affairs than anything else."

"How so?"

"Matt," she said flatly. "You're probably the last person I have to tell about road relationships. You meet someone nice, you connect right off the bat and fall in love for a couple of days or a couple of weeks. Maybe you even see each other again in some equally exotic locale. But eventually it comes down to letters or phone calls from the airport. 'Hi, I'm just switching planes. Want to meet for a drink in the airport?' " She reached a hand up and switched off one of the flashlights. "That's why I asked whether you stay in touch with people after a trip's over. What'd you tell me in Kathmandu about short-term memory?"

"I was talking about clients. I've got friends I stay in touch with." He thought about Brie. "Thing is, most of the letters I've been getting include marriage announcements."

Taylor laughed. "I'm a Puma client."

"Funny, but I haven't been thinking of you as a client."

"I'd like to keep it that way. I don't want you thinking I did this as part of the adventure. I'm guessing that goes on quite a bit—clients wanting a piece of the guide."

Matt paused to consider it. "It's happened. But lately it hasn't been the piece you might have in mind."

🏵🏵 14 🏵🏵

Sewing-machine Leg

Matt crept back to his tent shortly before sunrise, during a soothing break in the storm. The campsite was silent, no flashlights on in any of the tents, but something was shaking in the porters' quarters. Matt thought he'd give himself an hour or so of sleep before going over to investigate.

He spent a few minutes squatting in the puddle outside his tent, mopping out the interior with a towel that was still damp from two days before. The tent smelled of forest rot and mildewed clothing. He was laying out the mattress and quilted poncho liner when he heard the telltale zipper sound of a tent door. He peered over the ridge of his shelter and in the misty light could just make out Travis Dey tiptoeing toward the mess tent. Matt went back to his tasks only to be distracted by another tent opening. This time it was Morgan Bessman, wrapped in a hooded jacket and hurrying off in the same direction.

Matt lingered a moment to see if anyone else would appear—chiefly Buzz or Audrey, with or without weapons. He thought about Taylor and smiled to himself. Who was he to be telling anyone how to wait out a Himalayan rain?

Rolled up in the camouflage poncho liner a short time later, he could feel sleep coming, but Lopsang's urgent whispering put a quick end to it.

"Matt, come quick. We have big problem."

Matt threw the cover off in frustration and shot his head out the doorway. "Now what?"

"The porters," the *sirdar* said, glancing over a shoulder. "They leaving."

Two hours later Matt and Jake were breaking the news to the group. "We managed to talk a few of them into staying, but the others have already left." Matt swept his eyes around the mess tent, taking facial readings while everyone toyed with their oatmeal. "Purbu and the kitchen staff are still with us. And Lopsang's out right now locating replacement porters."

With Barbara back to her jogging routine, Matt had breathed a sigh of relief knowing that Tulo was gone. That still left him with a dozen suspects, but most of them were in sight just now. Candice and Kaylee were, by all reports, down by the river, bathing.

"But why did they leave?" Doug asked from the foot of the supply-box table. "Was it a question of money? After all, two dollars a day . . ."

"That's the going rate," Jake said. "If we offered to renegotiate every time there was a problem, we'd only make matters worse for the next trekking group."

"Jake's right," Stu Sinotti grumbled. "Good riddance to the lot of them."

"Look," Matt said, eyeballing Stu. "It had nothing to do with money. The porters are paid at the end of each stage—each day's walk. We don't have an official contract with them like the climbers have with their Sherpas, so it's not unusual for lowlanders to quit when the weather turns bad—especially under the kind of conditions we've been experiencing."

"We shoulda sicked Taylor on 'em," Karl said, laughing as he extended an arm around her shoulder. "Lady lets a smile be her umbrella and still doesn't get a drop of water in her mouth."

"That was yesterday," Taylor told the table, briefly meeting Matt's gaze. There'd been little sleep for either of them, and she was looking a little pale. "I think that sore throat thing is finally catching up with me—"

"Why did we hire lowlanders in the first place?" Buzz

said. "I don't understand why they weren't properly outfitted for these conditions."

The doctor's outburst took Matt by surprise, and Stu
spoke to the question. "First of all, it's common practice
to use lowland porters for the initial stages. But what's
more important is that they *were* equipped with proper
footgear and blankets—which most of them probably sold
off for a few rupees back in Trisuli. In any case, they
would have only been with us for another few days. Once
we reached base camp, they would have been let go."

"So where were the replacement porters going to come
from?" Audrey said, without a hint of anger or undue
concern. She seemed well-rested if somewhat somber.

"From pretty much the same places Lopsang's going
to be visiting," Matt replied. "From nearby homes and
villages. He'll go back to Thanget if he has to." A wave
of relief spread through the group. "The difference is we
wouldn't have required as many as we need now because
our equipment load would have been lightened. We'll
have to wait and see how many Lopsang's able to round
up."

Buzz almost came to his feet. "And what if he can't
find enough to carry everything?"

Travis said, "I could carry a few more pounds if I had
to."

"I'm up for it," Doug added. "And so is Chris,
right?"

"I guess," Chris said, gazing up from his plate.

Buzz snorted in Travis's direction. "Can I pay you
two dollars a day to carry my pack, Travis? You seem
to have an interest in my things."

Travis swallowed hard. "I only meant—"

"I'm getting sick and tired of all your optimism, you
know that?"

"Jeez, chill out, people," Chris muttered in a disap-
proving tone.

"No, we should all be encouraged to speak our
minds," Dee-Dee offered, loud enough to be heard over
several separate conversations. "Group dynamics under
these—"

"Dee-Dee," Maury interrupted. "Later, babe, okay?"

Matt waited for things to simmer down. "No one's

going to be asked to carry extra loads," he said in the calmest voice he could summon. "If we end up with too few porters to move our supplies to base camp in one trip, then we'll have to do it in two. Word will spread once we're there and we shouldn't have any trouble hiring as many carriers as we need. We can always hire the climbers' Sherpas to come back for our loads." He gave everyone a moment. "In the meantime we're just going to have to make the best of it."

"Might be a good day to move the tents to higher ground," Doug suggested in an energetic voice.

Travis said, "Good idea."

"More unflagging optimism," Buzz said, looking back and forth between Travis and Morgan. "Bet you two'd like nothing better than to be bogged down here?"

Morgan blanched. "What's that supposed to mean, Buzz?"

"If the shoe fits, Morgan."

"Asshole!" she fired back, and the table fell silent. Morgan dropped her face in her hands and cried for a moment; then got up from the table and rushed out of the tent.

"I guess we're adjourned," Jake said while everyone was busy studying their plates of oatmeal.

The rain let up enough to allow everyone to spend some much-needed time outside the tents. The men shaved and the women did what they could with their hair. Doug and Chris shoveled a trench around their tent, then began to do the same for the Delong and Bessman tents. Candice took Morgan, Dee-Dee, and Maury on a tour of the local flora. Neither Buzz nor Travis were anywhere to be found, but Jake was off looking for them.

Purbu entertained everyone with tales of the abominable snowman, which he called *temu* rather than yeti. Few people realized, the cook explained, that several varieties of *temu* had been glimpsed in the Himalaya. First there was *thelma*, a small apelike creature some thought the Assam gibbon. Then there was what the Sherpas called *dzu-tch*, an eight-foot-tall eater of cattle. And finally there was *mih-tch*, or *miti*, the man-sized thing of the snows, whose body was covered with red shaggy hair.

Matt made use of the lull to wring out his bag and wet clothes and break down his tent. Figuring on re-pitching it near the now near-vacated porters' lean-to, he had Fiberglas-frame poles and plastic couplers in hand when he spied Barbara emerge from her tent in shorts and sweatshirt and commence a series of warm-up exercises.

"Barbara, aren't you coming on the yeti hunt?" Taylor yelled from the mess tent, where Stu was organizing a fanciful search-and-seizure mission.

"We need a mountaineer's eagle eyes," Audrey encouraged.

"Walkin's better for you than runnin'," Karl thought to point out. He and Audrey were sporting Puma caps. Everyone was carrying a ski pole.

Barbara touched her toes and bent her torso side to side. "Which way are you taking them, Stu?"

Stu said, "Toward Tato Pani. I thought we'd explore that drainage about two miles back. Lots of rhododendron. Looks like decent yeti-hunting territory."

"I'm going out the other way. But maybe I'll double back and catch up to you at the drainage," Barbara told him.

Matt had stopped to listen to them. He watched Stu and the trekkers move off, then swung around to Barbara, who had her nose pressed to her right knee. From a folding chair in front of the adjacent dome tent, Kaylee was also watching her. "Maybe I'll join them," the cowgirl climber said after a few minutes had gone by. And the next moment Kaylee was on her feet—a broken-spine paperback set aside for a ski pole—and making for the trail at a brisk pace.

Matt dropped the tent poles and made a one-hand grab for his hiking shoes, stuffing plastic couplers and shock cords into the thigh pockets of his fatigues.

"Barbara," he called out, hopping on one foot while he tied his shoe, "you want company?"

"Love it," she told him, somewhat breathlessly. She jogged in place while Matt struggled with his other shoe.

He asked for five minutes to move his gear under the porters' tarp. "You're going to run in those?" she asked. pointing to his trousers when he finally trotted over to her tent.

Matt imagined the snares any number of suspects could be laying out for Barbara in the woods. "I'll be fine," he assured her. "Boot camp."

Barbara shrugged and started off at a slow pace along the trail to Paldol. "I didn't know you were in the service, Matt," she said after they'd covered an eighth of a mile or so.

"I wasn't," he told her, dangling his arms while he ran.

"Then what was that about boot camp?"

Matt frowned at her back. "I meant scout camp."

The trick was to get in front of her, he decided. It was also going to be a contest, considering the pace Barbara was setting. Matt considered himself as strong a walker as the next guy, but he'd never been able to work up much energy for running. Especially the high-altitude sort. Barbara, consequently, was soon leaving him farther and farther behind.

Rain had left a shine on the rhododendron and laurel, and mist was swirling in the upper branches of the oaks. Barbara's plan was to run north for about a mile, then return to camp and continue south along the Tato Pani trail. Matt wasn't sure he could go the distance. He didn't foresee much chance of trouble north of camp, however, so he began to relax somewhat, pacing himself.

Barbara hit the turnaround way ahead of him, which enabled him to turn short of the mile mark and hold the point for the run back to camp and for a short distance along the Tato Pani trail. They were perhaps a mile and a half out—Matt trailing by thirty yards—when Barbara broke stride and began to stagger forward. Her knees were bent and she had both hands clasped at the back of her right calf.

Thank God for cramps, Matt thought, already slowing down.

A ten-foot length of rotting tree trunk crossed the trail not five feet from where Barbara was pawing at herself, going into quite a frenzied dance now, Matt realized as he closed on her.

He didn't see the bees or hornets or whatever the hell they were until he was standing on the log with the things swarming all around him. Barbara tore past him with a wild-eyed look, screaming, "I've been stung!"

He pivoted on a foot and ran after her, flailing his arms at his winged assailants, dimly aware of Barbara's continued cries. She stopped in the middle of the trail to stomp her feet and agitate her salt-and-pepper hair with both hands. "I've been stung, Matt! I'm allergic to them!"

Matt got half the word *allergic!* out when his right thigh went white-hot in pain. Reflexively his hand slammed against his thigh and the broken body of a large bee tumbled out of his pant's leg. Follow-up explosions shook his left leg at thigh-and-calf level and he swatted again, and again, two more dazed insects falling onto his sneakers. The goddamned things had *flown up his pants!* he realized, unbuckling the fatigues and pushing them down around his ankles.

Barbara might have thought him a madman or a sexual deviant had there been time for it; but her eyes were already beginning to swell closed—from stings or histamine reaction to them, Matt wasn't sure which.

"Have you got a bee-kit with you?" he asked, hitching up his pants and trying his damnedest to ignore the burning pain in his legs. "Pills—anything?"

"Back at camp," Barbara said weakly, down on her ass in the wet dirt, arms wrapped around quivering knees.

Matt thought through a rapid calculation: they were scarcely a mile from camp. Allowing for trail conditions, that was nine, ten minutes at a fast clip. But could Barbara run it? And just how long did she have before the reaction grew critical?

"I've had anaphylactic reactions to stings," she told him, standing up with his help. "My windpipe closed up once. They had to shoot me up with Adrenalin."

"Can you run?" Matt said, gritting his teeth.

She shook her head in a confused way. "It might make it worse, bring it on faster, I don't know."

He gazed about the surrounding forest, suddenly aware of the stillness, the power inherent in the damp greens. Down slope, through conifers and birch, the Chilime roared dully in the trench it had worn through pink-granite bedrock. "Well, we can't just stand here. You've gotta give it a try, Barb. I'm right behind you."

She nodded, regarding him through puffy, narrowed eyes, and set off at a forced pace. Matt's leg's throbbed under the fatigues, aching where cloth and swollen skin made contact. He felt light-headed, bombed, as his own body grappled to combat the insects' toxins with its own chemical releases.

Barbara ran half a mile before she collapsed, wheezing. "I can't breathe!" she managed, in an eerily high-pitched voice. "Matt!—"

Her hands tore at her throat, then she went completely limp. Her face was tinged with blue, and her eyes were rolling back in her head.

Matt stooped down to gather her in his arms; but he soon laid her back down on the ground, steeling himself for what he knew he would have to do. In the five minutes it was going to take to carry her back to camp, she would die, and all the artificial respiration he might bring to bear wouldn't open a swollen windpipe.

On hands and knees he began to search the damp ground cover for a stick he could hollow with his camper's knife. A tube! he shouted to himself, fixing the image in his mind's eyes. A straw! A pipe stem! . . . Then he recalled the plastic tent-pole couplers he'd shoved into his pockets.

Brie had worked for a company that manufactured ventilators for technology-dependent children. She had told him about a nurse friend of hers who had once performed an emergency tracheostomy—was that the word?—with a kitchen knife and the shell of a Bic ballpoint pen. First you had to feel for the ridge of the larynx, then drop your finger to the soft hollow of the neck just below the voice box . . .

Was that it? he asked himself. *Was he remembering correctly?*

"Barbara," Matt said, showing her the coupler—a three-inch-long tube of hard plastic—"I've got to do this—do you understand?" Her breathing was an ungodly rasp, but he thought he saw recognition in the slits that were now her eyes.

He positioned her shoulders over his thigh to hyperextend her neck. Then he opened the knife and traced a forefinger down her larynx. He lowered the knife and hesitated; tried again and hesitated again. On the third attempt he made a rapid but careful inch-long horizontal incision through the skin just above the points of her collarbones.

Blood immediately welled from the cut and his eyes went wide in panic, fearing he'd nicked a major vein, or—*Christ!* an artery. He slipped the blade of the knife into the wound and felt it contact the fibrous tissue of the trachea. He shuddered and began to saw a gash through the gristly pipe. When the pool of blood bubbled and drained somewhat, he knew he'd made an opening. Gently he tried to insert the coupler into the wound, but it wouldn't go in. Blood ran in rivulets down both sides of Barbara's neck; blood stained his fingers and the blunt end of the coupler.

At a downward angle, he remembered all at once. You couldn't push the thing in straight without risking damage to the trachea's rear wall!

He laid the coupler against his thigh and quickly beveled one end of the plastic with a knife pass that sliced open his fatigues and the skin under them. He inserted the beveled end at a downward angle into the wound and forced it through. Instantly the dark blood around the coupler frothed.

He put an ear to the tube then pressed his head against Barbara's sternum and heard her lungs filling with air. The color returned to her face and her eyes blinked.

Matt leaned back on his hands waiting for his heart to find a rhythm it could live with. Like a zombie, then, he picked Barbara up, allowing her head to dangle over his forearm, and carried her the rest of the way into camp.

🏵🏵 15 🏵🏵

Rock Bottom

Next time you decide to perform an emergency cry-cothyroidotomy, Buzz had told him, *slip the tip of your knife between the tracheal rings.* He had taken hold of Matt's fingers and pressed them to his own neck, showing him what to look for. *When you get the blade in, you give it a twist.* The anesthesiologist added a ratcheting sound effect. *And carry a beveled trach tube with you. A little more blade with that knife of yours, and you would have killed her.*

Well, Matt thought, he hadn't exactly been going for a merit badge.

Barbara was alive and well inside one of the North Face domes, where Buzz was repairing the damage to her neck and starting her on a course of steroids. The blood loss hadn't been too great, but any blood loss at high altitude posed a risk, so Buzz was recommending that Barbara be evacuated, or at the very least carried back to Thanget to recuperate there from the dozen or so stings she'd suffered. Had the anaphylaxis not been limited to laryngeal edema, Matt's attempt at traching her would have come to nothing.

"A medevac isn't practical," Jake was telling Kaylee and Candice now. "The closest radio station is back on the Bhote Kosi, a day's walk north of Syabru. In the time it'd take to get there and arrange for a chopper to put down at Thanget or Tato Pani, we could have her back to Trisuli.''

"Isn't there a STOL strip in the Langtang?" Kaylee asked.

"Yeah, but it'd be the same thing." Jake's finger found the mountain range on the map he'd spread on the mess-tent table. "That's three days of serious walking."

Candice planted her elbows on the table and leaned over to study the map. "So you think Thanget's our best bet."

Jake nodded. "If her condition deteriorates, I go for help. If she recovers—which Buzz seems to think she will—she's still close enough to rendezvous with you in the Ganesh."

Kaylee nodded. "He says she could be back to full strength after a few days of rest."

Fat raindrops were striking the peaked ceiling of the mess tent and a cold wind was flapping the front doors, but Matt—sedated under 50 mg of antihistamine—was oblivious to most of it. He'd swallowed two of the pink-and-white pills after giving Barbara an injection of epinephrine from the bee kit she carried and dosing her with Benadryl.

Jake and Buzz had turned up fifteen minutes later, and the physician had removed the life-saving, tent-pole coupler Matt had installed in Barbara's neck.

"I still don't feel right about you taking her back to Thanget, Jake," Candice said. "Even if we are sharing the permit, Barbara's more our responsibility than yours."

Jake shrugged it off. "We wouldn't even be here if it hadn't been for your generosity. Besides, you heard Barbara: she's worried about jeopardizing the climb. It's important to her that you get to the top of Pabil—with or without her."

We've got to demonstrate just how hard-core we can be in the face of setbacks, Barbara had written in the note Jake had read to the climbers. *We've already had two accidents and we're not even on the mountain yet! I don't want to give our critics ammo by scuttling the climb before it begins. You* have *to go on—with or without me.*

"But what about your own group?" Candice pressed.

"Lopsang and I can look after everyone," Matt said, yawning.

"Besides, we'll have a better idea of her condition tomorrow. Even if I leave Thanget the day after tomorrow, I should be able to catch up to you this side of the high pass." Jake snorted. "We don't even have porters yet. You might still be here."

"Uh-huh," Matt said. "We go tomorrow if the weather clears. The group needs a change of scene. We can cache the gear and take just enough to erect a camp in the meadow."

"What makes you think you'll be strong enough to walk?" Jake said.

Matt said, "I'll crawl out of here if I have to."

Jake explained that he was going to take two of the few remaining porters with him to carry the litter Stu and Purbu had built for Barbara. Matt said he would cache a tent and food supplies for Jake and the porters to use on their return trip.

He found Karl and Taylor waiting for him when he hobbled out of the mess tent—the yeti hunt called on account of rain. The stings he'd received on thighs and calf were raised circles three inches across, but what hurt most was the cut he'd opened in his leg when he was beveling the end of the coupler. The throbbing had ceased, but his muscles were sore and the lymph nodes in his groin were swollen. The antihistamine had eased the itching but filled his head with smoke and cotton.

"Congratulations, hero," Karl said, passing him an umbrella. "You saved her life, buddy."

"What a guy," Taylor said, smiling. She took a look at Matt's naked legs and sucked in her breath. "Nasty-looking bites."

"You must have been right behind us when it happened," Karl said.

Matt cut his eyes to him. "Did Kaylee catch up with you?"

Karl tugged at his ponytail. "Was she out there, too?"

Taylor said, "I even think I heard Barbara scream, but I thought it was some kind of bird. Stu had us listening for yeti in the rhododendron."

"But you didn't have a run-in with the bees."

Karl and Taylor looked at each other and shook their heads. "But listen, you," Taylor said, sidling up to him, "if you don't give me that interview now, I'm never going to speak to you again."

Matt waited until Jake and the porters had carried Barbara off before heading out to pay the bees' nest another visit. He took along a quart of kerosene in a plastic squeeze bottle—to saturate the nest if necessary.

It bothered him that the group had passed over the log on the way in without incident; and that he'd stepped over it two more times on the round-trip to the potato-field camp—in the rain, admittedly. Then Stu, Taylor, Karl, and Audrey had stepped over the thing not ten minutes before Barbara had been stung. So what was it about Barbara that had so enraged the nest? Matt was certain he had seen her leap over the log; in fact, he was the one who had been fool enough to actually stand on it. But the bees were already out by then—and not just a few sentries, either, but a small air force.

And where had Kaylee been? She claimed to have changed her mind about joining Stu's group and was walking down to the river instead.

Matt had to take her word for it. And he supposed the break in the clouds could have accounted for the change in the bees' behavior. But nothing seemed accidental any longer—especially where Barbara was concerned.

The cloud forest was quiet under a cool drizzle, cathedral still in the high-canopied feeder gorges, mosses and lichens glistening in ambient white light. Matt stopped six feet short of the fallen tree and squatted down on his heels to regard it. The trunk was eighteen inches in diameter if that, gone nearly to soil where it lay across the trail in a slight depression that trapped water. A few bees were buzzing in and out of the log's open end; but every now and then one could be seen emerging directly from a spot topside where the bark had rotted away.

Matt aimed a thin stream of kerosene at the topside egress and half a dozen large-bodied bees made a sudden angry appearance. He gave the nest a moment to settle down and duck-walked to within two feet of the log, right thigh aching where his shorts chafed one of the bites.

Centered in a curve of porous brown wood was a neat circular hole—perhaps half an inch overall—where something had been forcefully driven down into the log at a ninety-degree angle. Matt risked another few inches and could just make out several faint spoke-like impressions radiating out from the hole.

He understood at once that the hole and spokes had been made by the aluminum tip and basket of a ski pole. The kind most of the Puma trekkers were using as walking sticks.

"Do you have to keep doing that?" Taylor asked, piqued by Matt's compulsion to poke his head out of the tent doorway every ten minutes. "Is there something in particular you're looking for, or are you just feeling a need to get your face wet?"

Karl had stopped by during one of Matt's brief EVAs, but he had turned down an invitation to come in.

Matt reverse-crawled to the center of the tent and tried to get comfortable. "It's not raining."

Taylor set aside her handwritten notes and stared at him. "So it's a kind of weather-person thing, is that it?"

Matt took a breath. "I'm just restless, is all. The antihistamines are wearing off. Maybe I'm coming down."

"And maybe I should get Buzz to prescribe some more."

"Forget it."

Matt reached for Taylor's notebook and picked up where he left off.

It has been raining steadily for the past forty-eight hours, he read. The soggy, puddled area that is our camp is perhaps the only level clearing between Tato Pani—hot springs—and the pastureland a day's journey north of here, below Paldol's glaciated flanks. We're some ten meters above the Chilime— it's white-water tumult everpresent—in a narrow band of hardwood forest, in an eldritch band of hardwood forest, an eyebrow of forest, of prelapsarian forest, a silent mossy place—bosky?—full of

*cloud ghosts, land leeches, lichen-covered rock
grottos—*

Matt set the book aside, unable to concentrate on anything but his emerging suspicions about Kaylee McMahon. Once again she could be placed at the scene of the
crime. Barbara had seen her the morning of the aborted
run in Thanget; Matt had seen her enter the cloud forest
ahead of them before the bee attack. Perhaps Kaylee was
harboring a grudge that had nothing to do with Barbara's
sophomoric China prank? It could have had something to
do with Barbara's diplomatic connections. Maybe Kaylee
thought Barbara's reputation as a top-notch climber was
undeserved; that it was only the political influence that
expedition leaders took into account when selecting her
for a team. Kaylee could have been passed over for those
very climbs; and now it was payback time.

Matt realized he should have questioned Ang Samden
Sherpa about the afternoon of the Jeep accident. Kaylee
said she'd been with him while Candice was off shopping. But then Candice could have been lying about the
shopping excursion. The two climbers could have been
in it together. What had Kaylee said about the imminent
Pabil ascent: *It's not K2. Shit, the* two *of us could do it
if we have to.*

Sure, Matt thought, that could be it. They never wanted
Julia or Barbara along in the first place. The idea of feminist camaraderie was a sham, a fake. They'd gotten
themselves out to Vajra Yogini and disabled the Toyota's
brakes, just so they could do away with Julia and Barbara
and climb Pabil alone. . . . Climb an inconsequential
peak in the Ganesh Himal, alone.

He was giving himself a headache.

"Not very good, is it?" Taylor said.

"Huh?"

"My writing. It's still rough, remember."

Matt glanced at the notebook. "Oh, no, it's not that.
I'm just not in a reading mood." Taylor picked up the
book and leafed through it. Then she began to read one
of the passages aloud.

Unless, Matt thought, there was some more fiendish
explanation. Pabil, after all, was only a warm-up for Ev-

erest. And all four climbers were in the running for the upcoming American expedition. So maybe the accidents hadn't been staged to thin out the Ganesh team; maybe they'd been staged to eliminate some of the top contenders for the Everest climb! Which meant Candice was now in as much danger as Julia or Barbara had been!

"You're not even listening to me," Taylor said, as Matt shoved his head through the nylon door flaps.

And just in time, he observed. For Candice was at that very moment sauntering down toward the river with towel and toiletry kit in hand.

Alone.

"Matt," Taylor repeated.

And there went Kaylee, not a moment later, something surreptitious about her movements. "I gotta go," Matt said, aggravating the soreness in his legs with a quick about-face.

"Go where?" Taylor asked.

"Hunting," he said, and was gone.

Moving as quickly and quietly as he remembered how, Matt paralleled the path the two climbers took down to the riverbank. He was a minute or so behind Kaylee, but he arrived at the water's edge in time to see her grab Candice's shoulders from behind and twist her around into her arms.

Candice let go of the tube of biodegradable soap she had clutched in her left hand and brought her right to the back of the shorter woman's neck. Candice's motion tipped both of them out of sight behind a smooth hemisphere of quartzite rock.

Matt rushed forward until he had them in view again.

Successful, as luck would have it, in stopping just short of showing himself.

Candice and Kaylee were still struggling, but now he could see if not hear their laughter. What he'd taken for an assault was in fact a loving embrace.

And there were few things that beat a passionate kiss in the great outdoors when you'd been trapped inside a tent for two days.

🏮🏮 16 🏮🏮

Decamp Decomp

Twenty of them were sitting around the mid-morning fire when Matt walked over. Some were eating *tsampa*—a roasted barley concoction ground to powder and cooked up as a porridge. Others were wolfing down potato pancakes and yak cheese. And still others were smoking cigarettes and *chilims* in cupped hands, sizing him up with dark pirate faces.

"Do they understand the terms?" he asked Lopsang.

"Oh, yes," the *sirdar* said, "they understand well."

Matt scanned the group of mountaineers, recognizing a few of them from Tato Pani. They were dressed in woolen long coats, brown jackets, britches, gray *topi* caps and military berets. Some wore Tibetan boots and some wore Chinese high-top sneakers. There were Fu Manchu mustaches and Charlie Chan beards; off-center noses and jagged scars across knobby cheekbones. To a man they wore ornately sheathed *khukris,* which had been warmed in coals and tucked into broadly striped cummerbunds.

"I want their word they'll stick with us all the way to base camp," Matt said. "The ones who remain at base and carry back to Thanget can earn half pay for days spent at camp and half pay for the day it will take them to return to their homes from Thanget." He waited for Lopsang's translation; the men were whispering to each other, nodding their heads.

"They are agreeing to this. Most of them want to stay until Thanget."

"Good," Matt said, showing an appreciative smile. "Then tell them we will supply sun goggles, cook stoves, and tarps for shelters; but no boots or snow gear."

Lopsang nodded. "They are understanding this."

"And they've brought enough food?"

"They have, Matt."

Matt blew out his breath. "All right," he said, feeling less like he was about to embark on a high-altitude crossing than a bandit raid on some mountain citadel, "I guess we're in business."

The Puma group now had twenty-five porters where it needed forty; so Matt directed that the nonessentials be cached temporarily and left for the second trip. He tasked two of the loyal Tamangs to watch over the supplies, and—after the usual haggling over basket-load weights— had the mountaineers under way by ten o'clock.

Stu, Lopsang, and the climbers, leading the kitchen staff and the ten trekkers, had a two-hour lead on the porter train, with instructions to break for lunch on the Nepal side of the log bridge that spanned the Chilime and terminate the stage in the alpine meadows below the high pass, at an altitude of some 14,500 feet. The route would take them into Tibet for a short distance; then veer back into Nepal as it followed the west fork of the river toward the glacier that flowed from Lapsang Karubu's southeastern face.

The sky was a low ceiling of white light, but emptied of rain. Matt's legs had ballooned overnight as a result of the stings, but he was able to walk out most of the soreness—walk it out of awareness.

He was still beating himself up for sneaking up on Candice and Kaylee, and for the conspiracy he'd invented to fit the facts, such as they were.

Hell, Kaylee hadn't been the only one carrying a ski pole, he told himself. Stu, Taylor, Audrey, and Karl had all been out there in the woods, and any one of them could have accidentally punctured the log while they were out on their yeti hunt. As the next one in line, Barbara had run smack into the angered bees. End of story.

Even if someone had made the hole deliberately, where

was the guarantee Barbara would be stung? And who, if anyone, had prior knowledge of Barbara's allergy?

The trail north emerged from the cloud forest an hour out of camp; it wound through tall grass before crossing the river, then rose sharply along the treeless, rock-strewn slopes above the Chilime's notorious notch. The river was a vertical white tumult there, ice cold and treacherous as it roared out of Tibet. At a backward glance Matt could see down the length of the valley, clear to the Trisuli, with the luminous peaks of the Langtang Himal floating above dark striations of clouds.

On the Tibetan side of the river the mountainside trail was barely a foot wide; but it improved as it reentered Nepal, then split and split again at the foot of the meadow until there were any number of upward western routes to follow. Paldol, Lapsang Karubu, and Ganesh I, V, and VII towered over the grassland basin in a horseshoe of sawtooth rock and ice.

Matt stopped alongside a mani wall to place a stone atop the heaped tablets. *"Om mani padme om,"* he muttered, at a loss for what else to say. It was a prayer formula that seemed to work for the porters; maybe it would work for him as well.

He prized binoculars out of the side pocket of his pack and aimed them west. High up in the meadow the tents were bits of orange, blue, and red, widely scattered across uneven ground. Patches of melting snow lay on blue-green bunch grass, feeding black water pools. The land beyond was boulder-strewn moraine, a gray river of rock and rubble that ascended in a long snow-covered curve to wild, windswept heights.

It worried Matt that Kaylee and Candice weren't in camp when he arrived; everyone else was, however, and the two climbers showed up soon enough, explaining that they had gone up valley to see if they could catch sight of Ang Samden and the Sherpas. Lopsang ventured that the liaison officer—taking advantage of the relatively good weather—had made a push for the high pass.

Matt searched out a place for his tent and had to settle for an area of lumpy grass on a severe incline. In the end he elected to pitch the tent across the angle rather than with it, willing to find himself hammocked in the morning along the downward-facing side rather than drained of blood from the knees up.

The trekkers were all in a similar fix, except for Maurice and Dee-Dee who had managed to locate the one flat spot around. Courtesy of the climbers, Audrey Dey— giving her husband wide berth—now had a tent to herself.

Matt ambled over to the duffel drop in the porters' camp to run a check on the supplies—specifically the medical duffel, which contained the oxygen tank and regulator. The waterproof bag was open, and Buzz was nearby attending to blistered feet. Most of the highlanders had left for the caves in which they would pass the night, but a few had remained behind to help themselves to the cigars Karl was passing around.

By late afternoon a chill wind had kicked up, forcing everyone into turtlenecks and sweaters and quilted vests. Running shoes were exchanged for lug-soled or low-impact boots, and headgear ran the gamut from Puma caps and wool fedoras to earmuffs and crocheted stocking caps. In the thin air and unobstructed light Matt could see just how haggard the group looked after the Chilime ordeal. Forced to list everyone in order of fitness, he would have put Doug, Karl, and Chris at the top; Dee-Dee, Travis, and Buzz somewhere in the middle; and Taylor, Morgan, Maurice, and Audrey at the bottom.

But fitness alone was no guarantee of safety at high altitudes, where biophysical and psychological changes could affect the strongest climber. Nearly everyone was suffering from headaches, lassitude, and mild nausea—what the Andeans called *soroche*, or mild altitude sickness.

Stu Sinotti was his usual ursine self, and the two climbers had acclimated well. Itching legs notwithstanding, Matt was feeling reasonably strong—if obsessively troubled by the trek's continuing setbacks.

He took his morning thoughts with him into the mess tent that evening and kept mulling them over while Pasang and Num served the meal. A discomforting silence prevailed through the soup course, and by the time the *dhalbaht* was on the table, Matt thought there might be a mutiny. Even pressure-cooked, the beans and rice looked underdone and singularly unappetizing.

"I know it's not medallions of lamb," he said, "but carbohydrates are what we need for strength."

"Carb-loading," Stu seconded, shoveling a spoonful of the rice-and-lentil mix into his mouth. "Don't think about it: just eat."

"What I'd like is a nice, thick sirloin," Travis mused.

"Meat isn't good for you up here," Buzz snarled at him.

Travis met the anesthesiologist's gaze. "Neither's alcohol from what I hear."

"You're both right," Matt said firmly. "Meats and fats don't metabolize well. And alcohol acts as a diuretic."

"Man should have been a nurse," Buzz said into his cup.

"I predicted it would come to this," Dee-Dee announced suddenly, setting a cloth shoulder bag on the table. "I don't know about the rest of you, but Maury and I read *The Snow Leopard* before we got here."

She extracted several plastic vials from the bag and began to line them up in the center of the table. "I kept being struck by what he wrote about the food—a radish here, a cold potato there—and I thought, now there's potential trouble. So—" and she gestured to the arrangement, "—voilà. We now have curry powder, coriander, cumin, thyme, red pepper, garlic salt . . . A sprinkle of this and that and it's a whole new world of lentils."

Matt shot her a smile as the group applauded her foresight. Everyone was soon eating with gusto.

"Long as no one's got an allergy to spices, huh, Buzz?" Matt said around a mouthful of white rice.

"Amen," Buzz enthused. He's been hitting the *rakshi* all afternoon and was pretty well shit-faced.

Stu seemed to pick up on Matt's thought. "You'd think Barbara would have had sense enough to keep that bee kit with her when she ran."

Buzz purposefully dropped his fork. "It happens all the time. Christ, I've known patients who were carrying around epinephrine that was three years past its expiration date. Stuff's got a very limited shelf life." He took a sip from his mug and laughed. "Like marriage."

Matt saw Morgan's face tighten in the harsh light of the Coleman lantern. "Well, at least she knew she was allergic," he said quickly, hoping to keep the conversation on track. "Coulda been the first time she ran without it."

Buzz directed a scowl at his wife. "There's first times for everything."

Matt cleared his throat. "Anybody else have any allergies they want to confess to?"

"We knew about her allergy," Kaylee said, including Candice by gesture. "Once when Barbara and I were climbing in Chile, the same thing almost happened. It was hornets that time. God, they did a number on one of the Chilean guides."

"Of course," Taylor said. "I remember seeing a picture in *National Geographic* of the guide's face after the attack. Poor man looked like he'd gone ten rounds with a heavyweight."

"You know, Buzz, fuck you," Morgan said. "I swear, you're getting paranoid in your old age."

"If you'll all excuse me," Audrey said, as she got up and left the tent.

Chris lowered his head. "Here comes the buzz crusher. Man, I don't ever want to get married."

"That shows good sense, lad," Buzz said, raising his drink to the teenager.

Morgan shot to her feet. "Don't you tell him that!" she said. "Just because you've forgotten what it takes to make a marriage work—like love and *trust*."

Buzz flashed her an ironic grin. "Oh, I'm sure there's a lot of love and trust going on in this group." He gestured broadly to the table. "Why, we're a regular family, aren't we? Matt's our father figure and Dee-Dee supplies the spice. We've got Karl for jokes and *Travis* for love interest."

"Stop it, Buzz!" Morgan said. "You're drunk."

Karl looked up from toying with his food. "What I need's something to help me sleep, not spices for the food."

Buzz broke out of his staring match with Morgan to slap the pockets of his vest in search of something. "Here," he said. "I've got something to add to Dee-Dee's little display." He inserted an amber medication vial among the spice bottles. "Halcions—to make us all rest easy with our problems."

Doug restrained his son's eager hand. "You've been sleeping fine," he said.

"I wouldn't take those if I were you," Stu said. "Tranquilizers and high altitude don't mix."

Buzz waved a hand at him. "Nonsense. Proper sleep is as essential as 'carb-loading' and fluid intake. Think of the pills as spices, Stuart." He laughed. "Besides, we're at fourteen thousand five hundred feet. You really think any of us are going to sleep tonight?"

"I know one person who won't," Karl said under his breath. But he neglected to say just who that might be.

Buzz Bessman was correct about one thing: At high altitudes sleep was an elusive state. And when sleep did arrive, it was often fractured by episodes of irregular breathing or weighed down by ponderous dreams. Matt's dreams that night were like roulette mandalas in which he was consistently missing the mark by one number.

He woke up with his face pressed against the cool sidewall, body scrunched into the corner of the tent, nothing but the thin floor and the compressed fill of his bag between him and the cold, rock-hard ground. The Thermarest had sprung a leak somewhere along the line and was little more than a half inch of rigid corrugations now.

Matt's breath hung in the cold air as he and Lopsang discussed a game plan for the day. Pasang brought burnt-tasting tea over to the porters' encampment, where the mountaineers were heating their *khukris* in reanimated coals and coughing God knew what from their lungs and throats. The *sirdar* volunteered to lead the group downriver to retrieve the cached supplies and bulging bags of trail garbage the trekkers had collected. Matt had considered pushing on to establish a high camp below the pass but thought it a better idea to allow for a further day of acclimatization. A layover would also give Jake—and perhaps Barbara—a better chance at rejoining the group on the near side of the pass.

The porters were off by six-thirty, calculating a mid-afternoon return. Matt had Num and Pasang spread word of the layover plan while they were delivering wake-up beverages to the group.

The sun eventually broke through rapidly moving

clouds and the day grew warm. By noon most everyone was shedding clothes and looking for shade. Candice and Kaylee gave a lecture on mountaineering, employing crampons, pitons, carabiners, and ice axes as visual aids.

They made for an entertaining duo, and listening to them Matt couldn't imagine either of them doing anything to cripple a fellow climber or sabotage an expedition. Although maybe they were just a bit *too* happy under the circumstances; too blasé about undertaking the Pabil climb alpine-style should Barbara fail to show for one reason or another.

Both of them had been aware of Barbara's allergy. But then, Barbara's condition was apparently common knowledge to anyone who read the *Geographic* article Taylor had mentioned.

Just as Julia's driving habits were well known.

Matt turned it over in his mind while he was laying clothes out to dry on the bunch grass in front of his tent. He heard Karl give a yell from lower down the meadow and turned to see him gesturing to something lower still. He had his binoculars out by the time Karl drew near, fanning a fedora at the shit-eating grin on his face. Matt focused the glasses on a distant file of colorful figures, then tipped them down from his eyes to show Karl a gloomy look.

"That's right, amigo," the Texan said. "The Italians have arrived."

Carlo was wearing wool trousers, a ribbed sweater by Lothar, and mountain boots by Asolo. His sunglasses were Ray-Ban, and Matt guessed he had ordered the wristwatch from Sharper Image. His group was similarly attired. Several of them were sporting umbrellas, and a few seemed to have been assigned personal porters, who tailed them like golf caddies.

Carlo's hazel eyes scanned the campsite and went on to appraise the meadow's black-water springs and undulating, uninviting surface. "Well," he said after a long moment. "It looks like you found the only flat ground."

Matt traded looks with Karl and smiled thinly at the Italian. "There's always the moraine," he said, jerking a thumb over his shoulder. "You put a couple of rocks together and build yourself a nice, comfy bed."

Carlo snorted derision. "An American joker." The group's porters were gathering a few feet behind him, acknowledging Matt with their laughter. "I think we're going to set up our tents just over here," he added, indicating the unoccupied ground between the trekkers' tents and those of the climbers. "We have platforms for our tents, so we don't worry too much about the uneven ground."

Matt sucked at his teeth for a moment. "I don't think so."

Carlo smiled. "Look, Matt—you are Matt, right? You don't understand. This ground is our place. This is the place our group always uses. There is water close by; the views are best for photographing." He paused for a moment. "We stay here three nights. You are here for one." He turned to glance at his porters. "And we have the majority, no?"

Karl voiced a rodeo sound. "If this dude don't take all!"

Over the top of Carlo's razor cut and the capped heads of the Tamangs, Matt could see Lopsang and the wisecracking replacement porters humping into view. He ventured that the two groups had taken different routes from the Chilime fork.

Karl saw them and tapped Matt with a sideways elbow. By now the Tamangs were turning around to regard the *khukri*-toting strangers with wary looks. Some of the lowlanders were actually backing away, wide-eyed with concern.

Carlo turned to the sudden chatter; his expression was dismayed when he swung back around. "My God, who are these people?" he asked Matt. "They look like bandits."

"No," Matt told him, savoring the moment. "Those are our porters."

"So you made him give you his Thermarest?" Taylor said, from her side of the tent, bare legs in a yellow cone of light.

Matt shook his head. "I didn't threaten him. I just told him we wouldn't put up a fuss about their sharing our camp if he surrendered the mattress. I guess he saw some logic to it." He grinned in recollection. "Anyway, I gave him mine."

🏵🏵 17 🏵🏵

Nightmare Pitch

"Just try for ten steps, then stop and take a few deep breaths," Matt said, bending over to lessen the pack's weight on his hips and shoulders.

"I'm never going to make it," Taylor said, tugging at the collar of her sweater as she leaned her weight on the ski pole. "My feet feel like they've been through a bastinado." Her face was flushed from rapid breathing. "I can't believe it," she added, swallowing hard, "I'm going to be the last one into camp."

Matt glanced up the notch trail in time to see Morgan overtaking one of the overburdened highland porters. Further along, Stu and the climbers held the point. "It's not a race. It's one foot in front of the other. Don't think about anybody else. We've all had off days."

Taylor put a hand to her forehead. "And my head is throbbing. Am I a candidate for the paper-bag trick yet?"

Matt pretended to appraise her. "I don't think so. Just give yourself a minute to rest."

Quick but fleeting relief for high-altitude headaches could sometimes be gained by breathing into a paper bag, as Matt had had Morgan do. Inhaling low concentrations of carbon dioxide dilated the blood vessels in the brain, increasing circulation. He had learned the technique in Bolivia from a seventeen-year-old Aymara Indian pick-

156

pocket who worked the Altiplano train between Cuzco and Puno.

"How high are we?" Taylor managed.

"Maybe fifteen five."

"And you said we were going to make camp at sixteen, right? So that should be five hundred feet from now."

"Five hundred in elevation, yeah. Problem is we've got a few ravines and gullies between here and there."

Taylor showed him the whites of her eyes. "I'm not taking one downhill step. And if I do, it's going to be in the direction of the Chilime."

Matt grinned. "Ready to go home, huh?"

"Oh, screw you," she said, shouldering past him. "I just don't like being last."

Matt allowed her a good lead before moving out. The sun was merciless, but a stiff wind was cooling the sweat on his face and rippling the sleeves of his parka. For an hour now they had been contouring a scree slope above the moraine, inching southward below Paldol's north-face snowfields toward the saddle. Below, the frost had vanished from the sunny side of the meadow, although Matt suspected a couple of inches of fresh snow would await them at high camp. He still could make out the bannered peaks of the Italian tents, rising above the pitted black boulders that littered the moraine-meadow interface. He thought if he listened hard enough he could hear strains of Rossini over the intermittent water-rush roar of unseen avalanches.

The view north across rockfalls and glaciers to the massifs of the blue-backdropped Ganesh was enough to stir feelings of unbridled vitality or reduce one to a state of existential despair. The problem was one could never predict the effects of altitude, and where one day might bring revelation, there'd be confusion the next. So Matt had to content himself with a half-and-half mix, a mood swing with each separate upward push between breath-catching breaks.

Taylor was waiting for him around a twist in the narrow trail. Clutching the ski pole, gasping for breath while the cold wind attacked her hair, she looked wild-eyed and beautiful. "I didn't really mean that about turning around."

"I didn't think you did," Matt told her, scooping a handful of crystalline snow from a rock shelf. "Just your day to get schizzy."

"Well, why not?" she said defiantly. "We can't have Buzz using up everyone's share." She blew out her breath and straightened her back. "You know, it's your fault I'm last. We've been staying up too late. I could barely drag myself out of my bag this morning." She smiled dreamily. "I felt like I could lie there forever."

No one had been eager to get under way. Particularly since the day's stage entailed some four hours of strenuous walking to gain a mere two thousand feet in altitude. Even the porters had been grumbling. Most of them would have preferred a 2:00 A.M. awakening and a double-load push for the saddle over to a two-trip hump with single loads to an intermediate camp.

A few of them were still complaining about it now as they edged along the trail, their *dokos* topped off with loads of firewood carried up from the Chilime bivouac.

"I should have taken Buzz up on that Halcion," Taylor was saying. "Travis and Karl took some."

"No wonder they were slow getting started," Matt muttered. "Maybe I'll record their Cheyne-Stokes breathing and play it back for them. Once they hear how that sounds, my guess is they'll pass on swallowing tranks."

Taylor blanched somewhat. "Am I breathing like that—just shutting down when I'm asleep?"

"It's nothing to worry about. You're feeling all right now, aren't you?"

"Who can tell up here?" She set off with small uphill steps. "I mean, Buzz looks like he's ready to kill someone. Before, it was just anomie. But now entropy's taking over."

"Which someone?" Matt asked.

"Morgan's behaving like a genuine asshole. I think I would have moved out on her like Audrey did." Taylor finally glanced over her shoulder. "You should donate your tent to Buzz. Then you wouldn't have to concern yourself with talk about our sleeping together. Nobody's fooled, anyway."

Matt nodded. "I figured. But I'm supposed to be working, Taylor."

"The responsible sort. A first for me."

"I don't want everybody to start thinking I'm distracted all of a sudden, or that we're off on our own separate trip." He shrugged. "We might have to wait till Kathmandu to make it a night."

"Just like with the flowers, huh? Well, not if you surrendered your tent to Buzz we wouldn't."

"I could always sleep in the mess tent," he said, smiling.

She stopped for breath. "The mess tent . . . The mess tent's going to become a shelter for wayward spouses before this trek's through."

Matt lifted his sunglasses to his brow. "About Morgan and Travis . . . Are they, uh . . . ?"

"Why, Matt," she said in feigned surprise, "you want me to *gossip*?"

"Yeah. I guess I do." He thought about mentioning the predawn activities he'd witnessed in the Chilime camp.

"You mean are they an item." Taylor toyed with the moment. "In a word, yes." When Matt didn't respond, she said: "But then you can never tell when and where you're going to meet someone, can you?"

Matt leaned over to kiss her.

"Um," she said, "warm lips on a cold day. What d'you say we call it a stage right here? Spread out the bags, snuggle . . ."

"Did you get *any* sleep?" he asked, rubbing warmth into her upper arms.

"I tried after you left. But I just laid there wide awake with about a thousand things from my past crowding in on me. I start out thinking about where we are—how far away we are from everything—and before I know it, I'm thinking about all the mistakes I've made. The messes I've created, the opportunities I've missed. Introspective masochism. Then after about an hour or so of that, I'm planning all the changes I'm going to initiate when the trek's over." She gave her head a tight-lipped shake. "I mean, why wait for New Year's eve?"

Matt put his arms around her, and they stood there for a moment with the wind howling about them. "Is that like why wait for Kathmandu?"

She leaned back to study his face. "You tell me."

* * *

The snow at sixteen thousand feet was pure white and laced with ice; above the sheltered bowl where they made camp, it swirled like spindrift against a draining sky. A few of the stronger porters had arrived ahead of the trekkers and were on their way back down the scree and talus for second loads before the stragglers had even dropped their packs.

Matt and Lopsang decided against erecting the mess tent and prevailed on Purbu to ready his tent-to-tent rapid delivery service one more time. No one, Matt assured the cook, was likely to have much of an appetite. Tea, pressure-cooked noodles, and slab chocolate would probably fit the bill.

The sun was behind the peaks when the porters trudged back into camp. The temperature had dropped thirty degrees, and the crusted-over snow crunched beneath their sneakers and knee-high boots. While the porters were hurrying off with their parcels of firewood, Matt and Lopsang counted the numbered basket loads and draped the pile with a tarp.

Mist filled the entire lower portion of the pass from the Chilime to the glacier-driven erratics that marked the terminal moraine. The surrounding peaks were obscured by twilight gray clouds.

Lopsang glanced at the sky and ran the zipper of his coat up to his chin. "Storm coming," he said, hunching his shoulders inside the down baffles.

Matt breathed warmth into his hands and cupped them around his nose. "Long as it holds off one more day."

"Oh, now this is ridiculous," Taylor said, poking a fork at her noodles. When she ultimately inverted the bowl entirely, not an overcooked strand was disturbed. She laughed in astonishment. "God, what's Purbu using for cooking oil—Krazy Glue?"

Karl set his bowl aside to contemplate it.

Matt refused to look at either of them; but when a twirl of his fork stirred not one or two noodles but the entire mass, he burst out laughing. "What we do," he said, drying tears against the sleeve of a wool shirt, "is get

Purbu to guy a goat when we get across the pass. Time for Puma to spring for some flesh.''

''I'm just going to imagine the taste,'' Karl said, having another reluctant go at the bowl.

They were dining in Taylor's tent, which was toasty from body heat and candle power. Outside, the temperature was down another fifteen degrees and there wasn't a star to be seen.

''You make the other side of this mountain sound like heaven,'' Taylor said, nibbling at a corner of her chocolate bar.

''Compared to here it is. Strong afternoon sun, beautiful views of the south faces of Pabil and Lapsang. It's grazing land for yaks. There's even a cheese factory.''

''Yak cheese, goat meatballs,'' Karl said. ''That's a little bit of heaven all right.''

They were discussing the prospects when angry shouting broke out from the other side of camp. Matt put his head through the door flaps and listened. He couldn't make out all the words, but Buzz's voice and intent were clear enough. A minute went by before the Bessman tent was zipped open. Morgan crawled out and sat in the dark for a moment; then she stormed off to what used to be the Dey's tent but was lately the sole property of Travis. She and Travis exchanged a few words at the door, but instead of going inside, Morgan stood up and made straight for Taylor's tent.

''Make room,'' Matt said, back inside once more.

Morgan wasn't a moment behind him. ''I can't stand one more minute of it,'' she began, sniffling and patting her tear-streaked face with the tips of her knit gloves. ''I have to move out.''

Matt and Taylor traded looks. Matt was about to volunteer his tent when Karl did it for him. ''Hell, amigo, you could bunk with me. Or wherever,'' he added, cutting his eyes to Taylor for an instant.

Morgan shook her head. ''I don't want to put you or Karl out.'' She looked at Taylor. ''Taylor, I was hoping you'd let me stay with you until Buzz and I work things out.''

Taylor's mouth fell open.

''Just until we work things out, Taylor, please.'' Morgan sighed wearily. "Look, we're all adults here. You know what's been going on, and I guess you all think I've been acting like a class bitch."

Everyone made an effort to respond, but what emerged were indistinct mumbles.

"Well, I really don't care what anyone thinks," Morgan went on, angrier. "I'm just not cut out for this kind of macho outdoor adventuring. This trek was Buzz's idea, not mine. I agreed to come along, but—I'll be honest with you—I've resented him for it. Travis was willing to listen to me bitch about it, and, well, I didn't intend for anything like this to happen." She glanced at everyone.

"Where's that leave you and Buzz?" Matt wanted to know.

"I'm going to tell him to fuck off in the morning. So can I stay here or not?" she added after a moment of uncomfortable silence.

Taylor showed Matt an anguished look. "Well, sure, I guess. But what about your bag and everything?"

"I was hoping you could get them from my tent."

Karl hid a laugh of disbelief; then slapped his knees. "Well, I got three of those little pills left if anybody wants one. Travis already gobbled up the rest." Morgan held out a hand for one. "Sure?" he asked Matt with a smirk. "Gonna be one cold, lonely night."

Matt's wristwatch alarm went off at 3:30 A.M. Awake since two o'clock, he was ready for it. On every other morning of the trek he could trust the kitchen assistants to rouse him, or failing that the porters' hacking; but the early morning awakening for the high-pass stage required an artificial prompt.

"Fucking three-thirty in the morning," he muttered.

He reached overhead and switched on the flashlight, the yellow beam illuminating the vapor of his breath. His teeth began to chatter as soon as he unzipped the mummy to retrieve thermals, pants, and shirts, which were sandwiched between the bag and the full-length mattress. He dressed as quickly as he could, slipping his hands into cold gloves, his feet into cold boots, and strapping on gaiters. Then he stuff sacked the bag, rolled the air out of the mattress, donned vest and parka, and back-crawled into the night.

The world was black and white under a starless sky, with frozen flurries swirling in on the wind.

A fire was going under the kitchen tarp and several of the porters were squatting around it, warming hands and knives on the coals. Purbu had water boiling, but both of his assistants were still asleep, huddled in sleeping bags draped across flour sacks and garbage bags. Lopsang wandered in behind the glare of a headlamp and joined Matt for a cup of tea. Stu walked in a moment later and took his cup over to the fire.

"Weather is bad," the *sirdar* said. "We leave right away and cross before snow. Otherwise . . ." He made a plosive sound. "We here for two, three days more."

"We're here for the duration," Stu amended.

"No way we're going to miss our window," Matt told him. "But I want us prepared for storms on the pass. Lopsang, remind everyone to leave their sleeping bags and mattresses out of their duffels. We'll pack them with the mess tent, medical bag, and emergency rations." He turned to Stu. "How's that sound with you?"

"A change of clothes."

Matt added up the list. "All that goes with the lead porters, understood?"

"Okay, understood. Sleeping bags, mattresses, dry clothes, mess tent, medical bag, emergency food." Lopsang's smile revealed a gold tooth. "But we get over pass, no problem. Even in snow."

Matt initiated a street handshake routine with him that set the porters laughing. He lit two of the Coleman lanterns, carried them over to the tent area, and snugged them down in the snow. Taylor, Morgan, Karl, Doug, and Chris were already collapsing their tents. Candice and Kaylee were close by organizing their own gear. Matt doubted that anyone had slept; but the group seemed functional if somewhat dazed, running on anticipation adrenaline.

Matt thought: You could test what you were made of against the midnight darkness and stinging snow.

"How was your night?" Taylor whispered as he walked by.

"Cold and lonely. How 'bout yours?"

"I'll tell you about it," she said.

Dee-Dee appeared bundled up in a fleece-lined coat; Audrey's made her look like she'd been inflated. Matt made a move to help with Audrey's tent when Pasang tapped him on the shoulder. "Come quick," he said, loud enough for Audrey to hear. When it was obvious the Tamang was headed for the Dey's dome, Audrey said, "Travis? Travis?"

She was one step ahead of Matt in reaching the tent and scrambling through the door. Matt shined his flashlight on Travis's face.

"Oh, my God, Matt, what's wrong with him?"

Travis's eyes were half closed and his breath was coming in shallow gasps. Vomit was pooled on the tent floor inches from his face. "Pasang!" Matt said, reaching outside the tent for the Tamang's trouser leg. "Get Stu and the doctor over here—*chito!* Quick-quick!"

Audrey was stroking her husband's hand and talking to him in a controlled voice. Travis was babbling and seemed unable to coordinate the movements of his hands. Matt backed out of the tent and dashed for the medical duffel. He put the flashlight between his teeth and dug around inside for the oxygen tank, regulator, and respirator mask. Buzz and Stu were inside the tent by the time he returned; Audrey was outside, pacing the frozen snow with her face in her gloved hands. The lanterns threw long shadows across the camp and lent a surreal element to the scene.

"Trav, can you understand me?" Buzz was saying. "Travis, I want you to try to sit up. Can you do that?"

"Let's get the oxygen running," Matt said, passing the green tank to Stu.

Stu extended the mask's plastic tubing and began to fiddle with the tank's regulator valve. "Oh, for Christ's sake."

"What?" Matt said.

Stu threw the tank aside. "The goddamn valve's come open. It's empty."

Matt grabbed the tank and shone his light on the zeroed gauge. "What the fuck—"

"We could try two hundred and fifty milligrams of

Dexamethasone,'' Stu said. "Just to see if we get a response." Buzz nodded.

Travis was barely conscious, shaking as though in the throes of palsy. Matt ran down the symptoms in silence: shortness of breath, nausea, vomiting, decrease in mental acuity. Acute Mountain Sickness. Cerebral edema, maybe. "Is it AMS?" he asked at last.

Buzz said, "The symptoms are right. But I can't be certain."

"What about a Valium overdose? Karl told me Travis ate two pills last night."

Buzz shook his head.

"We go with our best hunch," Stu said, tugging at his beard. "We've got to get him down mountain— immediately."

Matt asked if they could risk carrying him over the pass and descending on the other side.

"I'd advise against it," Buzz told him. "You're talking about a two-thousand-foot gain before a five-thousand-foot descent. He could become comatose. I'm sure the Italians have oxygen—possibly even a hyperbaric chamber. I think that's our best course of action."

Matt worked his jaw. "Stu?"

The naturalist nodded. "I agree."

Matt watched the two of them. "We need to talk," he told Stu, nodding to the door.

Candice and Kaylee were standing with Audrey a few feet from the dome. The rest of the trekkers were huddled near the cook fire. Matt and Stu walked to the perimeter of the white light.

"We've got two choices," Matt began quietly. "If we can't carry him over the pass, then he either goes down alone or the whole group goes with him." He held a palm out to the flurries. "But if we all go back down, the trek could end right there. Another couple of days of being socked in by the weather and we're going to have a lot of unhappy campers on our hands. Plus, I think there's a good chance the porters will skip and strand us up here."

"No, the group goes across," Stu said after a moment.

"Good. Now, as to which one of us takes him down . . ." Matt showed Stu a narrow-eyed look. "By rights it should be me. Everybody's got to know that their safety comes

first and that Jake and I are willing to see to that personally. But we've got some problems with that. First off,
Jake's already gone. If I go, there's a chance they're
going to feel shit adrift out here." He paused, then added:
"Which probably wouldn't have been the case if you
hadn't worked so hard at alienating everyone."

Stu snorted but said nothing.

"But there's even better reasons for your going: You're
fluent in Nepali, and I know you've handled cases of
cerebral edema. You're also a damned strong walker,
and you've crossed this pass before. That means if Travis
recupes, you can lead him over."

"Assuming we don't get snowed in."

"That's the gamble."

"And suppose he needs to be evacuated completely?"

Matt nodded. "I'm ahead of you. You take two of the
Tamang porters with you. As soon as you hit the Italian
camp and get Travis on an oxygen flow, you dispatch
one of the porters to Thanget with a full note of explanation for Jake."

Stu gnawed at his mustache. "Jake might not be
there."

"He'll be somewhere between Syabru and here," Matt
said. "But if the porter isn't back in two days, you make
a judgment call on Travis and either take him over or
take him back."

"And leave you people without a lecturer? What about
that unhappy group you were worried about?"

"I'm going to run this conversation down for them. If
they feel I made a wrong choice, it's my head on the
block with Jake, not yours."

"I can live with that," Stu said.

"Yeah, I figured."

Buzz was directing an opthalmoscope at the engineer's
eyes when Matt returned to the tent. Lopsang had been
directed to choose two Tamangs for the carry down to
the Italians' meadow encampment, and Stu was off gathering up his gear. As expected, Audrey announced that
she would be going with them.

Matt had no intention of asking Buzz to accompany
the Deys, and was surprised when he volunteered. "I

know I came on this trip looking for adventure,'' he told Matt, ''and God knows I've had my fill so far—especially with Travis.'' He glanced at his near-comatose patient. ''But I'm a doctor before I'm anything else. Including a jealous husband.''

Matt regarded him from across the tent. ''I can't stop you, Buzz, but I can tell you that no one'll think you derelict in your duties if you choose to stay with the group.''

''But I'm a doctor,'' he repeated.

''There are three doctors down there,'' Matt said, gesturing in a vague way. ''And Stu is perfectly capable of taking care of Travis between here and the meadow. You're on this trip as a client, not as a team physician.''

Buzz considered it for a moment. ''All right,'' he said finally.

They got Travis bundled up and tied to a makeshift stretcher; then Matt dropped the tent and stowed it with Dey's gear. Purbu put together a food bag that would see the five-member party through a week if need be. Matt had a final talk with Stu while the group filed by with soft-voiced good wishes for Travis. Audrey stood alongside the stretcher the entire time, both hands clasped on her husband's mittened hand. Matt had never seen her looking so strong and determined.

The eastern peaks were outlined by the thinnest band of yellow light as the highland porters began their ascent to the saddle. The group followed, led by Lopsang, Candice, and Kaylee. Only Doug and Karl lagged behind to watch Stu, Audrey, and the stretcher-bearers leave, heavy snowflakes dancing in the beams of their flashlights and headlamps.

''I don't see why we couldn't've carried him over the top,'' Karl was saying. ''We're s'posed to drop down to twelve thousand over there, aren't we?''

Matt nodded in a distracted way. ''Doctor's orders. He didn't think Travis would survive the trip.''

Doug grunted. ''Guess Buzz had his own good reasons for wanting Travis evacuated.''

◫◫ 18 ◫◫

Rapid Decline

A pre-dawn departure from high camp normally ensured a trek across hard snow; but since there was no sun that morning to soften the crust, it wouldn't have mattered what time they left. Even so it took the group four lung-burning hours to reach the saddle—an ascent that might have taken six had it not been for the yaks.

The yaks had overtaken them halfway to the pass and broken a winding trail through avalanche debris and thigh-deep snowdrifts whipped up during the night. The shaggy beasts were burdened both sides with woven sacks and baskets, and driven by three *gopalas*—cowherds—who sauntered uphill with a lazy grace, hands clasped behind their backs, grunting commands to their small herd. The lead animals wore red collars and brightly colored tassels that dangled from their ears.

Matt gave each of the *gopalas* a pair of goggles and gladly surrendered the point to the bushy-tailed cattle. Two of the males were carrying loads abandoned by deserting highlanders on the way up.

The pass was marked by a huge stone cairn, behind which Matt gathered the group and passed around chocolates and trail mix. The peaks on either side were lost in a dizzying welter of snow. On the landmark's flatstone ledge, the porters left flowers carried up from the valley floor, securing them against a whistling wind with small rocks gathered from the windswept saddle itself. Kaylee took photos of Candice in Grand Design gaiters and double boots, along with a few shots of Buzz in his Eddie Bauer mustache antifreeze.

The adrenaline-high everyone rode to the col was bolstered by a sense of accomplishment that almost made up for the exhaustion, the frigid wind, the concerns for Travis, and the treacherously steep descent that now faced them.

"So much for paradise!" Karl shouted in Matt's ear as they were regarding the snow-covered caldron of swirling mist on the far side of the saddle.

"Can't be much worse than what's behind us!" Matt told him.

"We don't follow yaks from here!" Lopsang yelled into his other ear. The *sirdar* pointed off to the left, where Matt assumed there was a trail buried somewhere beneath the snow. "Base camp this direction. We stay high on ridge and drop down later on."

"You lead," Matt said. "I'll take the rear."

Candice and Kaylee walked by without a word, and Karl—showing a comical leer—fell in behind them. Matt held the rest of the group back and motioned the porters forward. "Three more hours to base!" he told everyone, with a silent prayer that it wasn't snowing five thousand feet below.

He'd spent the first hour of the climb blaming himself for Travis Dey's condition, berating himself for negligence and irresponsible behavior. Where his full attention should have been given over to the group, he had focused instead on the climbers, reading paranoid conspiracies into the accidents that befell Julia and Barbara. And when he wasn't wrapped up in imagined intrigue, he was wrapped up in Taylor instead of doing the job he was paid to do. Jake was right about him after all: he had become addicted to trouble.

Taken together, the headaches, the loss of appetite, the personality changes, and lassitude would have suggested the onset of Acute Mountain Sickness. Travis could have been kept behind in meadow camp to acclimate; he could have been sent back down to the Chilime camp if need be. Jake was still down there; Jake could have taken him over the pass and there wouldn't have been any cerebral edema.

If that was what it turned out to be.

Doc Bessman wasn't sure.

Guess Buzz had his own good reasons for wanting Travis evacuated.

Matt tried not to dwell on Doug's statement. But the harder he fought it, the larger it loomed. Buzz wasn't sure: Travis's symptoms *read* like cerebral edema. But goddammit, Matt told himself, Dey *was* acclimated. Certainly as acclimated as any of them. Sure he'd complained about headaches and he had no appetite for Purbu's noodle and vegetable amalgams, but he was no different than the rest of the group on that score. Nor had he seemed confused or especially fatigued; and if anyone had been experiencing a personality change, it was *Buzz*, not Travis.

And just how the fuck had the oxygen-tank valve worked itself open?

After the yaks had taken the point, Matt had asked Morgan how Travis seemed when she had stopped by his tent on her way to Taylor's.

I can't talk about this, Matt, she told him in-between breaths.

"I just want to know if he was all right, Morgan. Did he seem confused by what you were telling him? Did he seem *different*?"

She had whirled on him then, eyes concealed behind dark glasses, nostrils flared in anger. *He told me I couldn't sleep with him. He told me we were going to have to go back to being friends. So, yes, Matt, I guess he did seem* different!

Shuffling by him now at the top of the pass, Morgan looked dead on her feet.

"Into the valley of death," Maurice Delong quipped as he took a sideways step down into the snow. Dee-Dee was a few steps behind him, beaming. "The high pass! We made it, Matt!"

"The trek from hell," Chris muttered, while Doug urged him along with a fatherly hand.

Matt motioned for Taylor to fall out of line. "Matt,

I'm really worried," she said after Buzz had filed by. "Is Travis going to be all right?"

"The Italians have a regular clinic down there. If it is cerebral edema, they'll be able to pull him out of it."

"If?"

"You said you had something to tell me. About last night," he added.

What little he could see of her face under the hood of her parka and snow goggles registered surprise; then concern as she looked down into the bowl. "Can't it wait till we get off this mountain?"

"What did Morgan tell you?"

Taylor's wave of dismissal almost tipped her into the snow. "Shit! I'd rather be on skis than wearing these damn boots!"

"Lean into the hill," Matt said.

She frowned at him. "Yeah, tell me about it."

Ahead of them the group was a colored convoy plowing through knee-deep snow. "So what about Morgan?" Matt said after they'd gained some distance from the saddle.

"She's a mess. Buzz said he wished he didn't have to see her for the rest of the trek, and then Travis told her she couldn't spend the night in his tent." Taylor paused. "God, if she had, maybe you and Buzz could have gotten to him sooner. I still can't believe how fast it came on for him. Morgan was pissed off at how rational he was sounding when he told her things were kaput." She laughed. "Downed out on Halcion but rational. That figures."

"This was before she came over to your tent?"

"No, later when she went back out."

"She went back out to his tent?"

Taylor turned around to look at him. "It must have been around ten o'clock. While *I* was getting her gear from Buzz. Which didn't thrill him any, I might add."

"And Travis was fine—at ten o'clock? Just downed out?"

Taylor nodded. "So she says."

They were still walking five hours later, and the snow was falling harder. There had been little in the way of communication save for when Matt would press forward or fall back to see how someone was doing, invariably meeting with terse replies—everyone down deep into their own thoughts, white for a backdrop, wind for accompaniment. No one was using the word blizzard, but he suspected that everyone was thinking it.

He had been looking forward to base camp as much as any of them—envisioning it: a flat camp with majestic mountain views, nestled in a narrow valley sheltered from the storms. A regular Shangri-la.

In front of him now, through horizontal snow, he could make out the yak-herders' stone corrals; but he didn't connect those with the quaint walls of his vision until his foot snagged on the exposed strap of a half-buried duffel. At first he thought the group had stumbled into some hapless climb team's hastily scuttled base camp, or that one of the lead porters had abandoned a load. But as he gazed around at the scattered equipment, the truth assembled itself, and he realized they had indeed arrived at their destination.

What was left of it.

Centered in one of the corrals was the North Face Dome Candice's team had entrusted to Ang Samden Sherpa. The tent was partially encircled by a drift of powder three feet deep. A smaller self-standing mountain tent was set up nearby, the rain-fly snapping in the wind like a poorly rigged sail. Still, there were no signs the camp was occupied.

Then Matt saw a flash of light appear in the doorway of the small tent. Lopsang said, "It is Gambu." He had a gloved hand to his brow. As Gambu approached, he did something that altered the flashlight beam to a red disk. The two *sirdars* exchanged light bows and *namastes*.

"What happened here?" Matt demanded.

The Sherpa looked up, shaking his head in a mournful way. "Ah, terrible bad story. We walk through very bad storm because Ang Samden is wanting very badly to cross the pass. Not too many porters are wearing boots and goggles and too many arriving down here with frozen toes and eyes. Snow blindness, yes?" Gambu glanced over his shoulder at the North Face Dome. "Ang Samden

is very, very mad at the complaining. He says porters are
not good porters, weak porters. They will make him a
bad name with trekking groups in Kathmandu.''

"So they deserted," Matt said.

"No, not desert," Gambu told him. "Big fight first."
He gestured to the exposed tops of cargo boxes and overturned baskets. "Everyone throw supplies everywhere on
the ground. No one is stealing," he was quick to explain.
"Just throwing supplies everywhere on ground. Then
leaving."

Matt and Lopsang traded looks. "They've left—all of
them?"

Gambu shook his head rapidly, dislodging snow from
the black bill of his staff cap. "Not all. Some still too
. . . snow-blind to move. They staying in caves." He
pointed north to a rocky slope, dimpled with small, dark
openings. "They eating some freeze-dry food with no
cooking in it.''

Lopsang asked in Nepali after Ang Samden Sherpa.

"Inside the big tent. But he is not coming out. He is
too dishonored.''

"You said some of the porters left," Matt interjected.
"We didn't meet anyone coming down from the pass.''

"No, no, they go long way around to Thanget through
Sathi and Gadrang before bridge falls.''

Matt's stomach dropped. "The bridge is out?''

"Since two days. Very, very much rain below.''

"What about the trails down to Sathi?''

Gambu threw up his hands. "Too much landslides.''

The three of them fell silent for a moment. Matt's eyes
swept over what was to have been base camp; then he
turned a glance at the trekkers, who were munching on
the *chapatis* and snacks Purbu had parceled out. "We
can't make camp in this," he said to Lopsang. "If the
snow keeps up we'll be buried by morning. We'll have to
drop further down—below the snow line.''

"No," Gambu said. "Very dangerous going that way.
Too many hours. You leave now and arrive nine, ten
o'clock.''

"Well, we're not about to go back over the pass."
Matt wiped snow from the goggle lenses. "What about
the caves? Is there room for our porters?''

Gambu surveyed the line of mountain men and shook his head.

"What if we climbed to the cheese factory?" Candice said. "Do you think they'd take all of us in?"

"They will," Gambu said. "But you must ask permission from the *rimpoche*—the head lama."

"At the monastery," Kaylee said.

Gambu nodded. "But he will let you stay. He will."

Matt looked back and forth between the two women.

"It means a climb back up to fourteen thousand feet," Kaylee said. "The monastery's just below Rajagang Glacier."

Matt gritted his teeth. "So we either stay here and get ourselves buried, or drop down into rain along unsafe trails with no chance of crossing the Manjet Khola."

"*Or* we reascend," Candice said. "We'll be beat, but at least we'll have a roof over our heads."

Matt dug his watch from the inner pocket of his parka. It was just two-thirty. "Do you think they can make it?" he asked, indicating the group with his chin.

Candice leaned over to peer at the watch. "We can be there by five. Six at the latest."

"We should go there," Lopsang said. "The *rimpoche* will let us stay."

Kaylee regarded Matt for a long moment. "You could put it to a vote, Matt. Let the group decide. Staying here won't kill us."

Matt thought a moment and shook his head. "It was my decision to cross today. I'm not going to throw it back to them all of a sudden."

The *sirdars* swapped looks. "What's your decision?" Lopsang asked.

"We go up," Matt told him. He cut his eyes to Gambu. "And tell Ang Samden he's coming with us."

🪷🪷 19 🪷🪷

Front *Stupa*

Lopsang hurried down the snow-drifted staircase that fronted the largest of the monastery's whitewashed outbuildings and followed his own footprints back to where Matt was waiting with the Puma group. "The *rimpoche* won't talk to us," he reported.

Matt was sure he'd heard him wrong. "Whaddaya mean he won't talk to us? He's *gotta* talk to us. Doesn't he realize why we humped up here?—"

"No, no," Lopsang cut in, hands waving, uncovered head hurling melting snowflakes. "He has a promise, a, a . . . How do you call it?"

Matt stammered, "Uh, uh," as though he and Lopsang were charades contestants.

"A vow?" Candice offered.

"A vow, yes," Lopsang said.

"A vow," Matt said, almost touching a gloved fingertip to his near-frozen nose. He directed a frown at the head Sherpa. "What kind of vow?"

"A not-speaking vow."

Matt's face went blank for a moment. "You mean he won't even shake his head yes or no?"

"He can't, no. But the other one—the servant . . ."

"The caretaker," Candice said.

Matt showed her a smile. "Can I play on your team next time?"

"The caretaker say we can stay."

Matt's shoulders sagged with relief and he relayed the good news to the group. Suddenly the snow, the altitude, the incipient darkness didn't seem quite so foreboding.

The three-hour trek had taken them two thousand feet up a narrow ravine, through stunted conifers and across snow-covered scree. The glacier that had carved the drainage still dominated its northeastern terminus. The monastery was set on a five-hundred-foot rise above an ice-coated river that flowed from beneath the glacial prow itself.

"We go this way," Lopsang said, gesturing to the trail his boots had broken across level terrain. He threw his pack over one shoulder and barked a few sentences at Gambu and a sullen Ang Samden. "Porters can stay in open area under cheese factory," he explained for Matt and Candice's benefit. He pointed to a grouping of mostly single-story buildings off to one side of the compound. "We can use these rooms. For guest lamas and monks."

The monastery's principal structure was a brick building perhaps thirty feet square, roofed with corrugated tin and capped by a smaller replica of itself. The few windows were wooden trapezoids and the doorways were carved. Three whitewashed houses formed an open courtyard below the building's front entrance. Below these was a cluster of narrow, earthen outbuildings with mullioned windows and slate roof shingles.

Adjacent to the cheese factory stood a small *chorten* on a kind of promontory that overlooked the valley, and resembled nothing so much as a truncated pyramid wearing a marshmallow-shaped crown. The entire compound was surrounded by prayer flags and a meandering wall of unmortared stone.

"The monks have gone to Kathmandu," Lopsang said as they were approaching the only two-story outbuilding among the lot. "To Swayambunath . . ."

"On a pilgrimage," Matt and Candice said at the same time. "See what I can do with a little practice?" he told her.

The eaves of the building were packed with saplings and bundles of brushwood gathered from the lower valleys. Lopsang tugged at a heavy door that opened on a dank and unlighted hallway. Matt went to his pack for a flashlight but the *sirdar* stayed his hand.

"No flashlights, or cameras, or cassette players. *Rimpoche*'s rules." He stomped the snow from his boots, stepped into the dark hallway, and emerged a moment later with two butter lamps. "We use these."

Matt touched a lighter to the thick wicks. "What about the gas lanterns?"

"Lanterns and stoves, okay," Lopsang said.

Off both sides of the hallway were doorless, musty cubicles, each equipped with a narrow plank cot, a bench seat, and a crude writing table. The alcoves and niches in the unpainted walls were bare. The short corridor emptied into a kitchen area that had a small, chimneyless clay oven. The roof beams and support posts were blackened from years of cook smoke. Directly opposite the entry hall was a short corridor that led to two additional rooms, somewhat larger than those Matt had already peered into.

He instructed Lopsang to see that Purbu's team was installed in the kitchen before he left to check on the porters. "And try to make them understand they shouldn't be superstitious about what happened to Travis," Matt thought to add. "It was just the altitude."

He figured on putting Karl, Doug, Chris, and Lopsang in the front rooms, and offering the rear ones to Dee-Dee and Maurice, and Buzz and Morgan. That would leave him looking for a room for Taylor, a spare for Morgan if need be, one for himself, and two more for Gambu and Ang Samden—unless either of them decided to stay with the cook staff.

Matt got six of the trekkers settled while Purbu was setting up his kitchen. The climbers had found suitable lodgings for themselves and Taylor in a second outbuilding, and Morgan jumped at the chance of a room to herself. Matt found space for the Sherpas in a large house not far from the cheese factory, and one for himself in a hermitage near the compound latrine.

On a low table in his tent-size room, Matt set down the butter lamp he'd found in the hallway and stripped out of his wet clothing, banging into walls and ceiling with each move. By the time he'd changed and spread out his mattress and sleeping bag on the plank cot, some of the feeling was returning to his fingers and toes. But even dry clothes couldn't thaw the frozen knot the storm had tied in his gut. His face tingled and the tops of his ears burned.

He returned through the dark to the trekkers' dormitory, thinking it could have almost been a midwinter Montana night, save for the incessant sound of wind chimes, snapping prayer flags, and a deep rumbling from the glaciated head of the valley.

The Puma group was gathered in the kitchen, sipping at mugs of Japanese noodle soup. Huge lidded pots dwarfed the three compressed-gas stoves Purbu had running at full operation. Matt accepted a mug and sat down on the earthen floor next to Karl and Doug. "Everybody all right?" he said in a discomforting silence. "All fingers and toes accounted for?"

"Nothin' dropped off that I care about," Karl muttered, getting a soup-spewing laugh from Chris. "Sure wasn't no walk in the park, though." There was a hint of anger beneath the Texan's friendly tone.

"I'll say it wasn't a walk in the park," Doug said a moment later. "In fact, I think we should count our blessings."

Matt took a deep breath. He hadn't expected everyone to be *cheery*, but he thought a touch of self-congratulations was in order. They'd crossed the pass intact; they were warm, dry, and sheltered now. "It was a lot tougher than it was meant to be," he said. "But sometimes you just have to chance it. I can't apologize for the snow, but I can tell you I would have held us over if I'd known it was going to be this bad."

"Twenty-twenty hindsight," Doug said.

"I don't feel dissed," Chris said, studying the ground between his unlaced sneakers. "I thought it was awesome."

Morgan narrowed her eyes at the kid. "Well, I don't think it was 'awesome.' I think it was damn foolish for us to cross that mountain." She glowered at Matt. "We're not mountaineers, you know. Most of us are business professionals. You might keep that in mind next time you're calculating the odds, Matt."

Matt nodded. "Okay. But normally you don't see this kind of storm till next month." It slipped out before he realized how defensive he was sounding.

"Don't listen to her," Buzz said. "It's a freak storm. And sure it was an ordeal. But that's why *some* of us are out here. We made it. We should be patting ourselves on the back instead of attacking Matt."

"Mr. Men's Adventure," Morgan sneered.

"I didn't think I'd even get over the pass," Taylor said, trying for an up note.

Dee-Dee and Maurice were nodding. "I'd do it again," she said.

"Oh, for Christ's sake," Morgan said.

Karl shook his head. "Not sure I would. But I think Matt made the right call in sending Travis back down instead of carrying him up and over."

Morgan stood up, displaying her anger. "I'm going to bed."

"Guess I'll turn in, too," Doug said, breaking a long silence. "You about ready, sport?" he asked Chris, who shrugged.

One by one the trekkers got up and filed out of the kitchen, leaving Matt, Candice, and Kaylee with the sheepish cook staff. "Fuck 'em if they can't take a joke," Kaylee said, frowning into her soup. "We lose our shot at Pabil and they have the nerve to complain about wet feet?"

Matt put his tongue in his cheek. "I'd rather hear about it now than at the end of the trip. We've still got sixteen days together."

Kaylee blew out her breath. "Chris had it right: 'The trek from hell.' "

Gambu reported that Ang Samden Sherpa felt unworthy of accepting the offer of a room in the outbuildings and preferred to continue his penance under the cheese factory with the spooked porters.

After Candice and Kaylee turned in, Matt discussed breakfast with the kitchen crew. It was time, everyone agreed, to break open the eggs they'd been carrying since Thanget and rustle up some omelettes for Puma's disgruntled trekkers. Purbu had a couple of peppers left,

more than enough onions, and fresh yak cheese was now
only a few steps away. Matt also assigned him the task
of finding a sheep to butcher as soon as the storm blew
over.

He spent a brief moment at each doorway on his way
out; then did the same in the outbuilding where Morgan,
Taylor, and the climbers were housed.

"Is that you sneaking around out there?" Taylor whispered from the darkness of her tiny room.

Matt said, "Just here to check the meter, ma'am." He
tiptoed in while she was lighting the lamp.

"I was hoping you'd stop by," she told him, up on
elbows inside the blue mummy bag. "The meter's reading way low."

He kissed her mouth, supporting himself on one arm.
She linked her hands behind his neck and urged him down
onto the hard cot. "So what are you up to—tucking the
group in?"

"Just seeing that everyone's breathing."

"God, after tonight why should you care? Just because
it's your job?" She studied his face in the flickering light.
"How were you supposed to know the weather was going
to turn evil?"

He grinned. "I'm paid to know."

"And how often do groups turn on you for not knowing?"

Matt rolled his shoulders beneath her hands. "It's usually only one or two people. But that's what got me out
of leading trips to begin with. I told Jake I wasn't cut
out to play den mother or shrink."

Taylor put her head down on an inflatable pillow and
stared at the low ceiling. "Any more than you're cut out
to settle down to a routine job."

"You're saying I need this?"

"Well, maybe not the Morgans and Dougs of the
world. But, yeah, the unanticipated storms, the close calls
along the trail. The affairs with exciting women." She
smiled, then yawned. "You're in your element. And
there's our trouble down the road: We're bound to end
up with an airport romance."

Matt stood up. "You better get some sleep."

"I already am."

"You warm enough?"

She patted his hand. "See? You don't make such a
bad mom, after all."

Most of the group slept late, nursing sore leg and lower-
back muscles. Wind-driven hail pelted the slate roofs and
worked its way around the edges of the wooden doors.
Reflected light from the snowfields spilled through the
windowpanes but did little to disperse a darkness that
seemed endemic to the place. A visit to the latrine meant
a fully outfitted trek through deep snow to a roofed-over
hole in the ground, footprints from the previous evening
filled in with crystalline snow. Pants and thermals
dropped, the temperature alone was enough to discourage
dawdling.

The omelette succeeded in lifting everyone's spirits
somewhat, and by noon Buzz, Doug, and Chris were actually outside having a snowball fight. The caretaker—a
shaved-skull Tamang in deep-red homespun robes—gave
those who were interested a quick look at the gloomy
interior of the *gompa*, with its carved ceiling beams,
Buddha frescoes, hanging drums, and prayer-flag print-
ing blocks. The walls were adorned with ancient swas-
tikas and depictions of dragons and elephants. Centered
on a low altar was a plastic bouquet in an ornate vase.

With Lopsang's help, the caretaker explained that
while Swayambunath was the ostensible goal of the pilgrimage, most of the monks had gone to Kathmandu simply to sell their scroll paintings to the tourist shops.

The head lama—the *rimpoche*—put in a brief appearance to appraise everyone from the monastery's elaborately carved entrance. Dressed in saffron and scarlet, he
had happy, puffed eyes and a dark, kind face stubbled
with silver whiskers.

Matt and Purbu spent an hour moving duffels from the
cheese factory to the dormitory rooms; then another hour
breaking trails between the outbuildings, devoting extra
effort to the one leading to the latrine. It seemed a sense-
less task given the continuing snowfall, but all the foot
shuffling involved gave Matt ample time to consider just
what he was going to do with the group after the storm
broke.

Candice and Kaylee were undecided about attempting an alpine ascent of Pabil. There was some chance their supplies had survived the mutiny and could be salvaged from the drifts at base camp; some chance, for that matter, that Barbara would show up within the week.

But Matt still had to arrive at a contingency plan for the trekkers no matter which way things went for the climb team. The rain, which delayed them in the Chilime Valley, had trimmed the days initially slated for base camp from eight to four. And now with word that the bridge across the Manjet had been washed out, Matt was forced to accept that the route home might entail a return trip over the high pass.

Later, pacing the porch of the cheese factory, he decided that any change in plans would have to await a reconnoiter of the lower valley. Until then he could keep the group occupied on day trips to the Rajagang and neighboring glaciers.

The slopes above the Rajagang were rumbling now, calving billowy avalanches into the glacial brook on the ravine floor.

"Thunder mountain," Karl said above the sound of the wind.

Matt turned to him as he was brushing large snowflakes from his shoulders. "How's it going, Karl," he said flatly.

The Texan raised his goggles and leaned his elbows over the porch handrail. "Listen, amigo," he began, "I didn't mean to come off so heavy last night about the pass. I was feelin' plain wasted is all. Halfway up the hill I started askin' myself just what the hell I was doin' out here. Who did I think I was foolin', you know. What the hell was I expectin' to find in Nepal that I couldna hunted down in Dallas with a lot less effort."

Matt acknowledged the apology with a grin. "No, I'm glad you said what was on your mind. Let's keep it that way, whichever way it spins."

Staring out over the ravine, Karl clapped him on the forearm. "You know, partner, you and I oughta have ourselves a regular blowout back in Kat. You know of any brothels in town?" He paused. " 'Course, you're probably not feeling as horny as I am.'' He looked to Matt for a reaction. ''You like her, huh?''

''Yeah, I do. I mean, shit, who the hell knows anymore? When the trip's over, she goes off on another assignment, and I end up in Malaysia or somewhere. We'd have a lot to work out.''

''Hey, if it's meant to be. Think of the places you'd be getting together in—Singapore, Sydney, whatever. Better than Miami. Besides, guy like you, I reckon you've got a coupla gals stashed here and there to tide you over in between meets.''

''You've got me confused with someone else.''

Karl laughed. ''Well, maybe. But take it from someone's who's just out of the corral, amigo: keeping liquid's the way to go. You settle down somewhere and you're buying into a heap of hard times. Before you even know what hit you, you got a bus load a bills to pay and somebody on the other side of the bed to answer to. It's no special effect, Karl's here to tell you.''

He edged a three-inch-high wall of snow off the railing. ''Seems like everybody on this trip's scorin' one way or another. Didn't I tell you I had the Deys and the Bessmans sussed the minute I set eyes on them?''

''You called it,'' Matt said. It got him thinking and he looked over at Karl. ''You knew Travis better than I did. You guys smoked some hash together, didn't you?''

Karl whistled. ''I'll say. I don't think Audrey took to it none. But that Morgan . . .'' He laughed. ''Well, maybe she was just feelin' wanton or something. Playing to both of them, Buzz and Travis. LA loose.''

''How did Travis seem to you on the walk up from the Chilime?

''How do you mean?''

''Did he seem confused, or apathetic?''

Karl gave it a moment of thought. ''He did seem kind of tired. But, hell, I wouldn't know the symptoms of Mountain Sickness if they came up and bit me on the ass. Why? What's on your mind?''

Matt made a thin line with his lips. ''I didn't see it happening. Usually there's some buildup to cerebral edema, but he was over into an advanced stage like *that*. I just can't figure it.''

"But didn't Buzz and Stu make the call?"

"Yeah, but they admitted they weren't sure it was edema."

Karl wedged a finger under the hood of his parka to scratch at his red-whiskered neck. "You're not thinking somebody spiked his noodles or anything, are you? 'Though between you and me I wouldn't put it past that little firebrand Morgan."

Matt shook his head. "I don't know what I'm thinking. First I thought it might be the tranquilizers. But you were taking them and they didn't seem to affect you any."

"Slept like a baby."

"Then I find the goddamned oxygen bottle empty. I checked it down in the meadow and it was fine. And the only one I know was into the medical supplies after that was Buzz."

Karl's mouth turned down. "Easy, Matt."

"I'm not accusing anybody. One of the porters could have fooled with the bottle for all I know. It's happened before. Besides, Buzz was right there for Travis. He was even ready to leave the group and take him downhill."

"Maybe he knew you were suspicious of him?"

"I'm not suspicious of anybody, either," Matt lied. "Anyway, Buzz sounded sincere. It wasn't a sudden case of conscience."

"Son of a gun," Karl said.

Matt forced an exhale. "This whole trip, man. First the Jeep accident, then Barbara, now Travis. I guess we're just running on bad luck." He closed his eyes and laughed. "The trek from hell. I'm going tell Jake to print it up like that in the brochures."

"Don't forget the dog." Karl screwed up his face. "Call the rest accidents, but I still think that porter, Tulo, did the dog. Remember what he said—'Karma *mo-mos*,' wasn't that it? He had it in for that pooch."

"Who didn't," Matt said. "Remember how Doug was complaining about Karma the night the three of us went into Syabru looking for beers?"

Karl's eyebrows beetled. "No, I don't recall that. But what the hell, Matt, the dog coulda got out of the tent on its own."

Matt considered mentioning the neat hole he had nearly fallen into, the snare that had almost felled Barbara, the ski pole imprint in the rotting log, Morgan Bessman's late night visit to Travis Dey's tent. But instead all he said was, "Definitely. That's exactly what happened."

By late afternoon the snow had stopped falling, and for five minutes the ragged clouds above the eastern peaks were patched with deep blue. Over dinner, Matt promised the group that Purbu was planning a special menu for the following night. The revised but scarcely finalized plan he offered for their approval necessitated relying on the abbot's generous nature for two more nights and continuing to use the monastery as a base of operations. Weather permitting, Candice and Kaylee would lead the group up to the Rajagang Glacier, while Matt and Lopsang scouted the lower valley to determine the condition of the trails and perhaps find some way of fording the swollen Manjet.

Everyone seemed agreeable, and Matt sensed the return of a semblance of group integrity. A few of the trekkers donned jackets and boots and went outside to watch for shooting stars; and Bimbahadur, the caretaker, entertained everyone with tales of local yeti sightings.

Thinking he should take out his maps and familiarize himself with the layout of the lower valleys, Matt was one of the first to say good night. He traipsed over to the little house feeling encouraged by the change in the weather.

He left the outer door ajar while he hunted for the fat candle that had become his light source since the butter lamp had burned itself dry. Then he closed the outer door and got the candle going. He had one hand cupped around the oxygen-starved flame and the other on the thumb latch of the door to his monastic cell when someone came through the outer door, stirring a breeze that snuffed the candle.

"Matt?" he heard Taylor ask.

"Right in front of you," he told her. "The one holding the dead candle."

"Did I do that?"

"Don't worry about it. I've got a lighter—*had* a lighter," he completed a second later.

"I was just trying to find you," Taylor said, realizing she'd knocked the lighter from his fingers. They bumped heads on the way down to the floor, but her groping hand finally seized on the thing. Matt handed her the candle and opened the door to the room.

The smell hit him immediately.

He yanked the door closed and whirled on Taylor, swatting the lighter out of her grip before she had thumbed the plastic tab.

"Hey! What's the matter with you? And what's that smell?" She sniffed and gagged. "It smells like gas."

"Yeah, the place needs to be aired out," Matt told her, reaching for the outer door handle. "Look, why don't we go back to your room instead of trying to squeeze into mine?"

"I just wanted to say good night," she said in a confused voice.

"Well, I'll walk you home."

He urged her outside with a hand at the small of her back, leaving both doors wide open behind him.

20

Grand Design

Matt sat on the cot in his aired-out cubicle contemplating the camping stove and the now-empty Gaz canisters someone had set up on the bedside table. He had passed a sleepless night in the cottage's other small room after walking Taylor back to her own quarters.

He thought he had a fair idea now of the scenario his would-be assassin had in mind: It was to have appeared as though Matt had been heating water on the stove. The stove canister had run out of fuel, so he had switched to a second, full one. Then for some reason he had changed his mind about having tea, only he'd neglected to turn off the stove. And later when he'd returned to his room and struck a match to light a candle or lamp—*fwhoom!* The well-sealed little room would have played host to a brief but possibly deadly flash fire.

Matt had seen just that sort of accident occur to campers replacing stove canisters inside a tent. The one believed to be depleted would leak just enough propane-butane mix to fill up the small space, and a moment after the stove was reignited, the unfortunate campers would find their tent engulfed in flames.

He loosed a snort. It wouldn't have worked. Which meant that whoever had selected him for flame roasting hadn't bothered to think things through very carefully. So either he was dealing with an amateur, or someone who didn't believe in fussing over details. The sloppiness of it irritated him as much as anything else.

And perhaps that was just what he was meant to feel. Maybe the effect of the gas trick was all in the set-up. Someone firing a warning shot.

He began to turn one of the canisters about in his hands. The neat holes his mystery guest had punctured through the thin metal skin of both tanks were uniformly an eighth of an inch wide and a quarter-inch long—the wrong dimensions for a camping knife blade or the thick tip of a hunting knife. Matt thought the shape of the punctures peculiar as well. Pointed at one end, the holes had flattened, somewhat parallel sides and a square-cut bottom. They looked something like tiny Washington Monuments.

It took half an hour of experimenting to finally determine the tool that had been used: the so-called "leather-punch" implement usually located on the underside of a Swiss army knife. He chuckled to himself as he slipped the suspect point of his own leather punch in and out of one of the holes, thinking maybe he'd judged his enemy too harshly earlier on. The choice of tools was fairly brilliant, since even Morgan Bessman was carrying a Swiss army knife.

As for who might have had access to the canisters, the answer was a simple *everyone*. The camping stoves and refills had been in plain sight in the dormitory kitchen. And as for who might have crept into the hermitage room: well, anyone at all. Any one of the previous evening's stargazers; anyone en route to or from the latrines; any one of the porters or Sherpas.

At first light he had gone out to inspect the trail that led to the cottage for telltale boot prints; but what marks hadn't been covered over during the night were undefined.

He composed a suspect list nevertheless, beginning with Morgan. She could have found Travis in the early stages of cerebral edema and, angered by rejection, deliberately withheld mention of his perilous condition. Could she be worried suddenly about being found out? And yet Taylor was the one who knew she had visited Travis's tent during the night.

Buzz was the far more obvious choice, if only in terms of motive. While Morgan may have been spurned, the anesthesiologist had been cuckolded. Still, why go after Matt now when the object of his rage had been effectively removed from the trek?

Unless all the accidents were smoke screens. Designed to so preoccupy him with the safety of the group members that he would forget to keep his own guard up.

Given the list of misadventures he'd been involved in in the past decade, he supposed there were any number of reasons to explain the *why* part of the puzzle; but the *who* remained a mystery. Buzz and Dee-Dee with their purportedly French surnames? Doug Makey, whose own son had described him as a government man? Candice, or Kaylee, alone or in concert? Karl, hiding behind the guise of a lonely, broken-hearted cowboy? Had the Texan all this time been using that hail-fellow-well-met smile of his to mask some unfocused homicidal urge? Lopsang, for that matter. The only people Matt could safely dismiss were the ones who had been left behind on the other side of the mountain.

By the time Matt left the cottage, the climbers had the Puma group assembled at the *chorten* for the hike up to Rajagang Glacier. East and south the sky was a cloudless, rarefied blue. The sun—recently appeared over the ridge—was warming the thin air, and Matt ventured that midday temperatures could hit eighty in the sunlight. Snow plumes adorned the surrounding peaks, and there was an almost sweet smell in the air when the wind ceased.

The trekkers were outfitted in full snow gear, noses coated with zinc oxide, ski poles at ready. Approaching them head-on, Matt found himself thinking about police lineups. One member of the group was not what he or she seemed.

Lopsang and Gambu were standing off to one side talking with Ang Samden Sherpa and a few of the porters. Matt surmised from the tracks in the snow that some of the naturally suspicious highlanders had beat an early retreat for home.

In the wake of his discovery, Matt questioned the wisdom of leaving the group to the care of the two climbers; still, a recon of the eroded trails lower down was essential, perhaps more so now than before. He thought he might rest easier with the arrangement if he could be assured the trekkers would be sticking together for the hike; and he was on the verge of discussing his concerns with Candice and Kaylee when a lone figure clad in blue and yellow suddenly appeared on the porter-cut trail that led down to base camp.

Doug screwed a telephoto lens onto his camera and aimed it at the distant figure. "It's Jake," he announced. A moment later, two porters surfaced into view behind him, over a dome of snow.

Matt asked for the camera and zoomed in tight on his friend. Jake had his head down and was moving with obvious difficulty. The porters, too, looked spent. "Jake!" he called through cupped hands.

The ravine repeated the call and Jake stopped short. He gazed in the direction of the monastery then waved an arm over his head and fell flat on his face in the snow.

"He's going to be all right," Buzz was promising Matt a short time later. Jake had been moved into Karl Tower's dormitory room and was sitting upright in Karl's sleeping bag now, sipping at a mug of hot soup.

"You feeling better than you look?" Matt asked.

Jake smiled weakly. "I'm feeling okay, if that answers your question."

The two porters who led Jake across the pass the previous evening had helped carry him into the compound. Matt and Lopsang had taken over from there, getting him into dry clothes and placing him inside the sleeping bag with a couple of hot-water bottles. Purbu had brewed soup for the near-frozen trio, two pots of which Lopsang ran out to the porters. Buzz had insisted on remaining behind to have a look at Jake; and while he was doing so, Matt sent the group up valley with the climbers and instructed the two *sirdars* to recon the lower trails without him.

"What possessed you to cross the pass last night, Jake?" Buzz wanted to know.

Jake took a long pull of soup and set the mug in his

lap. "The weather broke," he said, passing a hand over his mouth. "There was plenty of moonlight. I didn't want to miss my chance to catch up with you." His eyes never left Matt's.

"This is one for the books," Buzz said. "I mean, I've heard of tour operators going all out for their groups, but crossing a pass in the dark seems a bit excessive."

"That's Jake Welles," Matt said, concealing his bafflement.

Buzz grew serious. "How's Travis doing, Jake?"

"He's coming along fine. Audrey and Stu got him down to the Italian camp in record time and the doctors started an oxygen flow going. Audrey was apparently a real trooper. Anyway, he came around by midafternoon." Jake lifted the soup to his mouth. "Stu should be bringing everyone across tomorrow, providing the weather holds."

"Barbara, too?" Matt said, trying to keep a note of suspicion out of his voice.

"Barbara, too. She's just about back to strength." He nodded as Matt began to fill him in on how the group had ended up at the monastery. "Yeah, we met a couple of yak herders lower down who told us you were up here."

Buzz heaved a sigh. "All's well that ends well, I suppose. Though I do want to keep an eye on those two toes, Jake. Just to be sure you didn't suffer any frostbite."

"Thanks, Buzz, but I'm already getting the feeling back."

The anesthesiologist responded with a professional nod. "I'll leave you two to business, then."

Matt walked Buzz outside, where Ang Samden and Gambu were waiting to escort him up to the glacier. Back inside the dormitory, Matt bolted the door and hurried to Jake's bedside. "All right," he said, perching himself on the edge of the cot, "let's cut to the chase."

"Bessman's gone?" Jake asked quietly.

"All clear. What the hell's going on?"

Jake's eyes narrowed as he shook his head back and forth. "I showed up at the Italian's camp a couple of hours after Travis was carried in, so I only got to hear the story secondhand from Stu. Seems he was in critical condition by the time they got him down the mountain, but he didn't respond to oxygen. At first the doctors thought he'd suffered irreparable brain damage. At the very least they decided he'd have to be carried down to Thanget immediately. Someone suggested an IV drip with some added glucose to replace Travis's calorie loss, and all of a sudden he started to improve—even though he still wasn't responding to oxygen. One of the doctors got suspicious and ran a blood test for hypoglycemia. It turned out positive."

"Hypoglycemia? . . . Insulin shock," Matt said. "Was he diabetic?"

"That's exactly what the doctors thought. They figured he'd overdosed himself." Jake forced out his breath. "But he isn't a diabetic. Someone deliberately shot him up with insulin, Matt."

Matt swallowed hard. "Did he say that?"

"No, but it's the only explanation that fits the facts. He did take a couple of tranquilizers—he remembers that much. But he doesn't have any memory of what happened next. The Italians are certain he was injected with upwards of fifty units of a time-release insulin sometime around midnight."

"Certain how, Jake? Did they find evidence of an injection?"

"Not on his skin, no. Apparently the needle punctures are too small to detect or something. But nothing else makes sense, Matt. There's a ninety-nine-percent likelihood that someone injected him—probably with a pen injector. The effects are unpredictable in healthy people, so he could have died."

Matt stood up and paced to the center of the small room. "But whether he died or not, someone knew enough about it to figure we'd make a call of cerebral edema."

Jake nodded.

"What about Barbara? Is she coming over?"

"Her throat's giving her a lot of trouble."

Matt worked his jaw. "I tried my best not to cut her too badly."

"Hey, she's not blaming you, Matt." Jake said. "Fact is, she's hot to thank you—in person."

"A thank you'd do fine," Matt said.

Jake's smile disappeared. "Anyway, it's Buzz's malpractice that concerns me."

"I wouldn't jump to conclusions, Jake—"

"But who else, Matt?" Jake apologized for shouting and added in a more controlled voice: "He had a motive, he had the means. He's an anesthesiologist. He'd know about insulin."

"Yeah, I know it looks that way. But there're things going on you don't know about, Jake."

Jake folded his arms across his chest. "You're the pro here, is that it—after what happened in Mexico and Bali?"

Matt ran a hand down his face. "Lemme tell you about what I almost walked in on while you were coming over the pass. . . ."

They traced the events a dozen different ways, but at the end of each trail were left with only three knowns out of a host of uncertainties: Someone had tried to trip Barbara Bass with a walking-stick stake and a length of hemp rope; someone had almost killed Travis Dey with a midnight injection of time-release insulin; and someone had tried to incinerate Matt in his room.

Jake was no longer intent on dismissing the other incidents as accidents. The stronger Matt built a case for purposefulness, the more Jake was forced to reconsider. As circumstantial as it all sounded, there was in fact talk of brake tampering; there were in fact threats on Karma's life; evidence of an overturned stone, a *khukri*-sharpened walking stick, a ski-pole punctured forest log.

Matt was beginning to believe that a half-dozen crazed individuals had each played a separate hand in the incidents.

Buzz, though, remained their chief suspect; and Matt kept close watch over the physician's comings and goings within the compound after the group returned from the glacier. At the same time, he arranged for Karl to be moved into the unoccupied room in the cottage, so that Jake could have the cubicle adjoining Bessman's in the dormitory.

Lopsang and Gambu returned to the monastery just before sunset with news that the trails might be passable in a few days' time. The sudden warmth was melting the snows below, and the two *sirdars* thought the group should consider moving down to base camp. The *rimpoche* was beginning to tire of his unexpected guests. Besides, a quick survey of the climbers' snow-buried supplies had revealed that most of the boxes and bags were intact.

Dead on his feet by seven that evening, Matt passed on supper and managed a solid eleven hours of uninterrupted sleep. Barricaded behind the door to his tiny cell.

21

Tight Spot

"First you sneak off to bed last night without supper," Taylor said from the doorway to Buzz's room, "then you don't show up for breakfast. Are you avoiding me all of a sudden?"

Matt stiffened with surprise, but had a smile composed by the time he swung around from the physician's pack to face her. He was certain he bolted the outside door, which meant that he had inadvertently locked Taylor inside the dormitory with him. Getting rusty, he told himself. Very rusty, indeed. "Hey," he said, trying for a casual tone, "I thought you went out with Jake and Buzz."

"They're off somewhere with Lopsang and Candice," Taylor told him, suspicion surfacing in her brown eyes. "I was in Dee-Dee's room trying on her sweater." She plucked the alpaca wool sleeve away from her arm. "What do you think? She got it in Peru."

"Very fetching." Matt rubbed his hands together and took a step toward the door. "Well, what do you say we take a walk in the sunshine?"

Taylor didn't budge. Her eyes began to dart around the room. "What are doing in here, Matt?"

"Looking for an aspirin. Buzz told me he had a bottle in his pack but I sure as hell can't find it. Figured I'd just check his medical kit, but no luck."

She craned her neck around his shoulder to have a look behind him. "You're not going to just leave everything like this, are you?"

Matt regarded the score of vials and containers he'd been poring over a moment before. "No, 'course not." He squatted on his heels and started shoving the plastic vials back into the kit. "Everything but aspirin," he commented with his back to her. "Antibiotics, antihistamines, anti-inflammatories—"

"What's going on, Matt?" Taylor was down on one knee beside him, studying his face. "You're not looking for aspirin. I know you better than that."

Matt purposely froze for a moment, then resumed his task, zipping up the kit and sealing the Velcro straps that encircled it. "All right," he said, exhaling for effect. "You want the truth, I was looking for a Valium."

Taylor's dark brows arched. "A Valium," she laughed. "You're kidding me."

"I didn't want to make a big thing about asking the doc, you know, because I've been telling everybody to avoid them. But I haven't been sleeping well and I figured what the hell, what's a pill among friends."

"Among friends," Taylor said.

"Yeah, among friends." He stuffed the medical kit into the front pocket of Bessman's pack. "Anyhow, I couldn't find any."

Taylor was shaking her head in feigned disapproval. "Makes me think about the time I was having some work done in my apartment and I found out the painters were raiding my medicine cabinet for Percodans."

"You with Percodans?"

"Give me a break. I had two wisdom teeth pulled."

"Well, you know those tradesmen," Matt said, standing up. "Leave 'em alone in your house, anything goes."

Taylor stood up, rubbing floor grit from her palms. "Why didn't you just ask Karl, Matt? He's got a whole bottle of the things."

"Yeah, maybe I will," Matt started to say. Taylor was almost through the doorway when he put a hand on her arm. "Didn't Karl tell us he didn't have any left? At high camp, remember? When he offered one to you and Morgan?"

Taylor shrugged. "I just remember him telling Barbara that he always carried a bunch on high-altitude treks. In fact, he showed her the bottle and asked if she wanted any."

"Wait a minute, wait a minute," Matt said in a flustered voice. "He told Barbara he's been on high-altitude treks before?"

Taylor uttered a laugh. "You know, it's funny. It sounded like it slipped out. But, anyway, he didn't have to tell her the high altitude part of it."

Matt smoothed his hair back. "What are you telling me—they knew each other before this trip?"

Taylor stepped back to show him a look of annoyance. "You want to try a different tone?"

Matt glanced away from her. "Look, I'm sorry. I'll explain everything."

"You better."

"Just tell me how they knew each other."

"The ski circuit. Before Barbara started climbing. She used to teach downhill in Switzerland. She met Karl on the set of *On Her Majesty's Secret Service*. You know, the James Bond movie that had that one-shot actor—"

"What was Karl doing there?"

"He was one of the stuntmen."

Matt eventually got around to closing his mouth.

"Is there something weird about all this?" Taylor asked him.

"What's weird is that he didn't tell me." He took a deep breath. "When I asked him if he'd ever been at high altitude, he told me he'd done some skiing in the Alps. Some goddamn *stunt* skiing you're telling me. That's how he knows Italian. I remember he said, 'They're even worse when they're on skis.' "

Taylor had her arms folded across her breasts. "I'm sure Karl would have told you if you asked."

He looked at her. "I didn't want to ask him anything. I've been hearing way too much about his life as it is."

"He does talk a lot. But it's just because of the divorce. He can't get his ex out of his mind."

"But he said he wouldn't know the symptoms of Mountain Sickness if they bit him on the ass."

"What's strange about that?" Taylor said, watching

him. "I ski, and I wouldn't have been able to diagnose Travis's condition as cerebral edema."

Matt thought for a long moment before he replied. "You would've been wrong if you had."

"But I thought—"

He shook his head. "Someone shot Travis up with insulin, Taylor. At least that's what the Italian doctors think happened. That's why Jake nearly sacrificed two of his toes to get here last night. Travis's condition was just supposed to look like AMS."

Taylor put a hand over her mouth. "Oh, my God, Matt. Why?"

"I don't know why," he said, waving his arms. He stopped pacing to regard her. "That afternoon Barbara got stung. Stu had you looking for yetis, right? You, Karl, Audrey. You all had ski poles."

"So?"

"So I think someone deliberately stabbed a hole in the log where the nest was, knowing full well Barbara and I were right behind you on the trail. Somebody who knew all about Barbara's allergy."

"You think *Karl* did it?"

"They knew each other. He could have been chancing she'd get stung."

"But, Karl," Taylor said, refusing to accept it. "He's just a sweet, heartbroken good ole boy. He talks about you like you're bosom buddies or something."

Matt said, "I've been wrong about people before. Haven't you?"

Taylor looked concerned for all the wrong reasons. "Listen," she said in a placating tone. "Maybe you do need a Valium. I mean, why would Karl want to see Barbara hurt?"

Matt had resumed his pacing. "Karl could have overheard Tulo's remark about Karma *mo-mos* . . . He *knew* everyone would suspect the porters." He jabbed himself in the chest angrily. "He knew *I* would suspect the porters. Or I'd suspect Doug. It wouldn't matter."

"I feel like I should be taking notes," Taylor said anxiously.

"Travis was no accident, Taylor. Neither was Barbara. Somebody tried for her once down in Thanget and failed. Karl was right there to help her out of the woods when the snare didn't do what it was supposed to.''

"What snare? What are you talking about?''

"Karl could have found Tulo's broken walking stick. He could have had one of the porters teach him the hitch.'' He held Taylor's gaze for a moment. "Somebody tried for me, too. Earlier in the trip, then again the night before last.''

"The gas I smelled?'' she asked after a moment. "But you still haven't told me why, Matt. You said the Italians *think* it was insulin? That's not proof of anything.''

Matt studied his hands. "Some people buy themselves automatic rifles and climb towers. Maybe our would-be murderer needs an exotic backdrop. Maybe he's done this before on other trips. An accident here, a fatality there . . .''

"Not Karl,'' Taylor said.

Matt aimed a laugh at the ceiling. "I was so hung up on trying to find a reason for the jeep accident in Kathmandu I didn't see what was going on right in front of my nose.'' He turned to Taylor. "Maybe that's what started him off. He got a whiff of blood and decided to go to work.'' She was strangely quiet, hugging herself. "What is it?'' he asked finally.

Taylor looked up at him wide-eyed. "Karl wasn't on the mountain flight that morning,'' she said quietly. "He missed the flight. He said he spent the whole day in town buying souvenirs.''

Matt pulled on a wool hat and zipped up his vest. "Where is he? Have you seen him this morning?''

She swallowed and found her voice. "He's hiking up to the glacier. With Kaylee.''

Matt stopped to catch his breath as a small avalanche washed down the opposite face of the ravine. He had been pushing hard all the way from the monastery and his lungs and calves ached from the effort. The temperature must have been up around seventy in the sun and he was sweating profusely beneath parka and gaitered trousers; thankful for the cooling rush of spindrift that followed the avalanche. He took off his hat and stuffed

it into a pocket; then took a moment to clear the inside
and outside of his goggles.

A hundred feet below him the glacier's snout was pitted with rocks and dirt, its gray riverine surface glistening with melting snow. Water cascaded from the face
onto boulder-size chunks of ice and snow that had tumbled from the ravine walls. The debris had partially
dammed a brook that emerged from an ice tunnel under
the glacier's tongue. Elsewhere the world was dazzling
white, save for the exposed granite flanks and shoulders
of the surrounding peaks.

The avalanche was the fourth one he'd witnessed since
he began the ascent; perhaps the tenth or eleventh he'd
heard rumble down the warming slopes. The glacier itself
was making grinding noises in response to the sudden
change in the weather. Ice-blue holes and hollows in the
grainy snow competed with the sky for color.

Matt could see where the trekkers had made their descent to the glacier the previous day; but Kaylee and
Karl's prints told a different story: the duo had continued
to contour the scree slope above the lateral moraine.

Using his ski pole, Matt engraved a large arrow in the
snow at the trails' juncture to indicate the route he was
taking. Taylor was off looking for Jake now; but whether
she would find him and point him up valley before Matt
found Karl was anyone's guess. Matt only knew that he
had to catch the Texan before another convenient accident occurred.

He tugged the goggles down over his eyes and set out
following the two pairs of prints that disappeared around
the rib of the slope. There—below an ice-dammed cirque
lake or tarn high up on the mountain's western face—the
Rajagang Glacier made a sweeping westward turn. Behind a chimneyed buttress half a click further on, the ice
river was joined by a secondary flow originating from a
dark, hidden valley.

Matt burned uphill; by the time he reached the crest
he was panting so hard that his throat was raw. And he
was all the more dizzy for it as well. The tinted world
pitched for his protected eyes, canted left and right, and
played hallucinatory games with him. His breath mixed
with the wind, and he lost all sense of himself for a mo-

ment. The landscape was impossibly sized; the sky too close.

A short hike beyond the shoulder the footprints angled down to the lateral moraine and climbed the chunky side-wall of the glacier. Matt slipped off the day pack and took out his binoculars, training them on a dark distant spot on the snowfield at the foot of the mountain's west-face buttress.

Kaylee was lying on her side there, motionless, a length of nylon rope trailing out from her hip harness. She was wearing a yellow jumpsuit and two-tone boots. Troughs in the ridged surface of the glacier gave evidence that she'd been dragged a hundred or so feet from the spot where she had initially fallen. She was wedged tight against the wall of rock now.

Matt lowered the glasses in a rush and quickly toed into his crampons, securing them to the welts of his boots and strapping them tight across toes and ankles. He side-stepped down the slope and clambered up onto the mountain's groaning, frozen flow, trusting that Kaylee and Karl had probed the ashen surface for hidden crevasses. He took to their tracks at as near a run as he could manage.

He reached Kaylee fifteen minutes later; went down on his knees in the slush, fumbling out of gloves and woolen liners to lay two fingers against the skin under her jaw. Her pulse was slow but strong, and just finding it so dropped him back on his butt in exhausted, dazed relief.

He was reaching over to brush ice from her face when he spotted Karl stepping around the foot of the buttress. The Texan stopped to wave, then began to quicken his pace. With his red pants and jacket, his red hair and beard, he could have been a man-eating yeti.

Matt cradled Kaylee's head in his arms and called her name; he slapped her cheeks lightly and splashed ice water in her face. She stirred somewhat but didn't revive. "Kaylee," he tried again. "Kaylee, you've got to stand up." He put an arm under her and somehow got her to her feet, but she collapsed soon enough.

"Glad you happened along!" Karl shouted as he walked.

"Yeah, I'm sure you are!" Matt hollered back, having another go at the rag-dolled mountaineer.

"Really, Matt, I knew I couldn't carry her alone! Maybe the two of us, huh? What d'ya say?"

Matt waited until Karl was within range; then took a quick sidestep and punched Karl full in the face. The Texan went down but sat up after a moment, rubbing his chin.

"Matt," Karl said. "What a way to greet a pal."

Matt ignored him, positioning Kaylee so that he could hoist her into a fireman's carry. Karl was still down on the ice, reaching for something in his pack. Matt bent his legs and threw Kaylee over his back.

"Gonna have to ask you to set her back down, amigo."

Matt got off to a shaky start, stabilizing himself with the ski pole, crampons biting deeply into the uneven surface. "D'you spike her with insulin, too, Karl?" he asked into the wind. "Couldn't arrange for a gas explosion out here, huh?"

Karl laughed. "You're a sharp one, Matt, I'll give you that," he said, matching strides with him ten feet away. "But then again, so's this."

Matt turned his head under Kaylee's weight and caught sight of the drawn *khukri*. "That's not the one you bought in Kathmandu, so it must be the one you stole from Tulo." He was breathing hard, slowing down with each step.

"I have a preference for the genu-wine article, Matt."

"The one you used to sharpen a stake for that snare you set up in Thanget."

"Just smart enough to put two and two together, that Matt Terry. That's what they told me. And with a knack for landing on his feet against all the odds."

Matt adjusted his human load. "*They*, huh? So there's more than one psychopath involved in this?" By the time he saw Karl move, it was already too late; and a moment later he was looking up from a cold puddle, nursing a twisted knee. It hadn't required more than a shove from the Texan to send him sprawling. Nearby, Kaylee let out a low moan of pain and rolled over on her back with a splash.

"Let's not ruin a friendship over a woman," Karl suggested, flourishing the *khukri*.

Matt wiped the snow from his goggles. "Put that thing

away," he said wearily. "You haven't killed anyone yet. Suppose we make a deal to keep it that way."

" 'Fraid I can't do that, partner."

Matt rested his forearms on his spread knees, lowered his head and contemplated a zigzag of runnels in the ice. The glacier seemed to be moving beneath him. "What are you going to do, Karl—decapitate me?" he asked when he finally looked up.

The Texan adopted a thoughtful pose. "I'm jus gonna have to think on that one. You know, partner, I tried to make it easy on you back when in Syabru Bensi. Dug a little hole for you on the trail, hoping you'd just step into it and break a leg or something. Get yourself carried back to Kathmandu strapped to a bamboo litter."

Matt got to his knees and pulled himself upright on the ski pole. He leaned over Kaylee and tugged her into a sitting posture. "You gonna help me carry her down or not?"

Karl laughed again. "You jus don't get it, do you? Little Ms. Eight-Thousand-Meter's home. She's not leaving this glacier, Matt. Look, she's sound asleep anyway on what I fed her, so why not let her be? 'Course, if you're serious about cutting a deal for yourself, I'm willing to listen."

Matt tightened his grip on the lightweight ski pole and put everything he had into a roundhouse swing. Karl flinched, however, and the basket end swooshed through empty air an inch from his face. Matt's crampons held him fast to the ice, but Karl had the *khukri* raised against the return swing. The machete blade severed seven inches from the aluminum pole.

Karl said, "Whoops. There you go, partner."

Matt directed a defeated look at the hollow pole as he held it straight out in front of him like a sword. Karl's smile faded.

"You know, I like you, Matt. And I'm real sorry that the two of us had to end up on the same trail. I think we coulda been friends elsewhere."

Matt had begun to back away from him, casting wary looks over his shoulder at the glacial terrain. Karl was moving forward with the knife, desultory about it. Matt wondered if he could front-point him with the crampons;

step out of one of them and maybe wing it overhead like a bolo, count on some of the teeth to do a slasher job on the Texan's face. Trouble was, Karl wasn't giving him much in the way of bonus seconds. A backhand swing just then nearly batted the ski pole from Matt's hands.

"You know what, Karl? Next time I'm gonna have Jake demand psychiatric evaluations from every one of Puma's clients. Just so I know where everyone's coming from. I mean, what mental hospital awarded you a furlough for this trek?"

"You're branding me all wrong, Matt."

Matt risked a jab at Karl's neck. "What, it's some kind of fraternity initiation? A stuntman's thing?"

Karl showed him a grin that was all teeth. "Learned about that, did you? I went and shot my mouth off in front of Taylor. But, yeah, I did a bit of stunt downhill, some talus running. But what we got here's more like 'The Ganesh Sanction' than that James Bond flick, wouldn't you say?"

"I hope it pays well."

Matt barely got the words out when he felt himself falling. He did have time enough on the soft snow to catch sight of Karl's perplexed look; but the next thing he knew, he was weightless, then painfully snagged between jagged chunks of ice five feet below the surface, with snow drifting down on him from the lip of the crevasse, running up his sleeves and down his collar.

A long moment went by while the snow fell and Matt's body conformed itself to its new circumstance. He realized ultimately that he was wedged spread eagle in the narrow ice rift, tilted slightly to one side, with legs and hips held fast, the day pack crushed against his back. His chin and face had taken a bruising on the way down and his goggles were long gone, but he didn't think any bones were broken. Above him lazed a four-foot-long jagged wedge of blue sky with Karl's face at the center of it.

"How you feelin', partner?" The Texan's words echoed slightly in the near dark. "You really do have the knack, don't you? I was just searchin' out one of these for Kaylee when you happened along."

Matt swallowed to wet his throat. "Throw me the rope, Karl," he said, biting down mounting panic. "My hands are free; I can tie it under my arms.'' Once again he sensed movement, and far below him something cracked loose and fell into the blackness. "Get the rope, Karl. Quit fucking around."

Karl didn't respond right away. When he did, it was to palm a handful of snow over the lip. Matt squirmed and tried desperately to dislodge himself while the snow wet his face in a shower of crystals.

He shook his head madly. "Tower, you fuck!"

"I think I was saying that you had me all wrong," Karl answered at last. "Wasn't that it, Matt?"

"Fuck you!"

Karl dropped an exaggerated sigh into the crevasse. "You're too hard on me, amigo. I'm just a man doing a jog—a workin' stiff, just like you and the porters. I told you I tried to make it easy for you back on the trail, but no, you gotta keep landin' on your feet. Just like in Mexico, just like in Bali. The boys who ran the background on Puma warned me: they told me Matt Terry keeps steppin' in everybody's shit but he never falls down. Even now you're on your feet, ain't that so, amigo?"

Matt was keenly aware of his heartbeat; he could feel it thumping in his neck, hear it pounding in his ears. "Who sent you after me, Karl? Who's special operation did I fuck up this time?"

"You?" Karl said in a surprised voice. "Naw. You may have gotten in some people's hair from time to time, but I don't reckon anyone gives a good goddamn, really. No, Matt, I told you: It's no vendetta, it's just a job." He paused for a moment. "Hell, this whole sorry deal coulda been avoided if things had worked out in Kathmandu."

"After you messed with the jeep's brakes," Matt said.

Karl chuckled. "Yeah, I figured you got wise to that somehow. That's why I needed you out of the picture right quick. I coulda handled Jake without too much problem. But you—you're a regular waffle-soled gumshoe. A regular wilderness dick, aren't you? I could see you were suspicious of everyone, so I did my level best to offer you some diversions. Had you going with the pooch and Barbara's near miss in the woods, didn't I? You thought you had that poor fuck porter pegged.

"But then look what happens with Barbara the next time out. It was one hell of a long shot, I'll give you that, but I saw the bees' nest and I remembered about that allergy of hers. I knew she'd come joggin' right into them. Who coulda figured you'd end up saving her life? A regular boy scout, that Matt Terry.

"That's when I knew I was underratin' you. I saw you watchin' Kaylee and figured you might be thinkin' that one of the gals had it in for the others. First Julia, then Barbara. Or maybe Kaylee and Candice were in collusion, saving the Ganesh climb for themselves just to add a peak to their climb cards. Zat the way you had it scoped, partner?"

"Piss up a rope, Karl."

"I'd lay odds I'm right on the money. So I had to throw you off track again. Give you somethin' else to worry about. If I coulda gotten to Kaylee with the insulin, I would've, believe you me. But she wasn't interested in acceptin' any a my Valiums, and there was no way I was gonna lure her from Candice's side, if you get my drift—and I think you do. But it was easy enough to get to Travis and let you go on thinkin' that maybe Buzz or his spitfire wife had somethin' to do with it." He laughed. "I was a regular matchmaker on that one."

Matt fought hard to control his breathing. His legs were tingling and the cold was beginning to sap his strength. "You nearly killed him, Karl," he managed after a brief case of the shivers.

"Yeah, well, I figured him for a healthy guy. I gambled he'd come out of it on his own or down below with the Eye-ties."

"You oughta be g-grateful I didn't break a leg in that jeep," Matt said through chattering teeth. "Think of all the f-fun you would've missed."

Karl snorted. "My f-f-fun, partner, woulda been seein' all four of you go over the edge. Then there wouldna *been* a trek and I coulda had the two-fer I wanted. Just Kaylee to deal with then."

Matt closed his eyes and rested his forehead against the ice while the glacier continued to mangle him. "You were after the climbers all along."

"Just three of 'em, Matt, but, yeah, you got that right.

See, you gotta learn to play your hunches. Remember back in Casino Nepal? You kept playing against the wheel. I told you then: You gotta play to win.''

Matt took a minute to think it through, recalling what he could of Taylor's talk about the importance of the Ganesh climb; how the women had planned it as a separate venture, a way to display their integrity as a team . . . Only the accidents Karl arranged had nothing to do with the Ganesh climb. Karl was right: he'd been on the right track back in the Chilime cloud forest. ''It's Everest, isn't it? You're trying to make *sure* that Candice is the one to get the shot at the summit.''

Karl got to his feet and booted heavy clumps of snow into the crevasse, exposing another two feet of cloudless sky. ''Personally, Matt, I don't give a shit if an American woman makes it to the top or not. It's like Travis said at that little welcome fest back in Kathmandu: Mountin' em's more important than seein' 'em summit. But my . . . uh, employer doesn't see things quite that way.''

''Candice.''

''Candice? Hell, no. She don't know jack shit about this. I'm talking about her sponsor, Matt—Grand Design. Those boys figure it's goin' to be worth about ten million bucks in sales if they can get their gal standin' up on Everest displayin' that company logo.''

Absorbing it only sent his body shivering again. ''You think I was stupid enough to come up here without telling anybody about you, Karl? They know. Everybody knows.''

Karl peered over the rim of the crevasse. ''Things must be getting desperate down there, huh? We're up to the victim's you'll-never-get-away-with-this speech.''

''You won't,'' Matt bit out.

The Texan shook his head. Matt couldn't make out his face; only the silhouette of his thatch of beard and ponytailed red hair against the bright blue sky.

''You really think a car rental agency in Kathmandu is going to bother pursuing the details of that accident? Come on, Matt, you know better than that. And as for Barbara's run-in with bees or Travis's brush with the insulin reaper, what's anyone got on me or anybody else?''

"If I can put two and two together, the authorities can."

Karl sailed the *khukri* down past Matt's head; it struck the ice near his feet and rattled its way to oblivion. "Oops! There goes Tulo's knife," he said in transparent surprise. "See how easy evidence disappears out here? And what's one pen injector in Nepal but a needle in a goddamned haystack?"

Matt ceased his struggling with the ice to say, "What about now? You're just going to go back without us?"

"Hey, partner, you fell into a *crevasse*. What did I have to do with it? I didn't push you in. I didn't make you jump." Karl walked away from the rim, boots crunching the snow, only to reappear a moment later. "Besides, I'm planning to go down there and get help."

"You don't need any help, Karl!" Matt screamed. "Just throw me the goddamned rope!"

"No, I don't think I can do that for you. But I'll tell you what I will do: I'll make sure you have some company in your time of need."

Matt clawed frantically at the ice chunks, heaving his shoulders side to side, stopping only when he heard the return of Karl's boot steps. Wind whistled over the top of the crevasse, and the glacier stirred beneath him. Out of a deathly quiet moment, Kaylee came sliding down into the crevasse boots first, her crampons nearly grazing Matt's outstretched hand. He heard a snap of bone as her motionless body lodged itself not three feet from his grasp.

▣▣ 22 ▣▣

Peak Experience

"**H**e stayed right there with her while she died of exposure," Kaylee was telling Matt almost two hours later, sniffling and sobbing between sentences. Although it wasn't her own predicament that had brought on the tears, but the story she was recounting of a husband-and-wife climb team she had known back in her Mt. Rainier days who had fallen into an Alpine crevasse together. "Can you imagine what that must be like—to be there when your partner dies?"

Matt made a face at her even though she couldn't see him. "Christ, Kaylee, how'd we get over into this? I mean, there's gotta be something else we can talk about." Matt exhaled a breath cloud. "How about Alaska? Why don't you tell me about Alaska. I've never been to Alaska."

"Oh, God," she began on a sad note, "that reminds me of the first time I climbed McKinley . . ."

Matt shut his eyes and thumped his head against the ice. When she'd come to an hour before, she'd let out a scream that lasted a good thirty seconds. Matt wasn't sure if it was from the pain of her broken foot or the shock of waking up and finding herself wedged inside a glacier. Maybe some combination of the two. When he'd finally gotten her to calm down, to realize she wasn't alone down there, he guided her through the events of the past two hours, improvising when he realized she had no conscious recall of Karl's malevolent actions on the surface. Matt told himself there was no good purpose in telling her the truth. She was hurt, she was weak, and hell, Jake would certainly come to their rescue sooner or later. Karl had probably done something to erase their boot prints—walked backward down the length of the glacier gloving everything over, some sort of thing—but that was what the yelling was supposed to counter.

"Time," Matt said, interrupting her narrative after he'd checked his watch. The crystal was smashed but the mini light was still working.

"Ten minutes already?" Kaylee asked.

"You know what they say about time flying. Ready?"

"Jake!!" they yelled in unison, repeating his name several more times. It was easier than yelling *Candice*, and seemed to make more sense than yelling *ice!*

"Maybe we should switch to fire," Matt suggested a long quiet moment later, and Kaylee laughed lightly.

She was just inches out of reach of his left hand, contorted into a kind of sitting position, climber's helmet askew, with her hands between her legs and her left cheek pressed to the crevasse wall opposite the one he faced. She accepted, or was at least willing to believe for the time being, that she'd slipped in while walking with Karl, and that Matt—who'd happened along afterward—had gotten himself stuck when he'd climbed down after her. The fact that she was still wearing the harness and nylon rope seemed justification for Matt's thwarted rescue attempt, although she had spent a few minutes explaining how foolish he'd been to consider such a stunt. Karl, he'd told her, was bringing help from below.

"I don't understand what's taking them so long?"

Instead of answering her, Matt asked about her foot, which she said was numb now, like her fingers and most of the left side of her face. He wondered how many more hours they had in them before hypothermia set in. Kaylee insisted they could survive for days; they were well-clothed, and in truth the crevasse wasn't much colder than a meat locker. Rivulets of melted snow were trickling in from the rim. Of course things would get a whole lot worse during the night, but surely Jake and the others . . .

Matt had spent the hour or so before she'd regained consciousness thinking through the twists and turns that had landed him in the abyss. The one that existential hail of bullets had finally driven him into, thinking there was some advantage in cold storage concealment. The trek was supposed to have provided him with time to work out his dilemma about the road, to sort out just how it was he'd become a magnet for disaster. To determine whether there was something else out there for him now that disillusionment and paranoia had begun to sink in.

Who knew, though, maybe a crevasse in the middle of the Himalayas was the ideal place to pass a midlife crisis? *How I Spent Mine,* by Matt Terry, he thought. . . . There was even a way of looking at things that found him in the crevasse long before he'd started the trek, long before he'd arrived in Kathmandu. Numb, immobilized, grappling with the demons of the pit he'd stumbled into. A gray world of ice and shadow, a kind of limbo. A lovely woman and a bit of blue sky filled with lammergeiers just that much out of reach.

Maybe the truth of it was that no matter how hard you believed, no one was really coming to your rescue; that there was no warm indoor sanctuary waiting in the future, no soft-seated retirement chair with your name on it. That you had a choice between remaining wedged between a rock and a hard place, or clawing your way to the surface unassisted.

The glacier gave a low, resonant moan, and somewhere outside another snow mass avalanched. They'd been hearing them repeatedly the past hour, accompanied by loud gunshot noises in the ice below them.

"You tell me one now, Matt," Kaylee said softly. "Then I think I'll catch a little sleep."

Matt didn't like the sound of it. "Hey, who's gonna help me yell *Jake* if you fall out? Besides, you didn't finish the one about the two guys who fell into the crevasse with their supply sled." Kaylee made a sound that could have been a laugh. "What about Saint Bernards and brandy barrels?" he continued. "What ever happened to all the Saint Bernards of the world?"

Matt heard the glacier moan again and swore that the ice around his boots moved. He forced his brain to send a message to his numb feet and sure enough, he could wriggle one of them. "Kaylee," he started to say when the ice moved again and the crevasse widened perceptibly.

"Matt, it's moving!"

A cracking sound, almost like falling timber, commenced far off to the right and ripped through the glacier directly beneath them. And all at once Matt's legs were free. His hands pawed at the ice, trying for handholds as he slipped once, then again, losing a yard to his frozen tomb with each fall. Finally he succeeded in twisting his torso, spreading his legs, and digging the crampons into the crevasse walls. Then slowly he began to work his way up.

Kaylee was nearly free by the time he got to her, reaching out and grabbing a handful of her snowsuit. She had somehow managed to raise her arms over her head and had a double handhold on a knob of ice four feet from the surface. Her right foot was still sandwiched between two jagged blocks, but once Matt started stomping on them, they broke loose and tumbled down into the lower recesses of the dark rift.

Matt climbed until his hip was even with her shoulder; then got a hand under her arm and hauled her toward the rim. Her good foot and powerful arms took over a moment later and she completed the ascent on her own.

They crawled out of the crevasse into golden sunlight and rolled over onto their backs in the slush.

It was awhile before either of them could get their trembling limbs to function. Kaylee couldn't put any weight on her right foot; but with an arm around Matt's neck she could hop along with the best of them, and that was the way they left the glacier: arms around one another, wedded at the hip.

Matt found what remained of his ski pole and used it to poke for soft spots. Their morning tracks had disappeared in the strong sun, which had crazed the glacial surface into a myriad of serpentine streams.

The western face of the mountain had calved a huge shelf of snow from the hanging glacier that dammed the cirque lake, and now the whole cornice seemed in danger of collapsing. Twenty years back, in the Peruvian Andes, Matt had seen the eerie aftereffects of a similar collapse. A glacial dam had broken, deluging a highland valley with countless tons of water, mud, ice, and rock. The mountain tide had buried an entire village, leaving in its wake a boulder-strewn delta that the Quechua Indians had ultimately sanctified with thousands of wooden crosses.

With memories of that catastrophe in mind Matt considered abandoning the glacier and steering for the scree slopes of the sidehill opposite. But on reflection he couldn't see that the effort was warranted. The energy they'd have to expend ascending and contouring would take a toll; and more than that, there was no telling just how much water the ice dam contained. Enough perhaps to launch a wave clear up the face of the slope; enough perhaps to flood the whole of the ravine.

Matt's mind kept flip-flopping between alternatives. A backward glance revealed dozens of fissures and crevasses in the ice they had crossed only moments earlier. Recalling the avalanche debris damming the Rajagang brook, he wondered if these sudden rifts weren't the result of water pressure building up underneath the glacier itself.

They were approaching the trail juncture on the slope above the terminal moraine when Jake and a few members of the group ascended out of the hollow where a log bridge spanned the ravine. Gently Matt set Kaylee down on the snow. Candice charged up the hill and ran to her partner's side, taking Kaylee's face between her hands, encircling her with her arms.

Candice Dekker in her Grand Design parka and form-hugging snow pants.

"She's hurt," Matt told Buzz. The physician and Lopsang hurried over to Kaylee, while Matt motioned Jake off to one side.

Jake's determined expression changed to one of exasperated relief as he took hold of Matt by both arms. "My turn to say it: I hope you feel better than you look." He glanced out over the glacier. "What happened to you out there?"

Matt peeled a glove off and ran his tingling fingertips

over sore spots on his chin, cheekbones, and forehead. "Rebirth trauma," he muttered. He looked at Lopsang, the doc, and the climbers. "Where's Karl?" he asked Jake quietly. "Did you see him on the way down?"

Jake shook his head. "We came straight up from base camp as soon as Taylor found us. What happened out there, Matt?"

Matt ran his tongue over cracked lips. "You probably missed each other on the trail. Either that or he saw you coming and hid out till you passed. He's gotta be back at the monastery."

Jake tightened his grip on Matt's arms. "Did you fight with him? Tell me what happened?"

"Fight with him? Jesus Christ, Jake, the guy's a hired hit man!" He twisted out of Jake's grip and bent over to unstrap the crampons. "Didn't Taylor tell you?"

"She said Kaylee was in danger and that you'd gone up to the glacier. She made it sound like you were worried about Karl's inexperience."

"Karl's *inexperience*?" Matt snorted. "That's terrific, Karl's inexperience . . . She still doesn't want to believe it."

Jake's face twisted up. "But what's he—holy shit!"

It was the biggest avalanche yet: a section-by-section dismantling of the cornice below the cirque lake; a vertical storm that blasted them with a frigid wind.

"You've gotta get everyone to high ground," Matt said when the rumbling stopped. "I've been watching that shelf avalanche all morning. The whole works could come down." He shot Jake a look. "You've seen Yachay in Peru, Jake. I don't have to draw you a picture."

Jake's mouth twitched. By the time he snapped out of it, Matt was already on his way to the bridge. "Wait a minute, Matt, what about you?"

Matt stopped long enough to say, "I'm going after Karl."

"Please tell me you were wrong," Taylor said, stepping out of Matt's embrace to regard him. He had been walking for forty minutes when they encountered one another on the trail below the monastery. "Oh, God, your face—"

He restrained her hand. "I wasn't wrong. But why didn't you tell Jake what we talked about?"

Taylor looked away from him. "I didn't know what to say, Matt. I went over and over it all the way down to base, and I thought there was a chance you were mistaken." Her eyes found his. "Buzz and Candice and Lopsang were down there with him, so I just told him—"

"I know what you told him."

"Then they got to you in time? And Kaylee?" Matt assured her Kaylee would be fine once they carried her downhill. "I couldn't keep up with them," Taylor said. "I tried but my wind gave out."

Matt scanned the ravine. "And you didn't see Karl?"

"I didn't see anyone."

The guy really is some kind of yeti, Matt thought. He urged Taylor into the first of the switchbacks that led up to the monastery, filling her in on some of what had happened on the glacier. Taylor stopped half a dozen times to stare at him, more wide-eyed with each about-face.

At the monastery they split up to search the outbuildings. Matt went directly to Karl's room in the cottage and found it vacated. He checked the dormitory next, where Purbu and the cook staff duo were inventorying the food-supply *dokos*.

"Someone steal food," Pasang exclaimed as Matt entered the kitchen. "We missing potatoes, cheese, eggs . . . Some porters, maybe."

"How long ago?" Matt asked.

"Soon!" the cook said in near falsetto. "One, one and one-half hour."

But none of them had seen Karl.

In her room, Morgan answered no from behind a paperback. Chris and Doug weren't around. And over by the *gompa*, Maurice and Dee-Dee were too whacked on Ecstasy to remember whether they'd seen Karl or not.

"The caretaker thinks he saw him head up the ravine about two hours ago," Taylor reported when they rendezvoused in front of the cheese factory ten minutes later.

"No way," Matt said, glancing at his smashed watch by reflex. It was just two-thirty; the sun a jewel on the western ridge. "He's headed downhill if anywhere. D'you check out by the *chorten*?"

On their way to the mushroom-shaped shrine they ran
into Bimbahadur and Gambu. Gambu motioned to the
smiling caretaker. "He say *sahib* Karl went to glacier
with Taylor."

"With Taylor?" Taylor said. "But I'm Taylor."

"You not Matt?"

Matt growled. "I'm Matt. Karl is tall as I am. With
long red hair and beard. Red ski suit."

"He not doctor."

"No, he not doctor."

Gambu shot Bimbahadur a look of disapproval. "He
think Karl is doctor."

"What about the *rimpoche*?" Matt said. The head
monk was nearby, gazing out over the ravine. The caretaker followed Matt's look and said something to
Gambu.

"He say you cannot ask him," the *sirdar* translated.
"That one does not speak."

"But this is important," Matt argued, walking away.
"He'll understand." Bimbahadur gave chase, gesticulat-
ing in front of Matt's face. "He say you cannot ask him,"
Gambu repeated, apparently finding something comical
in the scene. The four of them were closing on the *chorten* now. The head monk heard them coming and turned
around.

"Just ask him, Gambu," Matt said. "Tell him it's
important. Tell him it's . . . Tell him it's a matter of life
and death." Peering over the wall, Matt could just make
out Jake and the group in the ravine below. Kaylee was
hobbling on one foot, arms draped over Lopsang's and
Candice's shoulders.

Bimbahadur was bowing apologies to the saffron-robed
abbot, hands at his chin in an attitude of prayer. But the
lama seemed to acknowledge Gambu's question. His only
response, though, was to turn his serene gaze on Matt.

Matt felt the blood rush to his head and began to sway
in place. Without understanding why, he took off his wool
watch cap and held it out in front of him. The *rimpoche*
accepted it with a nod. "That way," he said a moment
later, raising an arm in the direction of base camp.

Bimbahadur's mouth dropped open.

"Thank you," Matt said, backing away. "Thank you.

Namaste. A thousand *namastes.*'' He turned and trotted
for the wooden entry gate. Taylor followed him, pleading
with him to slow down and explain. ''I don't know why
he did it,'' Matt directed over his shoulder. ''I just knew
I had to give him something. A token.''

''But why the hat?'' she asked when Matt stopped short
of the stone wall. She was bent over akimbo, winded.

''Maybe he's got a head cold.''

Taylor straightened and scanned the downhill trail to
base camp. ''You'll never catch him, Matt.'' She swallowed and licked her lips. ''He has at least an hour start
on you.''

Matt had a foot on the wall and was tightening his boot
laces. ''He's wearing a pack, he's carrying supplies. I
can catch him.''

''But why do you have to? He can't just hop a plane
out of the country, Matt. The closest airport's in Kathmandu. You could get to a town and radio the authorities. Let them handle it.''

''Let them handle what?'' he asked, zipping his parka.
''Karl's the only proof I've got.''

''But the group can back you up.''

''Didn't you tell me I needed this—the extremes?''

''Not this.''

He allowed a grin. ''It's what I do, Taylor. And you
can quote me on it,'' he added from the far side of the
monastery gate.

🏵🏵 23 🏵🏵

Cliff Hanger

Half an hour along, the trail forked—one branch dropping down through a bit of fir forest to the yak-grazing lands around base camp, while the second stuck to high ground, disappearing over the ridge and eventually linking up with the main trail to the high pass.

Matt found the prints of Karl's size-thirteen Survivors in the wet snow ten yards up the high trail and followed them to the edge of a snowless expanse of jagged scree. But instead of continuing on to the ridge, he picked his way back to the trail junction, studying the prints as he sidestepped down the hill. The Vibram soles of Karl's Survivors—easily identified by a column of crosslike, toe-to-arch impressions—were easily singled out among the sneaker prints of the departing porters. The only other lugged prints were Jake's from the previous morning, but they were headed *toward* the monastery rather than away from it.

But why, Matt began to ask himself, would Karl make a retreat for the high pass knowing he would run into Stu and the Deys along the way? It would be easy enough to ready a story: that Jake had sent him over for one reason or another; that he was quitting the trek. And yet something didn't *feel* right. Matt recalled the sharpened stake and knotted rope Karl left him to find in the birch forest; the doubts he'd carefully planted in Matt's mind about

218

Buzz and Morgan Bessman. Diversion was his favorite ploy. Misdirection.

He began a more careful search along the downhill trail to base, and just at tree line—amid a confusion of sneaker and hiking shoe prints along seriously trampled ground—he located two careless half prints that could have only been Karl's. Headed *away* from the monastery. Jake, Candice, Taylor, Buzz, and the two *sirdars* were the only group members who had descended that far, and none of them wore a boot Karl's size. Plus, the stride was about right for a six-foot-three Texan moving at a desperate clip.

Matt hurried into the forest, allowing himself a bit of free-fall along the decline, slowing himself by reaching out now and again for an evergreen branch or a slender trunk. He was halfway to the floor of the ravine when he spied Karl some two hundred feet below him, perhaps an eighth of a mile out front. And despite his best efforts, his own voice betrayed him.

Karl stopped at the sound of his name and turned as Matt's call was echoing from the steep walls. Seeing Matt above him, he began to run—not toward the floor, however, but uphill toward the scree fields above the tree line.

As he followed, Matt caught fleeting glimpses of the sixty-degree, loose rock slope above the firs. *Did a bit of skiing, a bit of talus running,* he could hear Karl telling him on the glacier. And he realized suddenly that he would have to get to Karl before he reached the shingly scree. It was no contest, otherwise.

They were both fast approaching the uppermost trees— Karl maintaining his eighth of a mile lead—when the mountain at the head of the ravine loosed a prolonged roar that set the steep hillside quaking.

Matt swung around in time to see a huge cumulus of snow billow out of the glaciated basin beyond the monastery. At the same time the evergreens were bowed by an icy wind. Swept off his feet momentarily, Matt managed to grab hold of a tree stump and pull himself to his knees. He wiped the snow away from his face and scrambled upward from tree to tree as a ferocious, swelling tide of mud, water, and massive chunks of ice began to funnel down the ravine.

Boulders the size of Volkswagens careened into view, and explosive reports filled the suddenly frosted air. The wind tore at the trees and the quaking ground heaved and buckled. Toward the head of the valley, the violent water was displacing tons of rock and earth and surging higher and higher up the snow-covered slopes. Matt saw the *chorten* sweep from its promontory; two of the monastery outbuildings were inundated and instantly washed away. In advance of the tide rode a storm of wind-whipped snow and ice, a contained blizzard that filled the ravine from floor to ridge line.

Matt struggled upward, engulfed by a whiteout of swirling snow. The hillside below him was already underwater, the slope scoured clean of earth and trees. He could just make out red-suited Karl off to his right, slaloming through the trees at a seemingly impossible speed. Karl's sense of balance in the midst of the wind and snow was nothing less than astonishing. Bent severely forward at the waist, he was employing his arms as well as his feet and leaving Matt farther behind with each crazed and superhuman leap.

Matt raised his hands to his face against the snow and shouted, scarcely hearing himself over the deep bellow of the floodwaters. The hit man was actually headed down into the flood!

"Karl!" he tried again, snow-blind now but managing a slight, downhill correction along Tower's course.

Karl whirled on him once to return something that was more animal growl than articulated response. And then he was gone. In the blink of an eye. Vanishing among the overturned trees and newly exposed rocks and rising mud.

Matt stopped short in wonder, clutching onto long-needled branches while the wind died down and the snow began to settle. Only to hear movement on the slope above him. He pulled himself out of the forest tree to tree and glimpsed Karl bounding across the shingly scree a hundred feet above him. Somewhere along the way he'd gotten rid of his pack. Matt turned a double take in the direction of the forest where he thought he had seen Karl disappear. But if Karl had been above him all the while, who was the hulking figure in red that had growled at him? . . .

Matt let go of the question as he clambered out onto the rocks and reluctantly gave chase. The angle was so severe that nearly the whole of the left side of his body was pressed against the sharp, fist-size stones. Waves from the mud-brown, ice-chunked river were breaking high up on the tree line now, and Karl was making for the fractured cliff face that had loosed all the stone to begin with.

Matt leaped high, landed, and the scree slid like gravel beneath his feet, sending him back down to the level he'd started from. He regained his balance, leaped again, and the same thing happened, sending him a little closer to the eddying waters this time. Meanwhile Karl's practiced technique was carrying him uphill a few feet at a time.

Until the entire field began to slide.

Matt fell on his face and dug his boot tips in, churning them against the moving rocks and getting nowhere fast, like someone waging a futile upstairs battle with a down escalator. He recalled a time in his childhood when he'd nearly slid off a slate roof; he recalled other near misses and wondered if his life was about to pass in front of him. Just as the scree was doing.

Matt was spread eagled two hundred near-vertical feet above the newborn river when the slope finally came to a rest. He found what looked to be a bit of solidly-anchored rock and held on for dear life. Karl was ten feet above him, about thirty feet off to the right. Rocks bouncing down from the heights were impacting all around them.

"Wee, doggie, what a ride!" Karl said. "Real cliff-hanger we got goin' here, huh, Matt?"

Matt lifted his face from the cold stones. The Texan was lying on his right side in a visibly unsettled area of scree. His slightest movement seemed to set the stones in motion. "I should be enjoying this, Karl—seeing you like that. How come I'm not?"

"Aw, you can afford a smile, amigo. But this scree being what it is, I'd be careful about laughing too hard."

"I'm not laughing, goddamn you." The slope gave a

start and surrendered a yard to the river. "So why'd you light out, Karl? You could have denied everything. Said you'd gotten separated from Kaylee and me out on the glacier. By the time anyone found us—if they did—we wouldn't have been in any shape to contradict your story."

Karl laughed and the rocks beneath him moved, dropping him level with Matt, although still some twenty feet distant.

" 'Cause I knew you were gonna haul yourself out of that crevasse is why, partner. And I'm not wearin' the rabbit's foot you were born with. Figured I'd be better off gettin' myself back to Kat. Get my people to extract me before you or Jake showed up." He paused to study Matt's situation for a moment. "See you chanced on a piece of handhold there, Matt."

Matt risked a glance at the thundering river and tightened his grip on the rock. "Think you can make it over here?"

"Over there?" Karl laughed. "Matt, you are some kind of asshole. I dig a hole for you, I try to engineer a little gas explosion, I leave you in a fuckin' crevasse, and you can't stop being a boy scout. You're a caution, all right."

Matt looked to his left, where the trees began not thirty feet away. Four or five traverse leaps, he decided. Even if the scree carried him a hundred feet downhill, he'd be in the trees by then, with a decent margin between him and the water. "You're my evidence, Karl," he said, turning back to the Texan. "I want Candice to know what she bought into when she signed with Grand Design."

Karl shook his head. "Sorry to disappoint." Cautiously he raised himself on hands and knees and commenced a slow uphill traverse. He got all of ten feet before the scree gave, and he was breathing hard when he spoke next.

"A word of advice, Matt, from one adventurer to another." Karl was on his back just over the lip of a large concavity in the slope. "I've worked with some of the best in the field and I've come to learn that luck's a good part of any successful operation. And luck's what you got, amigo—in abundance, you understand? So I suggest you stop pissin' your time away with Puma Tours and get serious about yourself. Market that talent of yours, Matt. Turn pro. Advertise yourself as a finder of lost travelers, or just an all-around problem solver for people on the road. Instead of waiting for trouble to find you, go after it. Jake'll help you out. Hell, I'd even give you the names of one or two people to contact if I had time.''

Matt carefully rolled over onto his left side and looked down at Karl. ''Just quit moving around, you dumb shit. The water's already going down. We can wait it out.''

Karl chuckled. ''See, that's the thing about you. You know how to deal with clients. I never got the hang of the personal relations thing. My age I shoulda had an office gig by now. Instead, I'm still out in the field. Don't make the same mistake, Matt.''

Karl gently raised himself into a sitting position—a red-haired kid perched at the top of a sliding board.

''Karl! Don't do it!''

The Texan grinned. ''I told you 'bout evidence out here, Matt—how it just disappears.''

''Karl—''

Reflexively his hand flew out, but Tower was already halfway to the river. Matt watched him hit the water. Then the ice-strewn current had its way with him and he was gone from sight.

⊞⊞ 24 ⊞⊞

The Comeback Trail

Matt waited an hour before he let go of his handhold and rode the scree down to the tree line. He picked his way across rock and grainy snow to the high ground and found the trail to the monastery. The air remained chilled, and he kept well above the shadow line on the ridge until the sun set.

The glacial lake water had debouched from the ravine and gone on to wreak further havoc in the lower valleys. The denuded slopes below the monastery were strewn with erratics and enormous chunks of ice washed down from the terminal moraine. Much of the monastery compound itself was knee-deep in mud and glacial debris.

Later on, back in Kathmandu, Matt would learn that the sudden-draining phenomenon of glacial lakes was known by the Icelandic word, *jokulhlaup*, which meant "glacial leap."

Word of the catastrophe was slow in reaching the capital, but rescue helicopters were eventually dispatched to the village of Rajagang, which—while situated a good distance below the glacier—had been nearly wiped from the landscape.

The Puma group was on hand to meet the rescue choppers, having spent three days assisting in relief efforts in the area and sharing what little food there was to be had. No one in the group had been seriously injured in the flood. Jake had sent a porter across the high pass to apprise Stu of what had gone down on the other side of the mountain and instruct him to accompany the Deys back to Kathmandu. Matt and Jake discussed returning to the Trisuli by way of the high pass, but what with food in short supply and Kaylee McMahon's foot in a temporary cast, they opted in the end for a helicopter evacuation.

Matt never got his watch cap back, although the *rimpoche* did place a *yantr* around his neck just before he climbed aboard one of the helicopters. The rice-paper amulet had been inscribed, blessed, sprinkled with aromatic powers, wrapped with colored strings, and sealed with wax.

To keep your head safe from falling rocks, the lama had told him. Westerners, he went on to say, were exposed to many dangers in the world—especially longlimbed Americans who carried too much weight into the mountains.

Buzz and Morgan remained apart for the rest of the trip; but Travis and Audrey—after their ten-day return trek—were a couple again when Matt finally saw them in Kathmandu. By way of thanks for Matt's bit of lifesaving in the cloud forest, Barbara took him out on the town and extracted the promise of a visit to her home in Denver sometime soon.

Young Chris was deeply affected by the work that went into the relief efforts in and around Sathi. He told Matt that when the time came he was going to join the Peace Corps or something, instead of going straight off to college as Doug would probably want him to do. Hearing of it, though, Doug promised to back him if he still felt that way five or six years down the road.

Maurice and Dee-Dee turned in a ten-page trip evaluation before they even left Kathmandu, praising Jake, Matt, and Lopsang for their leadership and their handling of the unforeseen. They hoped someday to complete their thesis on "Stress and the Adventure Traveler," and hoped by then that Matt would be willing to share his thoughts and perspective. He told them to keep in touch.

Matt considered various ways of telling Candice what he had discovered about Grand Design's use of unfair means to ensure her a shot at Everest. There was no proof, of course, that Karl Tower had a hand in disabling the Toyota's brakes; in contriving a run-in with bees; in administering a near-fatal injection of insulin; in engineering a cold burial for Kaylee in the Rajagang Glacier. But with an assist from Taylor, who brought her memory and organizational skills to bear, Matt was ultimately able to present Candice with an irrefutable scenario.

As Karl had predicted, however, the authorities in Kathmandu weren't inclined to take Matt or Candice at their word. The rented jeep had already been repaired, and no one in the small village of Sankhu could recall the Americans' visit, or whether still other foreigners had been observed in the vicinity of the vehicle that afternoon.

In fact, the police were more interested in understanding precisely how and where Puma Tours had lost one of its trekkers to the flood—to the glacial leap—since the body of the westerner in question had yet to be found.

Taylor had her story and then some. She extended her ticket for three weeks after the others flew back to the States, so that she and Matt could avail themselves of some private time, which basically meant shacking up in the Oberoi and visiting places in the Kathmandu vale before winter blew in.

The editors at *Quest* were so impressed by what she sent in about the aborted climb and the Rajagang avalanche that they were ready to let her write her own ticket for a follow-up article. Although the magazine's legal department insisted on strict adherence to the facts and refused to involve themselves with unfounded claims about a plot by Grand Design to sabotage the climb.

Matt eventually let go of it and centered himself on Taylor. The three weeks proved that they could get along as well in the city as they had in the mountains, and when the day rolled around for them to kiss good-bye, neither wanted it to end.

"And you still think there's some future in this?" Taylor asked him as he was walking her to the departure gate. Tribhuvan was in its usual state of chaos. The flight was heavily overbooked, and Taylor had been bumped up to first class for the Bangkok leg. "After all, Matt, we're about to put a large ocean between us."

"There's telephones, telexes, video letters," Matt said. "Choose anywhere in Asia for your next assignment, and I'll be waiting for you."

"And in the meantime we get to romance each other over the phone."

Her look was skeptical and he turned her about in his arm. "We've already had the adventure part of it. And the sex part of it. So the romance is all we've got to nail down. I know it's ass-backwards, but it seems to be the way things work nowadays. Who are we to fight it?"

"I'm not going to fight it, Matt. But look how we're starting off." She made a broad gesture to the terminal. "We've already got an airport romance going."

He laughed, took her face between his hands. "And I'm already missing you. That's gotta count for something."

"Miss me enough to get on the next flight to San Francisco, then."

"Is that what you want?"

It was a long moment before she smiled back at him. "Okay. First we see if we can survive an ocean." She kissed him on the mouth, lovingly. "Tell me what you're going to do."

"I've got a few ideas, but I need some time to myself to sort through them."

"Time off to travel where you want instead of where Puma sends you?"

He shook his head. "Time off to sit still."

"Like Buddha."

He took off the *yantr* and slipped it over her head. "In lieu of flowers. And it'll keep you safe from falling rocks to boot."

She gripped a hand round the amulet. "But what're you going to use?"

He knuckle-rapped his forehead. "Fifty percent nickel," he told her, smiling.

Transformation took many forms, and it could often come from unexpected quarters.

His first mistake, he told himself, was in not leaving

Brie's lucky dollar at the shrine of Vajra Yogini—with the goddess who had convinced Manjushri way back when to drain the waters of Kathmandu's lake. But he had also erred in thinking the mountains were a good place to think things through, a good place to escape civilization for a time. For there was really no escape; Karl had proved that. Civilization and its manifold ills had followed them in, leaving as much garbage along the route as most trekking parties left. But that, too, was the way of the world.

Ecotourism meant leaving as little evidence of your passing as possible, but there was just no easy way to accomplish that. Not when evil traveled long-distance and could rarely be contained to any long-lasting benefit. We were all just passing through, and maybe the whole point was to have some effect, providing it was a positive one. The idea wasn't to hide yourself away in some remote corner of Asia, but to get out and leave a lasting though low-impact impression, to wait for the currents and chain reactions to spread that good around the world.

In some sense he felt as though he were emerging from the trip lighter than when he'd started; that he'd left some of his own garbage behind. He didn't imagine it the sort to despoil the landscape any—his own peculiar brand of 'sahib's prayer flag.' And what he'd packed out was a new sense of himself that seemed to grant him some control over his life.

It was good to be alive, even in a world of avalanches and floods. And for a time, he had had Taylor to keep him from the cold. Danger was what he did best. And maybe there was a way of making that work to other people's positive gain.

So when Jake asked him whether he'd made any decision about staying on with Puma, Matt told him yes—but under two conditions: that Jake would never take him seriously about wanting a desk job; and that his future assignments would be something more than adventure tours. Special assignments where there was some relevance or guiding principle—an environmental or ecological base. With some profit attached to it, of course. After all, Puma wasn't a charity.

And Matt wasn't exactly a crusader.

Jake—after a minute of reflection—told him about a group of concerned rock 'n' roll musicians who were looking for someone to design them a fact-finding tour of the world's beleaguered rain forests.

"Yeah," Matt said, "that sort of thing."

Candice Dekker and Kaylee McMahon would eventually return to Nepal to climb Pabil. As it turned out, neither of them would get a shot at Everest. But even so, an American woman would finally reach the summit of the world's highest mountain, and when she did, she wouldn't be outfitted in Grand Design climbing apparel.

About the Author

James Luceno has traveled extensively in Central America and has worked as a travel consultant in South America, Southeast Asia, and the South Pacific.